"Relax and enjoy the ride, Mr. Boss Man. It's fun."

As if to demonstrate, Sasha lifted her hand from the bar and jabbed both arms high in the air. "Woo-hoo!"

Even as they went in for another sweep at breakneck speed, he couldn't drag his eyes from hers.

"Cat got your tongue, John?"

A strange clunk rumbled through the mechanics, and his burgeoning smile vanished. "What was—"

Another rumble and the ride spun into freefall. Her hands ripped from the bar and she was flung into his side from the force of gravity whizzing around them. She smashed into his rib cage and the breath left his lungs. "Bloody hell."

Her gaze ran over his face to linger at his mouth. The desire to kiss her filtered through his mind. To show her who was boss and stop this damn power play she had going on. What was she doing to him? This was not the plan *at all*.

Dear Reader,

I am thrilled to introduce the first book in the new three-book contract I have signed with the Harlequin Superromance line. This is fabulous news for both you and me because it means we can continue to visit my most favorite place in the world, Templeton Cove! How can somewhere I created not be my favorite place? With each book I write set in this fictional U.K. seaside town, I fall more in love with its residents and settings. I am beyond grateful for your wonderful feedback, reviews and ratings for the first two books.

With the third book, I am introducing a brand-new hero and heroine. My heroine, Sasha Todd, runs the town's fairground. Funland has been in her family for generations before her grandfather sold it to the town's criminal mastermind, Kyle Jordon. Vowing to one day get the fairground back in her family where it belongs, Sasha thinks when Kyle is imprisoned her time to strike has finally come. Until the son nobody knew existed arrives in town...

John Jordan has plans of his own when he arrives at the Cove—plans to uncover his father's wrongdoings and publicly ruin the man who murdered his wife's killer and then abandoned their child. What John doesn't expect is an adversary in the form of beautiful Sasha Todd. Sparks fly from the beginning between these passionate, strong and determined individuals. Someone's going to get burned...and fall in love.

I hope you enjoy this third visit to Templeton Cove—the residents will be back again later in 2014 for their first Christmas adventure with you. Don't forget to bring the mistletoe!

I love to connect with my readers—please "like" my Rachel Brimble page on Facebook and/or follow me on Twitter. I am always there and love to chat!

Best wishes,

Rachel Brimble

RACHEL BRIMBLE

What Belongs to Her

ISBN-13: 978-0-373-60836-2

WHAT BELONGS TO HER

This edition published by arrangement with Harlequin Books S.A.

For questions and comments about the quality of this book, please contact us at CustomerService@Harlequin.com.

Printed in U.S.A.

ABOUT THE AUTHOR

Rachel lives with her husband and two young daughters in a small town near Bath in the U.K. After having several novels published by small U.S. presses, she secured agent representation in 2011. In 2012, she sold two books to the Harlequin Superromance line and a further three in 2013. Rachel is a member of the Romantic Novelists' Association and Romance Writers of America. When she isn't writing, you'll find her with her head in a book or walking the beautiful English countryside with her family and beloved black Lab, Max. Her dream place to live is Bourton-on-the-Water in South West England.

She is superexcited to have the chance to meet her readers and editors at the upcoming RWA conference in San Antonio, Texas. See you there!

She likes nothing more than connecting and chatting with her readers and fellow romance writers. Rachel would love to hear from you!

Website: www.RachelBrimble.com
Blog: www.RachelBrimble.blogspot.co.uk
Twitter: @RachelBrimble
Facebook: www.Facebook.com/RachelBrimbleAuthor

Books by Rachel Brimble

HARLEQUIN SUPERROMANCE

1835—FINDING JUSTICE
1869—A MAN LIKE HIM

To the many friends and family who continue to support me in my writing endeavors despite the lack of time I get to spend with you guys! You know who you are....

ACKNOWLEDGMENTS

This book could not have been written without the wonderful support of three very special romance writers, my intrepid critique partners: A J Nuest, Angel Nicholas and Vonnie Davis...no idea where I'd be without you!

I also want to thank my friend and U.K. romance writer Allie Spencer, who has supported me by answering many questions throughout my research for this book. Thank you, lovely!

Thank you to my agent, Dawn Dowdle, who continues to believe in my work, no matter how many times I doubt myself.

Finally, a huge thank-you to Piya Campana, my wonderful editor, who adores the love and laughter of the Templeton Cove residents equally as much as I do.

CHAPTER ONE

SASHA TODD STOOD ramrod-straight and narrowed her eyes as she studied the man standing near the bumper cars talking to a group of teenage girls. Unease rippled up her spine. Was one of them his daughter? Or was the son of a bitch edging in on forbidden territory? Uncrossing her arms, she pulled back her shoulders and strode forward, suppressed anger burning hot in her stomach.

When she was two feet away from them, one of the girls gave a delighted shriek and threw her arms around the man's neck. "Thanks, Daddy. You're the best."

He laughed. "You're welcome, sweetheart. Now behave yourselves. I'll be back at nine-thirty to pick you up."

The girl untangled herself from her father's embrace and waved, linking arms with her friend, her father's generous wad of spending money clutched in her hand. Her father stared fondly after her, before pulling a bunch of keys from his pocket and heading toward the fairground gates. Sasha released her held breath, heat pinching her cheeks.

She couldn't deny the proud smile he wore was one of a father who adored and cared for his little girl.

She sent silent thanks to God, relieved that her continual paranoia had been proven unsubstantiated once again. Happiness relaxed her shoulders, and she smiled as she surveyed the domain that would soon be entirely hers, excitement washing through her. She rounded one of the three Funland burger stands and came to an abrupt stop, her eyebrows rising in appreciation.

"Well, hello there." She casually appraised the handsome stranger standing at the Ferris wheel.

His dark, glossy hair and the gray five-o'clock shadow that brushed his jaw caught her interest... but it was the muscular forearms revealed beneath the rolled-up sleeves of his checked shirt, and the undoubtedly strong thighs covered with faded denim that reeled her in all the way.

Dance music pulsed from the loudspeakers at the corners of the bumper cars, and screams emanated from the roller coaster hurtling along the tracks above. Sasha's heart rate hitched higher. Lordy, the man was built. Inhaling a deep breath, she wandered closer under the pretense of cool nonchalance.

Tomorrow she'd face Kyle Jordon's asshole second-in-command and begin the task of taking back the fair from Kyle's criminal hands—but for tonight, she wanted some personal time. Some time to release the pressure of having to endure years of silent frustration. Frustration that had built to bursting if her earlier, misconstrued, father/daughter exchange was anything to go by.

She smiled. If everything went to plan, the fair would finally soon be back in the Todd family after Kyle had maliciously stolen it from her dying grandfather when he was in his most vulnerable and desperate state.

Exhaling, she concentrated on the satisfying sight of the stranger's taut ass. She tossed her hair over her shoulders, enjoying a rare rush of power. He stared up at the Ferris wheel as it slowly worked its romantic magic around the couples swinging to and fro in the brightly colored carriages. His jaw was a hardened line as he intently studied the ride. The man looked as though he wanted to spit at the joviality of it.

As she drew closer, the stiff set of his shoulders and the fisted hands at his hips swayed Sasha's confidence. Maybe this wasn't such a good idea after all. She glanced up at the ride. What if his girlfriend was up there alone and avoiding him? Or worse, up there with a new lover? A guy pitching for a fight was the last thing she needed added to her already teetering pile of problems.

Her smile dissolved and she shrugged on her manager persona. A potential fight brewing gave her no choice but to step in and cool the simmering fire before it had time to set fully alight. Sidling up beside him, she gave a loud, theatrical cough.

He turned, and his dark blue eyes coolly pinned her to the spot. She forced herself to stand still as his gaze languidly glided over her face, lingering for a moment at her lips. No smile lifted the corners of his mouth. No softness seeped into his hardened study.

She smiled even as her stomach knotted. "Hi."

He continued to stare.

Okay, so he's got that sexy, broody thing going on, but since when does a guy—any guy—leave me speechless? Say something...

"Well, you're all sorts of angry, aren't you?" *Great, Sasha. Just poetic.*

He lifted an eyebrow and turned his focus back to the ride.

She frowned and glared at his profile, feeling like an idiot. The guy needed to take a serious chill pill. Did he think he had a monopoly on being pissed off? *Wakey, wakey, mister, the entire human race holds a grudge of one kind or another.*

"I was only trying to make conversation. If you don't want to talk to me, that's fine." She shrugged. "I haven't seen you before and, as I'm the person running things around here, I thought you might appreciate a friendly word, a kind welcome. My name's Sasha—"

"I know who you are."

She stiffened. The deep, smooth lilt of his upper-class English voice filled her with equal measures of attraction and warning. "Pardon me?"

He faced her and crossed his arms across his broad chest. "You're Sasha Todd, exceptionally pretty and svelte manageress of this fairground, known so lovingly as Funland. You work for Kyle Jordon. Although, while Kyle's currently boarding at Her Majesty's pleasure in prison, you are undoubtedly forced to answer to his bull mastiff of a lapdog, the wonderfully charming and partially toothed Freddy Campton. Am I right?"

Sasha crossed her arms, mimicking his stance as irritation simmered inside her. "Yes, but who—"

"How do you feel about that, Miss Todd?"

"What?"

"Moreover, how are you going to feel knowing that from tomorrow, you'll be answering to me and not him?"

Sasha froze as his words filtered through her mind. What the hell did he just say? She uncrossed her arms and splayed her hands on her hips. "Is this some kind of joke?"

A flicker of amusement lit his eyes before he blinked and they turned cold once more. "No joke. From tomorrow you'll be reporting to me."

Panic and disbelief hurtled through her. *Who the hell does this guy think he is?* She huffed out a laugh. "I don't think so. Who are you?"

"Your new boss."

She grinned, hoping it would coerce some semblance of a smile to his lips and make him tell her he was kidding. "Very funny. You're a funny guy, Mr.—"

"You don't believe me?" His face remained unnervingly impassive.

Okay, enough was enough. "I asked you who you are. If you want to toss a revelation like that at me, the least you can do is tell me your name. Not that I'm likely to believe a word you say after this slightly creepy performance."

He uncrossed his arms and offered his hand, which she took without thinking. His hand enveloped hers. Warm, smooth and unnervingly large. Why did she have the sudden and unwelcome suspicion *nothing* about this guy was small or weak?

"John Jordon." He shook her hand. "Nice to meet you."

She stared into his eyes, her heart picking up speed. No, no, no. She swallowed in an effort to bring some saliva back into her desert-dry mouth. "Jordon? Are you telling me you're Kyle's son? His brother?"

He smiled.

She scowled as anger shot through her body with the speed of a freight train. Frustration and the enormity of what this meant turned her vision pink with rage. She slowly eased her hand from his and fisted her hair back from her face. "Well?"

"I'm his son."

She closed her eyes, struggling to maintain her equilibrium and not freak out. "As far as I was aware Kyle doesn't have a son or a brother." She opened her eyes. "I don't believe you."

His gaze locked on hers for a moment before it shot toward the crowds of people walking around the fair, laughing and shouting without a care in the world. "I'm his son whether you want to believe it or not." He met her eyes. "And I'll be here running things for the foreseeable future. So the sooner we get acquainted, the better."

"Get acquainted?" She laughed as her shaky self-control snapped. "You have no idea, do you? No damn idea whatsoever."

The anger dissolved from his eyes and was replaced with wary confusion. "About what? This place?"

"About everything. You need to go."

His brow furrowed as he stared. "That won't be happening anytime soon, I'm afraid."

Trembling, Sasha walked backward, opening the space between them. She shook her head. "You can't do this. You can't do this to me. Not now."

His frown deepened. "Do what?"

She waved her hand at him. "Do this. Turn up here. Say these things. I won't let you do this."

"Miss Todd—"

"I'm leaving." Her mind raced and her body felt strangely numb. "This isn't happening."

He put his hand out as if to touch her, hesitated and then dropped it to his side. "Wait. Just wait."

The stiff set of his shoulders slumped. "Maybe we should start—"

Sasha fled. She resolutely fought the tears that burned her eyes and blurred the crowds in front of her as she shouldered her way through. Her breathing grew labored and she rasped as if she had sharpened needles inside her chest. John Jordon. Kyle Jordon's son. He was going to take her fair. It was his. Not hers. Never hers.

She choked back a sob as the green, wrought-iron gates of the fairground came into view. Stumbling, she gripped them, shook them, wanting to rip them from their hinges. A scream gathered momentum, burning the back of her throat, and she dropped her head against the gate. *Damn you, Kyle Jordon. Damn you to hell.*

The gentle, firm grip of a male hand on her shoulder spun Sasha around. Her heart thundered as she stood poised for a fight. Under the light above them, John Jordon's eyes were soft with concern, the sculpted lines of his previously inscrutable expression somehow tamer.

She closed her eyes, stopping her traitorous tears in their tracks. "Just do me a favor and go away. Back to wherever the hell it is you came from."

"I'M SORRY, I can't do that." John slipped both his hands into his back pockets. The last thing he wanted to do was touch her. *Liar.*

He knew she wanted the fair, but no part of him

had expected the raw hurt and panic that showed so clearly in her eyes. This wasn't a woman prepared to do whatever it takes—this was a woman who was hurt…and angry.

For a long moment, she neither moved nor spoke. Just stayed where she was. Her slender shoulders, smooth and naked, rose and fell above the fitted confines of her bright yellow halter top. He struggled to drag his eyes from the length of her jet-black hair that fell in two gloriously thick sheets over her breasts.

He'd seen her from a distance all day and felt nothing. Yet, the moment she stood close, the full impact of her stunningly dark eyes and full, smiling mouth zipped a bullet through his chest.

He cleared his throat. "Miss Todd?"

Her sigh was loud and tired. She straightened and tipped her head back and looked directly at him. The tiny smudges of makeup beneath her eyes smacked John in the chest. God damn it. She'd been crying. He pulled back his shoulders and tightened his jaw. No, he had to be stronger than this. While he was in Templeton he couldn't be the man who looked out for everyone. He had to do what he came to do and then go home. "Look, maybe I shouldn't have delivered the news that way, but—"

"Are you here to take over from where your dad left off?" Her eyes were wide and cold. "That's all I want to know right now. Everything else I'll deal with tomorrow."

John ran his hand over his face. Tomorrow, he'd be better prepared, too. Her explosion had knocked him off-kilter, making him care. Tomorrow, he'd have it under control. He crossed his arms. "Yes."

"You're taking over the fair?"

"Yes."

She glanced past him toward the rides and noisy chaos of the fairground. Her jaw clenched. "I never even knew you existed." She met his eyes. "Kyle never mentioned a son to me or anyone else, as far as I remember."

John held her gaze, silently absorbing her unintentional insult.

Her eyes narrowed as she studied him; an intelligent light flickered brighter and then faded into their gorgeous depths. "None of my business, right? How did I know that was coming?" She gave a wry laugh. "Jesus, like father like son."

He flinched. She might as well have punched him in the gut. "I'm nothing like my father."

She lifted an eyebrow. "So you say. From the five minutes I've spent with you, you've already managed to piss me off as much as he did every damn day he was here." She raised her hands in defeat. "I'm going home. I'll see you tomorrow."

When she moved to brush past him, John touched her arm, stopping her. "I'd like to see you in the office first thing."

She looked pointedly at his hand on her forearm.

He released her, and she raised her chin. “Oh, I’ll be there. I’ll be there with freaking bells on.”

She stalked away from him. He released a low whistle from between pursed lips as his gaze glued onto the soft curve of her butt encased in black denim.

John’s father had described Sasha Todd as a ballsy, tough broad in need of a firm hand. He’d warned John to be wary of her. In the blink of an eye, she could be all soft femininity with the patrons, but in reality she was a fiery, spitting alley cat. He’d said that soft side of her was an act—the real Sasha Todd was apparently a hard-nosed businesswoman.

Two personalities—that’s what Kyle had said. Two personalities, each as scary as the other.

John drew in a long breath. Well, clearly he had a fight on his hands, but that was just fine by him. After years of self-control, of conservative containment within the walls of a private boarding school, Oxford University and then his own classroom, this teacher was ready to let off some steam.

He scowled as he strode back inside the fairground. If Sasha Todd thought she could direct any of her pissiness at him and come away unscathed, she’d better think again.

Like she said, he was Kyle Jordon’s son, and even though the bastard had abandoned him years ago—and now had the gall to ask for his help—little did she or Kyle know what John intended to do about it. John glanced around his father's domain. A fairground used as a cover for his illegal dealings—a place for kids and teenagers. The man was scum.

John scowled. Kyle might have thought it was time for a father-and-son reconciliation, but his son had other ideas. At last, John knew where Kyle was after years of speculation and silence. When his father finally made contact just six short weeks ago, he'd clearly thought the path to father/son love would be simple and John would want the riches and immorality his father thrived on. Unfortunately for Daddy Dearest, that was just the sort of perilous miscalculation that occurred when a parent vanished, leaving their children to drift through life without them.

John smiled. One way or another he'd right his father's wrongs…while royally screwing Kyle over and leaving the son of a bitch without a penny to his damn name.

CHAPTER TWO

SITTING ON THE balcony of her apartment in one of two ancient patio chairs, Sasha scowled at the view. The temperature was above average for July, but a slight breeze cut through the warmth and she pulled her pashmina tighter around her shoulders. The flickering lights of her beloved fairground taunted her in the distance, the sounds of laughter and rock music ringing in her ears. She wanted to punch something.

Kyle Jordon's son was there right now, no doubt parading around like he already owned the place. She cursed. *He does own it, you numbskull.*

Leaning forward, she picked up her wineglass from the upturned crate beside her. The cabernet sauvignon, warm and fruity, slid down her throat, ever so slightly mellowing her fraught nerves and barely controlled need to vent some serious anger.

Yet, she couldn't shake the feeling John Jordon was about as happy to be there as she was about his arrival.

Sasha struggled to get her emotions under control. She had to resist her instinct to worry about every damn thing before it happened. Her primal need to prevent evil before it could strike. Who was to say the guy wasn't there under duress? She glanced at her cell phone sitting on the table. Either way, she had a right to know why she hadn't been warned about his unwanted entrance. She had a right to demand some background information on the handsome enigma known as John Jordon.

Snatching up her phone, she punched in Freddy's cell number and focused once more on the fairground lights. Her heart beat hard as the tone rang ominously in her ear. She was just about to end the call when the line picked up.

"Freddy Campton's phone."

Sasha froze. Damn it. It was him. John-bloody-Jordon. What were the chances of him answering? She cleared her throat and sat up straight. Hell would freeze over before she'd let him get the better of her. "Is Freddy around?"

"Not right now. Can I take a message?"

"No. I'll catch up with him tomorrow. Thanks anyway."

"You know, if you're calling to ask about me, you could just come straight to the source. What is it you'd like to know, Miss Todd?"

She narrowed her gaze. The man's voice sounded more uppity and posh than ever. "My name's Sasha. Can we drop the *Miss Todd?* We tend to work on a first-name basis at the fairground. You know, circa the twenty-first century."

There was a pause before his breath rasped down the line. "I see."

Sasha glared. Was that a whiff of laugher or disdain in his tone? She'd bet a hundred British pounds on the former. "Are you laughing at me… Mr. Jordon?"

"John, please." This time he definitely laughed.

Her stomach knotted as a blush dared to warm her cheeks. She steadfastly bit back her smile. "Clearly, there are some things we need to get straight if we're going to start off as civilized individuals tomorrow."

"Meaning we're likely to get uncivil?"

The heat at her cheeks hitched up a notch. His voice was like liquid velvet, making the suggestion of incivility almost sexual. She shifted in her seat. "Fine. If you want our working relationship to start off on the wrong foot, who am I to argue? Could you just let Freddy know I called and that I'd appreciate a call back?"

"So you'd still rather ask him rather than me why I'm here?"

Damn it. She stared at the fair again. This man, with his smooth voice, handsome looks and, though she hated to admit it, masculine charm, was making her feel the need to fully arm herself before she set a single foot inside the fairground office tomorrow morning.

"Miss…Sasha? You still there?"

"Of course. I'm going nowhere." She picked up

her wineglass and drained it before reaching for the bottle. Strength in grapes.

He cleared his throat. "I need you to work with me. This isn't a fight to the death."

She sniffed. "That's what you think."

"Pardon me?"

Her hand stilled around the wine bottle before she released it and drove her clawed fingers into her hair instead. Clearly, more alcohol was not advisable. Her damn tongue was running away with her.

"Look, tomorrow's another day." She sighed and focused on dragging up a little dignity to battle her desire to poke out the man's eyes. "I'm just put out I wasn't told about your arrival. I'm sure tomorrow won't be as onerous as I'm thinking it will be right now."

"I'm quite a nice guy…sometimes."

She scowled. "And I'm quite a nice woman… sometimes."

He laughed and her stomach knotted again. Damn it, why were her guts going all stupid every time this man laughed?

"I need your help." He inhaled a heavy breath. "I don't particularly like that fact, but I'm man enough to admit it. Kyle told me you know the fair better than anyone. I can't do anything without you."

The humor in his tone had vanished, leaving behind a rough, masculine assurance that conflicted with his words.

Slow and steady wins the race, Sasha. Slow and steady wins the race.

She rose from her chair and approached the barrier surrounding the balcony. The swish of the tide lapping the beach a mile down the road drifted to her ears on the gathering breeze, and she inhaled. "And what is it you want to do exactly?"

"I can't tell you that."

Sasha closed her eyes as her heart turned to lead. Once again, she was fighting. The threat of another battle clinked like crossing swords in her head. "You know something, John?"

"What?"

"If anyone, including your father, had any respect for how long I've worked at the fair or what it means to me, they would've given me a heads-up about you coming. That didn't happen, so I'm wondering what you want from me. If you intend to do something with my…the fair, you should at least have the decency to tell me about it."

Her heart beat out the seconds of silence, broken only by his heavy exhalation. "Nobody knew I was coming."

She squeezed her eyes tighter. "I don't believe you."

"Nobody knew."

"Was this Kyle's idea? You turning up like a phantom menace?" She snapped her eyes open and choked out a wry laugh. "Stupid question. Even from behind prison walls, the guy likes to play the great puppet master."

"I am *not* Kyle's puppet."

His ice-cold tone sent an involuntary shiver down her back. The knee-jerk reaction to apologize lingered on her tongue, but she decided against it. The silence stretched until she was forced to say something. "Look, it's late and I'm tired. Maybe tomorrow I'll be a little more amicable. Let's just say good-night, shall we?"

"How well do you know my father, Sasha Todd?"

The soft, British upper-class way he said her name rolled down the phone line and licked softly over her skin. Why the hell did the man have to talk that way? Why couldn't he talk with the rough abrasion of some of the dock workers she knew at the harbor?

She pushed away from the barrier. "Not very well."

"Yet you've worked at the fair your entire life. He bought it from your grandfather. How could you not know him?"

Her heart hitched into her throat. "You know about that?"

"Yes."

"You know my granddad sold the fair to him? Do you know for how much?"

"Does it matter?"

Nausea whirled hot and heavy in her stomach and

she stumbled toward her vacant chair and collapsed onto it. "That matters to me more than anything."

"Why?"

Frustration surged through her. "All I've ever wanted is to get the fairground back where it belongs. It was in my family for generations and then my grandfather had a complete change of heart and let Kyle buy it for a song. Now you turn up and—"

"That's not strictly true, is it?"

"What isn't?" Her body trembled with suppressed rage.

"Your parents didn't want the fair. Your mother, your grandfather's daughter, is ashamed of it, isn't she? So, whether or not you ever get the fair back, it would've skipped a generation anyhow."

She gripped the phone until blood pulsed through her fingers. "So?"

"So what is it about the fair that makes you want it so badly? Does the need come from you or your family?"

"That's none of your business. I want it and, one way or another, I'll get it. Do you have any idea what it feels like to care about nothing else in the world but for the one thing out of reach? I really, really don't want to have to fight you, but if you refuse my offer tomorrow—"

"Your offer?"

"Yes, Mr. Snooty Nose, my offer."

Silence.

Her heart thumped loudly in her ears as she trembled some more.

"Fine. I'll listen to your offer." He blew out a breath. "And then I'll decide whether or not you still have a job."

The phone line went dead.

Sasha swallowed the hard lump of panic in her throat. *Whether or not I still have a job? Is this guy insane?* She snapped her phone closed and struggled to fight the horrible sense of foreboding stealing over her. She'd been aggressive, angry, dismissive and disrespectful—all things she'd been careful to avoid with Kyle and his cronies.

Stupid, stupid woman.

With an infinite amount of self-control, she'd bided her time and waited. Saved her money and kept a smile on her face so Kyle had no reason to push her out.

Now she'd snapped and a complete stranger had splintered her facade. He held the ability to rip away everything she wanted in one fell swoop. Why did John Jordon care why the fair meant so much to her? He didn't know her. He didn't know Templeton. He knew nothing.

She slowly stood on shaking legs and snatched the wineglass and bottle from the table. Even Kyle held a quiet, if not misplaced, fondness for the fair. The man was a criminal mastermind. A drug pusher and money-laundering bastard who'd finally been caught and thrown in jail, yet at least something inside him made people second-guess if deep down he was a decent man.

None of those same feelings emanated from his son. What John Jordon had in looks and physique, he lacked in warmth and understanding, which his father used unashamedly to blind people to his real motivations.

She opened the French doors and walked inside, welcoming the warmth of her apartment as a way of combating the chill of the unknown permeating her soul.

JOHN STARED AT the phone, heart beating steadily and mind messed up with a million conflicting emotions. Sasha Todd was something—or someone—he hadn't accounted for when he'd agreed to come to Templeton Cove. He hadn't expected a woman as beautiful as her to shake the deep and unyielding barrier around his determination to expose his father for the man he really was.

Worse, he hadn't anticipated the stark pain of betrayal reflected in her eyes when she stood in front of him, or in her voice on the phone. The little that Kyle's letters told John about the fair circulated in his mind on an endless reel.

Freddy was Kyle's trusted second-in-command, and John was aware the fairground was a legitimate cover for the crux of his father's criminal activities. Sasha Todd had a family history with the place. He remembered his father's words—"The chick works like a Trojan for shit pay. She should be out there living her life, not stuck in a small English seaside town like Templeton Cove. She needs to let the fair go, son. She needs to meet a decent bloke who puts a different kind of fire in her belly. Brings a damn smile to her face…."

"Who was that on the phone?"

John blinked and pulled his expression into a scowl as Freddy wandered into the converted barn that served as the fairground's office.

Freddy glared. "More to the point, why are you answering my phone and sitting at my desk?"

Irritation pulsed at John's temple and he tossed the phone at Freddy, who caught it deftly in one hand. "Sasha Todd just called." John stood. "I took care of it, so there's no need to call her back."

He walked to what was once Kyle's desk but was now his. The weight of Freddy's glare on John's back followed his progress. He whipped his jacket from the huge leather swivel chair. Even the size of Kyle's chair reflected the size of his damn ego.

The erratic shuffling of papers and the opening and closing of drawers made John turn and face Freddy. The man was checking over his desk in the manner of a dog hunting for blood. John shook his head as he shrugged into his jacket. "I haven't touched anything so there's no need to have a coronary on me."

Freddy grunted. "I don't like you sitting at my desk. Kyle never had any need—"

"Kyle's not here. I am." They locked gazes. "I'm leaving for the night. I assume I don't need to ask you if you're okay to close up."

Silence.

John tensed. He was more than ready for a showdown with the man who had only too clearly shown John his arrival at Templeton was as equally unwelcome as it was to a certain dark-haired, dark-eyed beauty.

Guilt over his harsh responses to Sasha Todd crept up his body, fuelling John's frustration. "Well?" He snatched his keys from the desk and stared directly at Freddy.

Freddy stared right back, his eyes bulging. "What's the game here?"

"Game? I'm not playing any game."

"I ain't going to lie to you. When Kyle was sentenced, I assumed the baton would pass to me."

"Why would you think that?" John raised his eyebrows. "Have you ever known Kyle to do the decent thing? Did he regularly reward his loyal followers for their hard work?"

Freddy straightened. "Hey, Kyle's been good to me."

"Really? So when did he suggest in any way, shape or form that the fairground was coming to you?" The seconds ticked by as Freddy glowered. John shrugged. "As I thought. My father doesn't give a crap about anyone. I would've thought you'd know that…being his right-hand man and all."

"I don't understand why Kyle's drafted you in to oversee things when he hasn't seen you for years."

"How much do you know about my relationship with him?"

Freddy leaned his considerable weight onto his fists on the desktop. "Not much, but—"

"Well, then, from now on, I wouldn't think too much if I were you. Until I know what's what at Funland and who the people are Kyle's got working here, I've no idea what will be happening in the future."

"What future? The fairground ain't going nowhere. Kyle wouldn't want anyone taking over who doesn't know the business like he does." Color seeped into Freddy's cheeks, and a vein zigzagged across his temple. "I saw Kyle only last week and he never mentioned your coming. He mentioned you in passing, nothing else. I don't buy that he'd want you turning up and changing things."

"You knew he had a son, though?"

Freddy's gray eyes turned colder than steel. "I've known Kyle for fifteen years and the first time he said a word about you was when I last saw him. You two estranged or something? Does he even know you're here?"

Resentment tipped like paraffin through John's blood, fuelling his constantly simmering rage against Kyle. "He knows I'm here. Did you meet my father in prison when he was there the first time?"

A muscle worked in Freddy's jaw. "Yeah. So?"

"And you met up again upon his release nine years ago?"

Freddy nodded, his gaze steady.

John stared. "And he never mentioned me in prison or after?"

"No."

"Then I guess I'm a big surprise to you in more ways than one." John smiled, even as his heart beat like a bloody hammer against his rib cage.

Freddy crossed his arms. "What's that supposed to mean?"

"Well, first, you didn't know about me, and then you find out Kyle has a son. I'm betting a bloody fortune you didn't expect his sole heir to speak and act like me, either, did you?"

"Your accent don't mean shit. I've met some pretty evil posh bastards inside prison. As for the rest of you?" Freddy's smile was slow and suggestive. "You scream of being Kyle's offspring. You've got a mean look in your eyes, no matter how much you might smile and want to make friends. People 'round here ain't going to take too kindly to Kyle's son turning up, regardless of what plans you've got for this place."

John slid a stack of files off his desk and pushed them under his arm. He grinned. "Worse than that, Freddy, my man, I'm not even sure what I've got planned yet, so people are going to wonder—or worry—more than ever what I'm up to, aren't they? See you tomorrow."

He strolled to the door and left it wide open behind him. It was nearing eleven and the fair was drawing to a close. The beat of a nineties dance track matched the stomp of John's boots as he made his way to his car. He unlocked it and slid into the leather seat of Kyle's Mercedes convertible. Placing the files on the passenger seat, his gaze lingered on the top file emblazoned with Sasha Todd's name.

"I've got my bedtime reading, Kyle. Let's see what other nightmares you have in store for me."

Drawing in a long breath, he yanked on his seat belt and gunned the engine. Time to get himself comfortable in his father's well-made bed.

CHAPTER THREE

SASHA LEFT MARIAN'S Bonniest Bakery with a vanilla latte in hand and gripped the handlebar of her bicycle. She waited for the road to clear and then steered it across to the other side. After parking her bike against the railings overlooking Cowden Beach, she lifted the lid off her coffee, and a plume of gray steam split the runners and dog walkers dotting the sand.

At 8:00 a.m. she would normally have been cycling through the fairground gates, the excitement of the day ahead running through her blood like oxygen. This morning, raw anxiety washed through her at such a rate she couldn't help thinking she'd be in danger of crashing her bike the moment she got back in the saddle.

She sipped her coffee and contemplated the last time she'd jogged across the beach. Who needed to run when she cycled everywhere she could? All day and half the night, she scrambled on and off rides, climbed ladders to fix broken overhangs or change lightbulbs. She smiled.

Not to mention the innumerable amount of times

she'd jumped on the carousel horses under the guise of accompanying a kid riding solo, while their mother rode with their toddler sibling.

Loving the local kids and wanting to make the park a happy, safe place for them was once again out of reach for the foreseeable future. How would the fear of history repeating itself ever go away if she wasn't in charge? How could she ascertain suspicious behavior from innocent if Funland was overrun with Kyle's criminal contacts? If only her family would join in the fight for their ancestral piece of history. How could they stand by and let something that had been in their hands for more than a hundred years slip into such undeserving ones?

Didn't they want the place made good again? To help her wash away the evil?

"That fairground won't run itself, you know."

Sasha quickly swiped at her face and pulled on a smile. "Hey, Marian. What are you doing out here?"

Templeton Cove's favorite—and scariest—baker stood beside her, holding Sasha's phone between her thumb and forefinger. "You left this behind. Thought you might need it…and a big ol' shoulder to cry on."

"Thanks." Sasha took the phone. "For the phone. The shoulder will have to wait. No tears today." She nodded toward the bakery. "You'll be overrun with angry customers wanting coffee and your famous honeycomb muffins in two seconds flat at this time of the morning."

Marian waved her hand dismissively. "You're more important. The girls can cope without me for a while."

"I was just about to head off." Sasha pulled her bike from the railing, but Marian pushed it back.

"Sasha Todd, talk to me. Now." Marian lifted an eyebrow and leaned her ample backside against the railing, pinning Sasha with her unrelenting stare. "I've never known you to be so distracted when my George was chatting with you. You know how that husband of mine relies on you young girls to brighten up his aging ego. The man's heartbroken over there."

Sasha laughed. "I've got things on my mind. Tell him I'm sorry and I'll make it up to him tomorrow."

"You think he's going to listen to me? He'll want to know what's going on with you…as do I. Spill. Now."

Sasha hesitated. If she said out loud what had happened between her and John Jordon last night, that would make the situation real, and part of her was still holding on to the hope that when she got to Funland, John would turn out to be nothing more than a figment of her imagination.

"Well?" Marian crossed her arms. "I'm waiting."

Sliding her coffee into the bottle holder on her bike, Sasha gripped the railing and stared ahead.

"Kyle Jordon's son turned up last night to take over the running of the fair."

"What?"

Inhaling a deep breath, Sasha turned. Marian's face had darkened to a worrying shade of scarlet and her eyes bulged wide open.

"His name's John." Sasha sighed. "And he speaks with some stupid posh accent as though he's a member of the Royal family."

"What?"

Sasha laughed at the pure disbelief on Marian's face. "Can't you say anything else?"

Marian blinked. "Kyle Jordon's *son?* Here? In Templeton? I don't believe it."

"Well, you'd better believe it. He's here and, from the little time I've spent with him, I've worked out he's dangerous. I'm not sure if he's 'Kyle Jordon' dangerous yet, but he's dangerous all the same."

She narrowed her eyes. "Did he hurt you? Threaten you? What did he do to make you think he's dangerous?"

Sasha glanced toward the beach. "I don't know."

"You don't know?"

She turned and pushed the hair back from her eyes, considering John Jordon and the unsettling effect he'd had on her mentally, emotionally...physically. She swallowed. "The man has more anger in the tip of his little finger than I've got in my entire body, so there's trouble on the horizon whichever way we look at it."

"I see." Marian looked toward the bakery across the road. "Does DI Garrett know he's here? We should call her. We've just gotten rid of one Jordon and another turns up." She faced Sasha again. "Did you know he had a son?"

She shook her head. "Nope. And he says Freddy didn't, either. I've got no idea what this is going to mean for the fair or Templeton."

Marian pushed away from the railing. "Well, whatever it means, DI Garrett should know he's here. I'm going to call her right now."

When she spun away, Sasha clasped Marian's arm. "Wait. I want to get an idea of what he intends to do first."

"But you said—"

"I know what I said." Sasha straightened and pulled her bike upright. "There's something about him that intrigues me. Something's just not right. He doesn't exactly look ecstatic to be here, any more than I am to see him."

Marian gave an inelegant snort. "How can anyone be right in the head if they're the product of Kyle Jordon's bodily fluid? Answer me that."

Sasha wrinkled her nose. "Seriously? Bodily fluid?"

Marian gave a hoot of laughter and patted Sasha's cheek. "Be careful and call me as soon as you know anything. DI Garrett should be told what's going on and she trusts my judgment, as I trust yours. The minute you tell me this man is up to no good, I'm on it." She brushed her thumb over Sasha's cheek. "I know what that fairground means to you and what it meant to your granddad. Watch your back, okay?"

Fighting to keep her composure, Sasha covered Marian's hand with hers and lifted it from her face. She squeezed the older woman's fingers. "I will. Now get back to the bakery before the inspector turns up because of a riot over honeycomb muffins, let alone anything else."

Marian smiled despite the lingering concern in her gaze. "I'm going. Just remember where I am."

Sasha saluted, and Marian hurried across the street. Once she'd disappeared inside the shop, Sasha inhaled a deep breath and drew a folded piece of paper from the back pocket of her jeans. She opened it and stared at her carefully typed letter to Kyle, offering him every penny she had for the fair. The amount included the money her grandfather bequeathed her from Funland's sale to Kyle seven years before, plus some savings.

Of course, there was still the glaring problem of the contract clause that gripped and twisted at Sasha's heart...confused and irritated her mind. Why had her grandfather written in a clause to say that the fair wasn't ever to be resold to anyone in the Todd family? She stared ahead at the growing numbers of locals and holidaymakers gathering on the sand to enjoy another day of the school holidays.

Why would you do that, Granddad? Why would

you keep something from me when you said so many times you wanted it back in the family?

It was a long shot, but she just hoped and prayed her suspicion that with Kyle imprisoned and her grandfather having passed, the clause would be deemed invalid. She tightened her jaw. Every hope was pinned on the money she'd accumulated being enough. She couldn't allow this clause to cut her dream to a million pieces. Her plan to ask Freddy to give the letter to Kyle when he next visited him had given her something to hold on to. She finally had a decent sum that even Kyle surely wouldn't outright dismiss.

Now John was here, and it was time to find out what his reaction would be to her offer. Clause or no clause. She slid the paper back into her pocket, straddled her bike and pushed onto the road. It was time to face the music…or maniac.

IT WAS ONLY eight-thirty when Sasha stowed her bike at the back of the fairground offices. She locked it to the iron bars of a sad, decrepit and very much disused kiddie ride before smoothing her hands over the rumpled cotton of her shorts. Rare self-consciousness overrode her, the same as it had in the bathroom that morning. Cursing, she tidied her shirt and ripped the band from her hair.

She shouldn't give a crap what John Jordon thought of her, but his gaze was unnerving and… baring. Yesterday, there were times he'd studied her with such intensity, she wanted to glance at her chest to see if her nipple had popped over the vee of her shirt. She couldn't let him see the way he made her aware of her body whenever she was within two feet of him.

Tipping her head upside down, she scrunched her hair before standing straight and swinging it over her shoulders.

Her long hair was the only thing she had going for her in the way of armor. If Kyle's son thought she hadn't seen the way his blue eyes swept back and forth from her hair to her eyes last night, he was a damn fool. Every man she knew was a sucker for her hair. Why, she had no idea, but it didn't mean she couldn't use the phenomenon to her advantage.

Everything else about her seemingly brought admirers straight back to earth with a hard bump within a few weeks. Their hair fetish soon cooled when they realized Sasha was more tomboy than girly girl…or else they sensed her discord, her wary apprehension of what might come next. She lifted her chin. One day, she'd meet a man with enough balls to stick around longer than a month or two.

She blew out a shaky breath and swept her gaze over the back of the office. *Just remember, you do fine and dandy kicking them out of your bed, instead of the other way around. Your way or no way, remember?* She narrowed her eyes as a blush heated her neck. Even though they never put up much of a fight.

Stepping across the short dry grass, the early-morning sun warming the back of her legs, she strode purposefully to the office and pushed open the door. Her heart beat hard, but her determination was on full-power. Steeling herself, she shot her gaze straight to Kyle's desk, expecting John to be sitting there ready and waiting. The chair was empty.

"God damn it." She released her pent-up energy in a whoosh of air from her lungs. She planted her hands on her hips. Now what?

The door clicked open behind her and Sasha spun around. Freddy wandered in, his ever-expanding waistline juddering with each step and his shaven head shining with perspiration. He closed the door, his brow furrowed.

Sasha stepped toward him. "You okay, Freddy?"

He turned. "You're late."

"Not officially. Officially my hours on Friday are nine to nine, remember?"

He grunted and walked to his desk. "Never known you to take any notice of what time of the day or night it is." He collapsed into his chair, his gaze wandering the length of her. "You looking for our new boss, by any chance?"

"Not particularly. He asked to see me first thing, that's all."

"He's outside."

Sasha glanced toward the glass doors. "Right."

"He's been here since I came in at seven-thirty. Christ knows what he's doing out there. He's walking around with this look on his face. A look that tells me he's Kyle's boy through and through."

She stepped closer to the desk. "And what does that face look like exactly?"

"Like he's a hard son of a bitch. You wouldn't think it looking at the pansy way he's dressed this morning, but I guarantee that bloke out there has a mean streak." He met her eyes. "Takes one to know one."

Unease rippled over her skin but Sasha smiled. "Yeah, well, you never scared me and neither did Kyle, so John Jordon has a long way to go to frighten me out of this place."

She marched to the door.

"You know something, Sasha?"

"What?" She faced him.

"Kyle's boy turning up like this changes everything."

She arched an eyebrow. "You think I don't know that."

"It changes things with the park, the staff, the patrons…and especially with me. I didn't work my ass off for Kyle to be pushed around by his damn son."

Trepidation furled in her stomach, and Sasha slipped her hand from the door handle. Freddy's eyes were colder than steel, his cheeks flushed red.

She curled her hand into a fist at her side. "He's trying to push you around?"

"Not yet. But give him time."

She smiled. Two against one was something to consider, surely? "Then maybe he needs to learn that neither of us will take too kindly to that."

Freddy stared, his eyes darkening. "I'm not your friend. Never have been. I work for Kyle and he ain't here no more, so it's a brand-new playing field. For all of us."

He shot her a final, loaded glare before picking up the phone and dialing.

Anger burned hot behind her rib cage. What the hell was going on here? One minute she thought the fair was within her grasp and her life was about to change for the better. Now she was facing not one, but two adversaries. Clearly, Freddy intended to lay claim to Funland, too.

She stared at his bowed head. She'd thought she knew Freddy and now it was abundantly clear she didn't. John Jordon, the other claimant, was an unknown entity entirely.

"Well, I'm glad we both know where we stand." She turned and shoved open the door.

Drawing in huge gulps of air, she marched past the rides, her gaze darting left and right as she searched for the best and most handsome target on which to vent her anger. She didn't have to go far.

Her nemesis sat in one of the dozen three-seaters, hovering above the platform of the dreaded Mixer.

John looked lost in thought, his stare following the progress of his hand as he wiped it back and forth along the seat beside him. Sasha's hormones surged to high alert.

When Freddy described Kyle's son as being "dressed as a pansy" today, Sasha had already guessed John would be wearing a suit, maybe even a tie, too, in order to add a flash of additional authority to their meeting that morning.

She'd been right about the suit at least.

What she hadn't expected was the way a black jacket and open-necked crisp white shirt looked on him. His dark brown hair, cut short and neat, chiseled jaw and lightly tanned skin only added to the overall confidence that exuded from his every pore.

Tiny flutters of excitement erupted in Sasha's stomach as she approached the steel steps. Her attraction to the man could be controlled. She'd had years of practice being in the driving seat as far as men were concerned. Her only weakness was the fair and she was no pushover with that, either.

She smiled. So he wanted to run Funland—and he wanted her help to make that happen, did he? He'd given her no idea what his plans were, or if the crime going on behind the scenes would get worse or improve.

Marian's suggestion of letting the police know John Jordon was in Templeton lingered in Sasha's conscience even as a worse, naughtier idea flittered through her brain. The only sounds were the seagulls diving to and fro overhead and the rush of passing traffic in the distance. By two o'clock, booming music, screaming and laughter would fill Funland, but right now, it was just her and John Jordon.

On the soft soles of her ballet flats, she climbed the steps and approached the control booth, her grin stretching as wide as the sun above her.

CHAPTER FOUR

THE MACHINE RUMBLED to life and John froze.

What the hell?

Gripping the lap bar, he hauled it up and stood. Sasha Todd gracefully skipped up onto the steel platform beneath the carriages. She was dressed in white shorts that revealed her long, slender legs and a simple red T-shirt. His breath caught. Did she have any idea how stunning she was?

She smiled, mischief glinting in her black eyes. "Sit down, John. Let's take a ride."

He blinked. "Are you crazy?"

"What's the matter? Don't you like rides?"

He tried and failed to muster some semblance of authority as the machine started to move. "No. Turn this thing off."

She quirked an eyebrow and curved her fingers over the back of the carriage. "Yet you want to run this place? You can't do that without knowing the fairground inside out. That includes the rides. Move over, I'm jumping onboard."

Their eyes locked and once again, his tongue stuck to the roof of his mouth. Why the hell did the woman managing the fairground have to be so physically arresting? God, he wanted to write about her. Describe her in words in a vain attempt to let the damn world know how unnervingly beautiful she was.

He lowered into the seat, steadfastly avoiding her gaze. He concentrated on keeping his pride in place and not giving in to the temptation to grip the bar again. The ride picked up speed and the carriage shifted as she hauled herself up and sat down next to him, pulling the lap bar down with her.

The distinct smell of something musky and sexy drifted as she tossed her long hair over her shoulders. The tendrils whispered across his cheek, and John closed his mouth, trapping the inconceivable urge to groan.

She wriggled her behind deeper into the seat and settled back with a sigh. "So…what's the plan today? Enjoy the fair? Cook the books? Fire me?"

Attraction gave way to irritation, fueled by the nonchalance in her voice. "You do realize this thing is moving, right?"

She shrugged and glanced around before focusing entirely on him. "Sure. Now is as good a time as any to get acquainted, don't you think?"

John swallowed. *Jesus, her eyes are ebony-black, like two huge pieces of jet.* He snapped his face forward. "Do you know something?" He slid his arm across the back of the carriage above her shoulders. "If you want to play some stupid game in a bid to annoy me, that's fine. I'm the one in control here, whether you like it or not."

"Is that so?"

He faced her. Her eyes blazed with anger, and he glared straight back. "Yes."

"This isn't about control. This is about me taking one look at you, sitting on this ride dressed for a wedding, and wondering how you think you're going to run this place."

He huffed out a laugh. "Wearing a suit dictates whether I'm capable of running the fairground? Wow, clearly you give me more credit for my clothes than my business acumen."

She scowled and her cheeks flushed pink. John fought the guilt that knotted his gut.

He hated being snappy with any woman, and with Sasha his hostility didn't sit well at all. The ride gathered momentum and they wove in and out for a few seconds. "I haven't got time for this. We're supposed to be in the office talking things out like adults."

"Adults? Adults don't hang up on each other mid-conversation."

"Adults don't talk to their bosses without respect. If you think you can speak to me the way you did last night, you'd better think again."

She glared. "You still don't get it, do you?"

"Oh, I get it. I get it completely. Kyle..."

The ride rumbled up another notch and the carriage shot forward with such force the remainder of his words were obliterated by the slipstream. *Holy crap.* They sped between the empty carriages at such speed, John had no choice but to slip his free hand onto the bar next to hers. He tightened his fingers along the back of the seat.

He glanced at her and scowled. She stared at his white-knuckled hand, her lips curved into a smug smile. She met his eyes. "All this tension and we've only just got going."

He glared, focusing on her mouth rather than those damn eyes. It soon became clear her mouth was no safer option, but what the hell else was he supposed to look at? His gaze drifted lower—to her breasts—and he yanked his eyes right back up. No. Anywhere lower was out of bounds. "I'm not talking business with you whilst riding a damn fairground monstrosity like this."

Her smile stretched to a grin. "*Whilst?* God, you are so British. Do you always speak this way or is it just for Freddy's and my benefit?"

"Look, I want to know how the hell… Oh, God." The ride lurched into an abrupt frenzy and took off at a speed to which no child under the age of sixteen should ever be subjected. John gripped the bar and held on for dear life.

Sasha's scream of laughter bore a hole the size of the damn cove into his ego, but he'd be damned if he let go. *Whoosh!* They sped in between the carriages, barely missing a fatal head-on collision with each maneuver.

"Relax and enjoy the ride, Mr. Boss Man. It's fun." She lifted her hand from the bar and jabbed both arms high in the air. "Woo-hoo!"

"Are you purposely trying to emasculate me?" he yelled over the whizzing and screaming of the ride's mechanical parts working at a ridiculous and feverish tempo.

"Emasculate you? Me?" She winked. "Never."

Even as they went in for another sweep at break-neck speed, he couldn't drag his eyes from hers. A smile tugged traitorously at his lips as adrenaline seeped into his blood. Her eyes were wide with childlike excitement; her bright teeth were straight and white with the sliver of a pink tongue barely showing within. He drank in the sight of her. God, she was something else.

"Cat got your tongue, John?"

A strange clunk rumbled through the mechanics and his burgeoning smile vanished. "What was—"

Her smile dissolved. "Oh, God."

The excitement in her gaze was replaced with horror. She slapped her hands hard to the bar and held on. Dread dropped like a rock into John's gut. This did not bode well.

"Here we go." She gritted her teeth.

"Go? Go where?" John looked ahead.

Another rumble and the ride spun into free fall. Her hands ripped from the bar and she was flung into his side from the force of gravity whizzing around them. She smashed into his rib cage and the breath left his lungs. "Bloody hell."

Instinctively, he dropped his arm to her shoulders, keeping her flush to his body for safety. He had no idea what he could do to protect her when it was clear an Amazon woman couldn't have fought the pressure that had spun her slight frame across the seat at forty miles an hour.

"How the hell do we stop this thing?" he yelled.

"I don't know." Her jaw was set in consternation.

His eyes widened as he stared at her profile. "You don't *know*."

"I thought—"

"No, Sasha. Thinking was the last thing you did."

"I know. I'm sorry." She turned.

John stared into her eyes. An apology from her was the last thing he thought he'd hear. Not today, tomorrow or ever. Her hair blew back and forth across her face, her brown-black eyes wide and beautiful.

He grimaced. "So, this isn't going according to plan, huh?"

Her gaze ran over his face to linger at his mouth. The ridiculousness of their situation gave way to physical awareness. The desire to kiss her filtered through his mind. To show her who was boss and stop this damn power play she had going on. His mouth went dry. What was she doing to him? This was not the plan *at all*. School was out for the summer and by the time the new semester started he'd be home and back at work where he belonged. Getting wrapped up in a woman, in Sasha, was not an option.

He tore his gaze from hers as they whipped to the other side of the ride once more. "I'll have to stop it."

"What? You can't. How will you get out of the seat, let alone anything else?"

Reluctantly, he slid his arm from her shoulders and attempted to lever an inch or two of space between them. "Try to pull away from me. Just a little so I can stand."

"Stand?" Her eyes widened to manic proportions. "Are you insane? Stay there. I'm not being held responsible for getting you killed."

He gritted his teeth and fought hard against the insistent pressure of the pulsating gravity holding them tightly together. His ass lifted about two inches before the ride shot off in another direction, landing him back on the seat with a violent shudder that reverberated up his spinal cord. "Bugger."

Her totally unfeminine snort and ensuing screech of hysterical laughter trembled through his body. They were well and truly glued to each other. His gut tightened as laughter tickled at the back of his throat. He turned and she looked at him with such delight, resistance was futile.

He tipped his head back and laughed harder and louder than he had in years.

SASHA COULDN'T DRAG her gaze from the totally masculine sight of his throat, faintly grazed with stubble, as the sound of his deep, toe-curling laugh hit her in the center of the stomach. The taut skin at his neck vibrated and the sensuous, joyous sound was captured on the wind and whisked into her box of memories before she could think to resist. She couldn't wipe the wide and undoubtedly stupid smile from her face.

He met her eyes. His shone with unshed tears. Bright blue like sapphires in the sun. Christ, what was she thinking? Sapphires in the bloody sun? She whipped her head around. She had to get off this damn ride. "Maybe we should try shouting for Freddy?"

"What?" He smiled.

Damn. He was more handsome than ever when he smiled. She closed her eyes. "Freddy!"

The screech of metal against metal ricocheted around them.

His laughter abruptly stopped and his body—so damn tight to hers, his biceps pushed her shoulder—stiffened. "What was that?"

She opened her eyes and stared ahead. Looking at him was far too dangerous to her game plan of throwing him totally for a loop—not that the plan was going all that well so far. "We're slowing down."

"But how? Wait. Did you know this thing would stop eventually?"

She shook her head and nodded toward the control booth. "Look."

He turned. The skewed image of Freddy showed behind the reinforced glass. "Thank God."

She screwed one eye shut and grimaced. "Maybe I shouldn't have—"

He stared for a long moment as the ride slowed before he lifted his arm from her shoulders and looked away. "You're right. You shouldn't have."

Realizing she was still pressed up against him without any need, Sasha hurriedly scooted away, leaving a foot-wide gap between them. Her heart raced. Had he just dismissed her? She looked at his hardened profile as he glared ahead at God only knew what.

"Do you know something?" She pulled back her shoulders. "I'm glad I did this. I wanted to see you knocked off-kilter for a while. You've no idea what it did to me, having you turn up here yesterday."

He turned. His eyes were midnight-blue with irritation. "And your response to that when you saw me sitting on this godforsaken ride was to pay me back by giving me whiplash?"

She bit back a smile. "Yes. Now I'm done."

"You're…" He shook his head and rolled his eyes heavenward. "She's done. My God."

They sat in strained silence as the ride took its merry time grinding to a halt. When it finally stopped, she leaned over and expertly released the mechanism locking the lap bar into place.

She shoved it upward, heedless of the fact he still gripped it. When his shoulders audibly clicked with the force of his arms almost leaving their sockets, she grimaced again.

"Sorry." She jumped from the ride and stormed toward the steps.

"Hey," Freddy shouted behind her.

God damn it. She turned. "What?"

He lumbered toward her. "What? Is that all you have to say?"

Heat pinched her cheeks. She'd acted recklessly. Anything could've happened. She and John could have been stuck on there. The circuit could've caught fire. She closed her eyes. "Just leave it, Freddy."

"What in God's name were you thinking?"

"She wasn't thinking, but that's my problem, not yours."

Sasha snapped her eyes open. John stood toe-to-toe with Freddy, their eyes locked in silent battle. Her heartbeat pulsed in her temple as the two of them faced off. She abhorred violence and hated anything remotely nasty or tainted. Why did things suddenly feel so much worse than they had since Kyle was locked up? Why had she started a fight with his son instead of playing nice and seeing what happened?

She cleared her throat. "Look, Freddy's right. I shouldn't have started the ride with no one controlling it. I was mad, and it was stupid."

After a few seconds, John nodded, his eyes still on Freddy. "There you go. She's sorry. Let's leave it at that. Sasha and I have somewhere to go this morning, so I want you to get the staff organized for opening this afternoon. Okay?"

Sasha stared. Going somewhere? Together? Alone? "Where?"

John glanced at her. "Just a minute." He turned to Freddy. "Okay?"

Freddy looked from him to Sasha, his suppressed anger showing in the reddening of his cheeks and inflating veins on his bald head. "Okay. I'll see you when I damn well see you then."

He flung a final scowl at her and John before stalking back toward the office. Sasha turned. John stared at her, his face a mask of angry determination. She swallowed. Her impetuous nature had once more turned around and bitten her in the ass.

"Well?" She forced her gaze to stay on his. "Where are we going?"

"Out."

"Out where?"

He released his crossed arms and closed the space between them. Standing at around six foot two, he towered above her five foot six.

His gaze traveled over her face. "I don't know anyone in this town. I don't know about any competition, tension or who the hell Kyle's enemies are. I need to know who, apart from you, is willing to pay good money to see me gone from Templeton before I've even had the chance for a cup of coffee in the local coffee shop. I want to know what I'm dealing with. You're the person to help me with that."

Unease rippled through her. "Why do you think I know Kyle's enemies?"

"You've worked here longer than anyone. You must know what he used this place for."

Revulsion swept a bitter taste into her throat. "I turn a blind eye to all that as much as possible. I hate what Kyle does. Hate it. I work here as manager only."

"You really expect me to believe that?" He shook his head. "I don't trust anyone with a connection to my father. That, unfortunately, includes you."

"How dare you."

He stared deep into her eyes for a moment before glancing over her head, his jaw tight. Sasha's stomach knotted with traitorous attraction. God, he looked like a model standing there, all dangerous and brooding....

He narrowed his eyes. "I dare, because it's beyond me how someone can claim to love something so much, but manage to tolerate a man who stepped on and then abandoned people whenever he wanted." His eyes were an icy blue. "Who are you, Sasha? That's what I want to know."

He turned away, and she gripped his arm. "Wait."

Anger seemed to burn from his skin, hot enough to scald her fingers through his jacket. Her hand slipped from his arm. A surge of unexpected sympathy rose behind her rib cage, and she quickly shook her head. "Nothing. Let's go."

He nodded stiffly before storming toward the office. Sasha remained welded to the grass. When he was out of sight, she released her held breath and slumped. Now what? She didn't want to be alone with him. That had never been part of the bargain. The frustration in his eyes from a moment before seeped into her conscience and lingered there, screaming with warning.

She sensed a pain as deep as hers in John…and that scared her. It took all her energy to fight the demons of her past and keep moving forward each day. She didn't need the pull of caring about someone else. Especially not Kyle's son, when it was Kyle who had unwittingly stopped her from bringing closure to her pain. Stopped her from winning a fifteen-year-old battle with Matt Davidson, the man who'd brought an end to her short-lived childhood.

She closed her eyes and her molester's face taunted her from behind closed lids. In a single summer, his actions had tainted the fair and tarnished what Sasha held dear. Well, sooner or later she'd make it hers and she'd make it a good, clean place for all its future visitors. She'd make it a magical, fun-filled adventure, as it had been before *him,* before everything *he* made her do.

Opening her eyes, Sasha exhaled a shaky breath and strode toward the office.

CHAPTER FIVE

SASHA FOLLOWED JOHN into the graveled parking lot outside the Funland gates with her chin high and her decorum well and truly restored. She'd grabbed her bag from the office while John gave a glowering Freddy a few instructions. The lack of information about their intended destination had infuriated her equally as much as a spitting and angry Freddy.

Her gaze wandered and then stuck to John's back as he marched ahead of her to his car. The temperature had risen and hovered at a pleasant eighty degrees. He'd removed his jacket and his broad, muscular back and strong shoulders shifted rhythmically beneath cotton as he strode forward. The guy's butt didn't look any worse in trousers than it did in denim—which initiated another tug on her already fraught nerves. Nerves that seemed constantly pooled in her damn panties.

He stopped beside a metallic blue Mercedes convertible and pointed his keys. Sasha stared in awed fascination as the roof slowly rolled backward into the open trunk with smooth, expensive precision. The cost of his car alone would probably keep her in rent payments for the remainder of the decade. She lifted her chin higher. His wealth wouldn't intimidate her. No doubt Kyle had kept his son well-cared for over the years. There was no pride in handouts as far as she was concerned.

When he walked to the passenger side rather than the driver's, her gait faltered. What was he doing? He opened the door and waved toward the seat. Sasha narrowed her eyes. If he thought a show of old-fashioned gallantry would penetrate her immovable anger, he'd better think again.

Yeah? So why are your cheeks hot and your stomach flying into a frenzy?

Forcing her eyes to his, she smiled. "Thank you."

"You're welcome."

She slid onto butter-soft leather, and the door closed with a gentle, moneyed clunk. He walked around the hood and slipped on a pair of dark sunglasses. "So…" He turned on the ignition and the car purred to life. "Where are we headed first?"

Deciding she needed to up her game, Sasha pulled on her femme-fatale persona and faced him. Whether or not she was letting down the entire female population, she had to at least attempt to get John off his damn sexy winning streak. She was seriously lagging behind and it rankled. Her defense was to always be in the lead as far as sex was concerned. It was vital. If she gave up a modicum of trust, things could get out of her control very quickly.

"Why don't we hit the town center first?" She smiled softly and looked at him from beneath lowered lashes. "I'm sure we'll bump into plenty of people I can introduce you to there."

He hesitated, a slight frown creasing his forehead. "You okay?"

"I'm fine."

"Only you've got a strange look in your eye."

Hah! She lifted an eyebrow. "Am I making you uncomfortable?"

"No, just concerned. You look as though you're sitting on something painful."

Her smile dissolved, and she shot him a glare before slumping back into her seat. "Just drive, will you?"

He threw the car into gear, and they left the parking lot. Sasha glanced at him from the corner of her eye. He wore the biggest smile known to man, yet instead of it annoying her, it made her want to smile, too.

"We're quite a pair, aren't we?" He grinned.

Wishing she could see his eyes and have at least a moderate idea of what he was thinking, she blew out a breath. "Meaning?"

"Well, we haven't stopped arguing or trying to outdo each other since we met."

"I'm not trying to *outdo* you. I'm trying to figure you out."

He glanced at her, one dark eyebrow rising above

his sunglasses. "And what conclusions have you jumped to?"

She scowled. "Who says I've jumped? Maybe my conclusions are spot-on."

He faced front. "Care to share them with me?"

Inexplicable nerves knotted her stomach as his smile vanished and his brow furrowed. It was pointless trying to deny how much more attractive she found the laughing, smiling John to the quiet, dangerous one.

She cleared her throat and focused on the road ahead. "I might be wrong, but I get the impression you're in Templeton under duress."

Silence.

She pressed on. "Am I right?"

He maneuvered the car through the traffic, his jaw tight.

When it was clear he wasn't going to provide an answer, Sasha's palms turned unusually clammy. "So, you're not going to tell me how you've found yourself in this unfortunate situation?"

"I don't know if it's unfortunate yet."

Curiosity sparked like a flint inside her. "I would've thought you'd have come to that decision upon our first meeting. I wasn't exactly welcoming. And then the decidedly chilly phone call...followed by this morning's fun and games—"

"Where you attempted a full-on assassination." He glanced at her. "There's nothing you or anyone else in this town could do that would be worse than what Kyle's done. Don't worry about your hostility toward me since I arrived…I'm not."

A strange sensation skittered through her chest at his clear dismissal of her actions…and her. Cursing the heat that struck her chest and face, she looked to the side at the passing facades of the pretty, pastel-painted Victorian houses turned bed-and-breakfasts. She blinked against the frustration burning her eyes. "Great, well, that's good. If there's any chance of this working out, we need to get along."

"You don't want this to work out."

She snapped her head around. "What?"

"Didn't you say you have an offer for me? For the fair? That means you want me out of here ASAP."

Sasha glared, wishing for a second time he'd remove his stupid glasses. Moreover, she wished they weren't driving this fancy bloody car with him in the actual, and metaphorical, driver's seat. "Yeah, and God willing, you want the same."

"I don't know what I want yet, so don't hold your breath."

Sasha curled her hands tighter around the straps of her bag in her lap. Her passion for the fair was so deeply seated no one but her grandfather and her best friend, Leah, could possibly understand what John Jordon's presence did to her.

The man confused her. Gave her zero to work with…or on. She had to figure out a way to break through his ice-cold veneer whenever they talked about Kyle. She'd made him smile a few times, which was one thing, but clearly anything to do with his father sparked a livid anger she'd be hard-pressed to break.

She couldn't lose this chance to make the fair hers again. Not now. Not after all the careful planning and waiting. She breathed deep. It was always best to tackle a challenge head-on. Not avoid the ugly and sit safe in the pretty. That achieved nothing. If she could figure out how much loyalty he had to Kyle, she'd know how much of a barrier John would erect against selling Funland to her—and how likely he was to find a way out of that godforsaken, and possibly devastating, clause. She swallowed. "I've got a question."

He glanced at her. "Hmm?"

"Why don't you call Kyle 'Dad'? Seeing he's summoned you here and kicked Freddy to the curb, I'm assuming your father trusts you, otherwise why would he—"

"Kyle called me here because he can't afford to trust anyone else. You and I both know he has enemies all over Templeton and beyond. I'm here because he's halfway up shit creek without a paddle. Believe me, if he could've asked anyone else to ensure all his loose ends were tied up, he would have."

"But you're his son. It makes sense he'd—"

"Son?" He eased to a stop at a red light. "He slept with my mother. That's it." He whipped his sunglasses from his face and tossed them onto the dash. "He's not my *dad*. That's the first and last time I hope to have to tell you that."

His glare was a strange, complicated mix of sadness and anger that struck Sasha's chest like a demolition ball.

"What the hell happened between you two?" she whispered.

His broad chest rose and fell beneath the tight stretch of his shirt as his gaze left hers and wandered over her face, coming to a stop at her mouth. "We'll never have enough time together for me to tell you what happened between Kyle and me so let's just concentrate on why we've been thrown together like this. Business, Sasha. We talk business only from now on."

She pursed her lips and turned away from his mesmerizing blue eyes, her body rigid with a nervousness she'd never experienced around his father. The anger emanating from John was in no way normal, yet she didn't sense any violence in him like she had in Kyle. In John, there was only sadness—and a whole dollop of a man recovering from huge betrayal.

The question was, what the hell did he intend to do about it? And would she get caught in the guaranteed and dangerous cross fire?

JOHN TRIED AND failed to level his breathing as he pressed hard on the gas and screeched away from the light. Damn Sasha and her incessant questions.

Her intelligent, far-too-aware gaze didn't help, either. Did she ever quit interfering? Or flirting? John inwardly cursed. Flirting? She wasn't flirting—he damn well *wanted* her to flirt. That was the crux of his frustration and he was more angry about that than anything Kyle had exposed him to so far.

He tightened his grip on the steering wheel.

God, he didn't want to shout at Sasha and he certainly didn't want to frighten her. He loved women. Loved the kids he worked with even more. His father had already seeped into his blood, turning him into someone he'd constantly fought so hard not to be. An angry, bitter man like Kyle.

The busy road caused him to stop and start in a long queue of traffic, bringing his nerves to the point of breaking. A tense silence hung heavy in the air, pressing on his chest and making him want to apologize as they slowed to a stop at a junction. He couldn't show her a single facet of the personality he left in Oxford. The funny, kind history teacher whom the staff held in high regard because "he has a way with the kids," or the guy who scribbled away at a Tudor mystery novel in his spare time. John smiled wryly.

God, he'd love to know what she thought of *that* John Jordon.

He sensed her study of him and turned. Her brow was furrowed, her eyes almost black as she stared with open curiosity. He snapped his eyes to the windshield and his armor slid into place with a resounding *clunk* inside his head. He'd been a good man, a good teacher and mentor for a long time. He liked that person and intended keeping him under wraps for the entirety of his time in the Cove. More and more people would soon know he was here and wonder why. He would find a way to leave Kyle without a penny of his immoral earnings and then leave.

Forging friendships—he glanced at Sasha—and starting to like people was out of the question. If he kept up the mystery surrounding himself, no one need know how he was venting an anger so deep it was shameful. The less Sasha got to know him, the easier he could leave town guilt-free because she had no idea who he really was and how much John actually cared about Kyle and the life he'd led without his only son.

Exhaling through gritted teeth, John swallowed his pride. One of them had to take the high road in the face-off growing at high velocity between them. "You're going to have to give me directions to wherever it is you think we should head first."

"What were you just thinking?"

God damn it. Can't she keep any thoughts to herself? Lord knows it isn't that difficult. "Nothing. Where are we going?"

"Fine."

He stole another look at her as she hitched her elbow on the door and stared toward the amusement arcades lit up like a mini-Vegas beside them.

She sighed theatrically, waved her hand nonchalantly. "You want to play it cool and not afford me the luxury of getting to know you better, we'll go to Marian's. Maybe she'll break you." She laughed. "Scrap that. I *know* she'll break you."

"First of all, no one is breaking anyone. Second of all, who's Marian? The idea isn't morning coffee at someone's house. I want to discover the hubbub of this supposedly quaint seaside town."

"Supposedly quaint?"

He edged the car forward in the slow-moving traffic. "I'll admit, on the surface Templeton Cove looks nice, picturesque, interesting even, but anywhere my father decided to live and work can't be any of those things once a person scratches the surface."

She scowled. "Templeton Cove isn't Kyle's creation, you know. The people who live here built this place. The decent people. The people who do their utmost to keep it clean, friendly and welcoming for the thousands of visitors who come every year. Not to mention the hundreds of people who live good, honest lives here. Your father was nothing more than a damn blemish on its crystal-blue horizon. And I for one say good bloody riddance to him."

John smiled. "Bingo. Something we agree on."

She glared. "We're not agreed on anything until I know for sure what you want. How can you expect me to believe you're not just going to pick up the illegal reins now Kyle's gone? Why else would he pass over Freddy unless he knew you were much more of a suitable candidate for what he had in mind?"

John's smile slipped. "I'm not here to pick up Kyle's reins."

"Then why?" Her eyes were hard, determined.

A horn sounded behind him, and she jumped. John snapped his gaze to the front. An empty gap of at least two car lengths stretched from the hood of his car to the junction. Cursing, he accelerated forward. "Which way?"

"Left."

He joined the main road leading into town. "So, who's Marian?"

"I assume the change of subject is your way of telling me to mind my own business?"

"I'm not answering any questions as far as Kyle's concerned."

She sniffed. "Fine."

The next few seconds passed in strained silence before John released a heavy breath. "Is Marian a friend of yours?"

She sighed. "She owns a bakery by the beach-front. We'll grab a coffee and I'll introduce you. If you've got any strength left in that muscled body of yours once Marian's finished with you, it'll be a miracle."

Muscled body? John savored the thought she'd noticed his body. At least it wasn't just him imagining the heat between them. He shook his head and smiled. "If you haven't managed to upset me, I don't believe for one minute this Marian can be any more of a pain in the butt. I'll be fine."

John glanced at her and raised an eyebrow. She shot him a glare before turning to look out the side of the car. Score to him. He'd only driven a few hundred yards when brown-and-white signs along the side of the road indicated the beach, thus leading him in the general direction without the need for further conversation. Pressing on the gas, he concentrated on looking for the bakery, rather than the continual distraction of Sasha's shapely legs showing beneath the hem of her white shorts.

He didn't have to look far. A long queue of patrons waited to get inside Marian's Bonniest Bakery. The shiny blue-and-white awning over the window boasted the owner's name in bold white letters. As he drew closer, the smell of coffee and sweetness, which could only be the result of jelly doughnuts, brownies and every other sweet treat known to man, teased his nostrils.

"And here we are." He pulled alongside the curb.

She sighed. "I am *so* looking forward to a cup of coffee...and this particular introduction."

She leaned to the side and snapped off her seat belt. The caress of her dark hair brushed his forearm where he held the stick shift. John snatched his arm away, but not before her perfume hit him. The soft, floral and incredibly feminine scent shouldn't have suited a woman so kick-ass, stubborn and mouthy as her, yet it did…perfectly. When his dick twitched in appreciation, he hurriedly removed his seat belt and yanked the keys from the ignition. "Let's go."

He snatched his glasses from the dash, opened the door and slammed it shut. He headed around the hood, but she was already waiting on the sidewalk before he had a chance to open her door. He dropped his outstretched hand to his side.

She stared at the bakery's facade. "This place is never quiet, so even though I haven't a clue what you're expecting to gain from talking to a few people, you'll have plenty to choose from." She pointed toward the queue, a wide grin displaying her beautiful teeth. "Let's wait in line, shall we?"

Still trying to figure out why she appeared to find the whole idea of him stepping inside the bakery so funny, John slipped on his glasses and followed her to the end of the queue. The line moved quickly as people ducked out of the shop and more entered. Four out of the five who came outside carried blue-and-white striped boxes as well as lidded cups of coffee.

"Seems everyone in town missed breakfast."

"Believe me, it's hard to leave Marian's with just the coffee you came in for. You'll find that out soon enough."

"I don't think so. I'm more a pastry-and-pie kind of guy."

She laughed. "Then you're a goner whether you like it or not."

"What do you—"

"See?" She pressed her finger to the window, and John leaned over her shoulder to get a closer look.

Struggling not to inhale the scent of her again, his gaze fell on the trays of golden-brown pastries and breads, crispy sausage rolls and slices of homemade, ridiculously loaded pizza. He swallowed. "They have a gym in town, right?"

She laughed and pulled back, her shoulder bumping the center of his chest. He purposely and cruelly planted his feet solidly on the ground, waiting to see what she would do. The flush of color that rose in her face sent a rush of hot male pride through his veins. He had her trapped between his body and the window. The seconds pulsed between them as he studied her mouth.

He couldn't deny Sasha had that *thing*. That special something that was effortlessly sexy in a handful of women—and made men want to dance around them in some strange prehistoric mating ritual.

She reached up and whipped the glasses from his face so fast they scraped painfully across his nose. He winced. "Hey—"

"No fair. You want to get all macho and moody on me, let me see your face." She pushed the glasses into his chest and shoved him away to stand in front of him, then turned her back to him.

Grinning, he stared at the crown of her beautiful head, took the time to study her amazing mane of jet-black hair that fell almost to her waist. Why did someone come to work at a fairground and leave their hair loose like that? His gaze traveled lower over her butt. Unless of course, she purposely left it that way for his benefit. It had been tied up into a high ponytail when they'd met last night....

"Stop staring at my ass."

He snapped his gaze up. "I'm not."

"Windows are reflective."

He turned to the window and their eyes locked in the glass. *Shit.* He shrugged. "Better I look and appreciate than don't, right?"

"Pervert."

She faced front as the queue moved forward and they stepped inside. Eight booths big enough to comfortably sit six people each lined a window at the far side, with tables scattered throughout, and a huge deli counter covering the breadth of the shop at the back. The atmosphere was relaxed and cheerful as bursts of laughter mixed with the chatter from the customers, and shouts and calls came from behind the busy serving area.

He pulled his wallet from his back pocket and slipped out a ten-pound note. "Why don't you grab us a table and I'll do the honors. What are you drinking?"

She tipped her head back and met his eyes. "Cappuccino would be great. Thanks. I'll be right over there at the front of the counter. I don't want to miss any of the action."

He frowned. "What action?"

She wiggled her eyebrows and left the queue. John followed her progress as she sashayed between the tables. She hung the strap of her bag on the back of a pine chair and sat, propping her elbows atop the gingham tablecloth. She intertwined her fingers and rested her chin on them, her dark gaze locked on his, a soft smile playing at her lips.

When his dick woke up again, John snatched his gaze from hers and approached the counter. The young girl serving was busy putting the change in the till from the previous customer. She didn't bother looking up when she spoke. "Yes, sir, what can I get you?"

"A black coffee and a cappuccino, please."

"Coming right up." She slammed the till closed and finally met his eyes. "Oh…wow." Her cheeks flushed a deep red before she turned and headed for the huge steel coffeemaker behind her.

Frowning, John slipped his glasses into the vee of his shirt.

"Well, hello there. And who might you be."

The woman who appeared in front of him tossed him a wide grin. She was ample in stature and, judging by the glint in her eye, intended to eat him alive. Straightening his shoulders, he held out his hand. "John Jordon. Nice to meet you."

Her smile vanished and the glint disappeared as

if a storm had blown in and snuffed out a candle. "Well, well, well."

John glanced over his shoulder toward Sasha as unease rolled up his spine. Her grin widened. He turned back to the woman behind the counter and dropped his offered hand. "Is everything okay, ma'am?"

She narrowed her eyes and crossed her arms, pushing her rather generous bosom to rest on top of them. "I don't know. We'll have to give it a little time before either of us knows, won't we?"

John raised his hands in surrender. "I just came in for coffee."

"Where's Sasha?" She ran her gaze over his chest. "You left her to run that fairground on her own? Or is that good-for-nothing Freddy Campton down there shouting the odds?"

Ah, so this is Marian. He smiled. "Marian, right?"

She didn't as much as lift the corners of her mouth. "The one and only."

Seconds passed before John tilted his head in Sasha's direction, keeping his gaze on Marian's. "Sasha's over there. No doubt enjoying the show."

Marian slid her gaze toward Sasha and the transformation in her demeanor was so ridiculous, John was struck dumb. Her face broke into a wide smile and her eyes lit with adoration before she dropped her arms and hastily wiped them on the towel hanging from the waistband of her apron. She waved at

Sasha. "I'll be right over." She turned to John and the smile vanished. "Go grab a seat. I'll bring your coffees over."

Giving up hope of a friendly exchange, John lifted his shoulders. "Great. Thank you."

He approached Sasha and stared at her. "Enjoying yourself?"

"Absolutely."

"I'm guessing you and Matron Marian are pretty close?"

Sasha laughed. "If she hears you call her that, she'll slice your balls off quicker than you can draw your next breath."

"Is that so?"

She grinned. "Yep. You're in for one hell…" Her gaze drifted to a spot behind him and her eyes lit up like they had lanterns behind them. "Oh, great. More company."

John spun around. Marian walked toward them carrying their coffees. Beside her was a woman with the reddest hair and greenest eyes he'd ever seen. If he thought Marian was prepared to eat him alive, the careful appraisal of this latest Templeton Cove resident left him no doubt she'd be more than willing to hold him down while Marian executed her chosen sadistic pleasure.

They stopped in front of him, and Marian glared. "Inspector Garrett, let me introduce you to Mr. John Jordon."

CHAPTER SIX

SASHA SWIPED THE tears of laughter from her eyes and pushed to her feet. Marian was one thing, but leaving John to cope with Inspector Garrett *and* Marian was too much to expect of any man, animal or superhero. She'd begun the day with plans to make John's welcome as uncomfortable as possible, but her fiasco on the Mixer and him making her laugh meant unnecessary cruelty was no longer part of the deal.

She stepped away from the table to stand at his side. She smiled. "Inspector Garrett. Nice to see you."

The inspector dragged her steady gaze from John's and smiled. "Hi, Sasha. Marian seems keen to introduce me to your friend."

A sudden and inexplicable need to defend John stole through Sasha. She didn't want to leave him to the wolves. Something about him intrigued her, interested her to the point she didn't want that tiny, unnamable facet of his personality quashed on his second day in the Cove.

Her sympathy was unnerving and she swallowed

hard against its implication. She waved her hand in what she hoped was a gesture of indifference. "John's…um… John's…"

"Why don't I help you out?" Marian placed their coffees none too gently on the table. "This, Inspector Garrett, is John Jordon—Kyle Jordon's son and heir."

Sasha grimaced. The entire bakery descended into silence, barely broken by the clatter of crockery and the occasional cough or snigger. Marian's booming voice was her trademark, the reason people warmed to her and loved her—but in that moment, Sasha understood why others dreaded her undivided attention. The queue of people turned toward the show, and Sasha's cheeks burned.

John, on the other hand, appeared nonplussed as he extended his hand to Inspector Garrett. "Nice to meet you, Inspector."

With her usual cool air, the inspector closed her hand around his. "Are you planning to stay long, Mr. Jordon? Or is this a flying visit?"

He raised his eyebrows. "Does it matter?"

Sasha whipped her gaze from one to the other. It was crystal clear as John stood unmoving in front of DI Garrett, his cool gaze locked with hers, he was Kyle's son. He was no more concerned by the inspector's perusal of him than Kyle would've been.

The inspector stared straight back, her intelligent gaze scrutinizing him. Sasha shifted from one foot to the other. Confrontation was never a good thing for her, regardless of the "don't mess with me" reputation she liked to project. Her persona had been forced upon her and maybe even branded her—but she also accepted, acknowledged and embraced it as if it were a powerful and protective coat of armor. Nothing and no one made her inferior to anyone or anything else.

Pulling back her shoulders, she shook off the vivid memories that never went away and stepped forward. She cupped her hand around John's elbow. "We just came in for morning coffee, Inspector. Maybe you'd like to join us?"

Inspector Garrett continued to look at John. "Your father was a known figure around here, Mr. Jordon. Known for the wrong reasons. I hope you're not going to give me any concerns while you're here."

"Am I being tarred with the same brush already? Just because Kyle and I share a name?"

The hairs on Sasha's neck quivered. The cool tone of his voice and stiff set of his shoulders screamed of Kyle, yet John's smooth, upper-class accent and undeterred self-confidence showed someone else entirely. Kyle was easily provoked, his temper a tangible and undeniable aspect of his feared potential for violence. Whereas John's relaxed, immovable stance showed an equitable man, open to reason and discussion. It drew Sasha to him with a force she neither liked nor wanted.

The inspector tilted her chin. "I'm not the kind

of cop who jumps to conclusions, Mr. Jordon. That doesn't mean the rest of the town won't."

He glanced over her head toward the spectators, then at Marian and finally at Sasha. She met his gaze and silently pleaded with him to back down. She didn't want him to fight the inspector but instead, sit with her and prove himself completely unlike Kyle. He briefly closed his eyes and dropped his shoulders. Sasha's heart picked up speed as she waited.

He faced the inspector and raised his hands in surrender. "Why don't you join us? Ask me anything you'd like to know. I've nothing to hide."

Marian sniffed. "Hmm."

Inspector Garrett shook her head. "I've no wish to harangue you, Mr. Jordon. Enjoy your coffee. Now I know you're in town, I hope I've no reason to be anything other than civil should we bump into each other." She turned to Marian and raised an eyebrow. "I hope the same goes for everyone else, too."

Marian opened her mouth, her cheeks flame-red with indignation. "But—"

"Because the people of Templeton Cove are good people." The inspector stared at Marian. "We don't judge without reason."

Sasha released her held breath. "Thank you, Inspector. I'll be working with John at the fair. Feel free to drop by anytime."

Inspector Garrett drew her gaze slowly over

John's face once more. "Thank you, Sasha. I might just do that. Nice to meet you, Mr. Jordon." She offered her hand.

John shook it with a curt nod. "You, too."

When Inspector Garrett gripped Marian's elbow and steered her toward the counter, Sasha mirrored the action by steering John to their table. She only released him once he sat. She slid into the chair opposite him. "Well, there you go."

He stared at her, his blue eyes dark with irritation. "What?"

"That's the reaction you're going to get around Templeton. Surely you didn't expect any different when you planned this little tour this morning?"

"How often did my father show his face here? Around town?"

His tone was cold, his eyes somber. The question hadn't been the first she'd expected. Didn't he want to know where Marian got off treating him like a second-class citizen? Didn't he want to know about Inspector Garrett? She lifted her shoulders. "Not much. He was either at Funland or off in his car somewhere."

"What about his business associates?"

Sasha felt a sudden disquiet and glanced toward the inspector, who stood at the counter waiting for her coffee. Marian shot Sasha another glare and she snapped her gaze to John's. "I don't know."

"You must know something."

"I don't."

Silence descended and the tension escalated. After a long moment and no sign of their coffees, Sasha pushed to her feet. "Let's go. I don't feel comfortable talking about Kyle here."

She made for the door, heedless of the stares of Inspector Garrett, Marian and the other pairs of eyes burning holes in her back. She shouldered past the queue of people filing into the bakery, her emotions torn. Why did she have to care about people so damn much? Why did everything come down to wanting people to be happy and enjoying themselves? When would she reach the jaded age of adulthood when she wouldn't give a crap about anyone but herself?

She shouldn't have backed up John—he was big enough to handle himself and from what she'd witnessed so far, nothing shook his cool exterior. She'd never know if he fought daily demons as she did, and for that she was grateful. She liked him, and because of that she prayed that once she had gotten the fair from him, he'd disappear as quickly as he had come. He tugged on something she'd thought stolen from her years ago. He tugged on her need for a man to care about her.

Swallowing hard, Sasha drew in a strengthening breath, drawing her protective cloak around her. The warm July sunshine hit her face as she stepped from beneath the shade of the bakery awning and leaned on the hood of John's Mercedes. Maybe the sight of her butt on his fancy, expensive car might break his cool. He emerged from the bakery and approached her. He didn't so much as blink to see her leaning on the hood of his car and instead stepped off the curb. He stood directly in front of her and the parked car behind him.

"Why did you leave like that? It would've been beneficial for us to face them out in there. Show it's us running the fair now, not Kyle."

She stiffened. "Us, John? Is that what you really think?"

"Don't you?"

His gaze bored into hers. Sasha's heart beat wildly, and her hands turned clammy. In all the time Kyle had run her and her granddad's lives, not once had he indicated they were on the same team, in even the smallest of ways. Funland was Kyle's, from the dirt on the ground to every lightbulb on every ride. Her heart twisted and she looked away. "Don't say things like that. You and I both know you couldn't possibly believe it."

"Why not? Hey..." He touched his finger to her chin, gently turning her face. "Why not?"

Heat assaulted her cheeks as a bolt of God knew what shot through her body on such intimate and gentle contact. What the hell was he doing? Why was he playing her like this? She pushed away from the hood and marched to the passenger side. More important, why the hell was she letting him? She fisted her hands on her hips. "Open the car. I want to get out of here."

She glanced past him toward the bakery window. She could practically feel the heat coming through the glass as Marian self-combusted inside.

He stared at her for a moment longer before pulling his keys from his pocket. The locks shunted open, and Sasha yanked the door and got inside. She pulled on her seat belt, her hands shaking. He slid in beside her, and the scent of musk and man rose between them, only to be torn away by the gathering breeze.

He turned the ignition. “We need to talk. Properly.”

“We will.” She stared ahead. “Right now I want to work. Funland needs me, John. The sooner you get that, the better.”

THE FOLLOWING NIGHT, Sasha entered the Coast Inn and approached the bar. It was Saturday night and the place was busy with patrons, but not so busy that she felt the need to turn around and leave. As desperate as she was to talk with her best friend alone, Sasha also wanted the cover of human bodies should John or Freddy decide they needed a drink as much as she did. This way she and Leah could make a dive for the back door with a better chance of escaping unnoticed.

“What can I get you?”

She plastered on a smile as the bar’s owner came to stand in front of her. “Hi, Dave. Can I get a glass of pinot gris for me and a merlot for Leah?”

"Sure." He turned to get the bottle of white out of the fridge. "Haven't seen you here in a while. You okay?" He filled her glass and placed it on a coaster.

Am I okay? Now, there's a question. She took a sip of her drink. "I'm great. Busy as always."

He eyed her carefully as he unscrewed the cap of the merlot. "Are you sure about that? I heard Kyle Jordon's son turned up."

She met his eyes for a moment before feigning interest in the black-and-white prints of Templeton Cove adorning the wall to the side of her. "Yep."

"And?"

She faced him. "We're working it out. I'm getting to know him and he's getting to know me."

He placed Leah's drink on a second coaster and lifted an eyebrow. "Marian said he's a good-looking chap and she's watching him. Do I need to watch him, too?"

Sasha smiled and slumped her shoulders. "No. I've got it under control. You can simmer down and tell Marian to do the same the next time you see her, okay?"

Dave winked. "You know we're only looking out for you."

"I know." She lifted the drinks from the bar. "It's appreciated, but John's all right…considering."

"Considering what?"

"Considering I'm still giving him the benefit of the doubt." She smiled. "If at any point I think the guy needs reminding I've got the whole of Templeton looking out for me, I'll let you know."

He laughed. "I'm always here. You know that."

She lifted her glass in a salute before turning and heading purposefully to a table as far away as possible from the small dance floor in one corner and the pool table and dart nook in the other. Despite her bravado with Dave, Sasha's heart hammered with nerves. John Jordon was far from "all right" as far as her body was concerned.

The man was a walking, talking magnet to her libido and that meant trouble whichever way she looked at it.

She was used to mental and emotional knock backs, used to people pulling her from her intended path, but John Jordon was a different challenge than any she'd faced before. His cool blue stare and bright, sudden smile jolted her. Made her waver, doubt and feel. She cursed. Even now, she wanted to smile because she thought of him.

He was…interesting. That was it. Interesting… and phenomenal to look at.

She sat down and stared into the golden depths of her glass, twirling the stem back and forth with her fingers as the past twenty-four hours played through her mind. Once they'd return to work after leaving Marian's, it became very clear, very quickly, both she and John had individually made the decision to keep their distance. It had been almost comical how they avoided each other, barely sharing more than a sentence or two for the rest of yesterday and all of today.

Freddy brooded and snorted his way around the fair, casting glares at her, John or anyone else in his line of sight. The atmosphere was stretched to breaking with the three of them biding their time to see who would cut the first inch and let some of the pressure escape.

Well, it won't be me. Not yet. I want to know what both of my opponents have in mind before I decide what to do next. One wrong move and everything I have planned will crash and burn.

The bar door swung open and Sasha lifted her gaze. Leah, her best friend of the past ten years, came striding toward her, seemingly in time with the drumbeat of the soft rock ballad blasting from the speakers. Her blond, short-cropped hair and dark-rimmed glasses belied her friend's soft nature. At five-three, new patients could've made the mistake of thinking Nurse Dixon a pushover...until she showed them who was boss with a syringe inserted into their bare ass cheek.

On a personal level, Leah was more cocker spaniel than rottweiler, but nobody would know that at Templeton A&E.

Her friend collapsed into the chair opposite Sasha, her brow furrowed and her cheeks flushed pink. "Wine. Fabulous."

Sasha raised her eyebrow as Leah downed a

hefty gulp and set the glass down with a satisfied smile. "Ahh, better. Much better."

"Good day?" Sasha grinned.

Leah pinned Sasha with a glare, her huge hazel eyes glinting with a trace of potential violence. "Just peachy. I had to sew up a kid whose father decided he didn't like the way his son was taking up so much of his mother's time. He thumped him and split his eyebrow wide open to prove his point."

Sasha's smile dissolved and she gritted her teeth. "You deserve a medal working in the E.R. I'd be more likely to inflict further injury than fix them up."

"Yeah, well, they train us to fight the urge to exact justice." Leah took another gulp of wine. "So, what's up? I love that we get to have a drink on a Saturday night." She smiled and shifted forward on her seat. "It's great you're actually doing something with your night off rather than working."

Sasha laughed. "You're not really the person to tell me off for the hours I work."

Leah grimaced. "Fair enough. So? What's going on?"

"On? Or wrong?"

"Ah."

Sasha inhaled a shaky breath and released it. "I've got a new boss."

"What are you talking about?" Leah frowned. "I thought you were going to give Kyle your offer this week. What happened?"

"His son turned up."

Leah's eyes widened. "You're kidding me."

"I wish I was."

"Kyle has a son?"

"Yep."

"Well, what's he like? Kyle in a younger, uglier form? If that's possible."

Sasha sighed. "I wish."

"Meaning?"

"Meaning, he's the handsomest man I've ever seen. All dark hair, blue eyes, built like a freaking model and about seven feet tall. He makes me feel..." Sasha shook her head. "Like a girl."

Leah's glass halted at her lips and she slowly returned it to the table. "Uh-oh."

Sasha closed her eyes, her shoulders slumping under the impending doom of any man stripping her off her tough, tomboy persona. "Exactly."

"What are you going to do?"

"I don't know." She opened her eyes. "He's barely said a word to me since yesterday morning and I've no idea what his intentions are. I was so close. So damn close to at least getting Kyle's attention back on my offer for the fair. Now this happens."

"What's his son's name? Have you told him about the offer?"

Sasha lifted her wine and took a sip. "John. And he knows about the offer. I told him. He also knows Mum hates the place and that I want it." She stared at her friend. "He asked me why Funland means so much to me. He said it can't be all about family if Mum wants nothing to do with it."

Leah's intense gaze softened with concern. "Your reasons are none of his damn business. All he should be asking about is the money."

"I know that."

Leah eased her hand across the table and grasped Sasha's. She squeezed her fingers. "He doesn't need to know what happened to you there. Your reasons for wanting Funland have nothing to do with anyone else. You've never felt you could even trust your mother to understand what happened and why you want to make it yours, let alone some bloke who's clearly shaken you up."

Sasha squeezed Leah's fingers in return before removing her hand to brush the hair from her face. "Do you think I'm mad?"

"Mad?"

"For wanting Funland. For wanting to make it good again. I know it's probably completely irrational but, for me, it's the only way to erase *him* for good."

"Hey..." Leah leaned across the table, her gaze intense and full of conviction. "That, my girl, is all that matters. If you owning Funland is the only way for you to deal with what happened to you, so be it. Don't let anyone tell you you're wrong. The animal who hurt you was one individual. One bastard who got away with hurting kids and then disappeared off the face of the earth. I believe you can make Funland an amazing place again. Don't give up, okay?"

Sasha smiled as relief she wasn't insane shuddered through her. "I'm so glad I've got you on my side, you know."

Leah grinned. "And I'm glad I've got you on mine. Between us, we've got enough baggage to fill an airport lost-property department, but who cares as long as we've got each other's backs, right?"

"Cheers to that." Sasha clinked her glass to Leah's and they each took a sip. She lowered her glass to the table and sighed. "It's weird. He almost frightens me."

She frowned. "Who? This John guy?"

Sasha nodded.

"You don't think he's dangerous, do you?" Leah's gaze darkened. "I don't want you working there if for one minute you think—"

"No. Not in the way you mean. I've never..." She swallowed. "I've never felt such an instant pull to someone in my life. You know what I'm like with men, what I've *made* myself like with them. He's... different." She smiled softly. "I kind of like him."

Leah raised her eyebrows and leaned back. "Wow."

"I know. No idea why I should." Sasha shook her head. "He should be on my hit list, for crying out loud, but there's something about him. I don't think he likes Kyle any more than I do. I think he's hurting, Leah. Really hurting...like me."

"You mean…"

"I'm not saying he's been sexually abused. I'm saying he knows hurt, real hurt. He's got that… thing. That anger, that open wound, and it comes off him in waves."

For a long moment, Leah said nothing, and Sasha tried not to squirm under her friend's scrutiny. Eventually, Leah smiled. "I think this guy is here for a reason, but be careful. Just because he stirs something inside you, doesn't mean he's not his father."

Sasha released her held breath as unease quivered up her spine. "I know." She drained her glass. "Drink up. Tonight we'll have some fun and come Monday morning, I'll feel better. I'll be back to normal and ready to find out for sure what John Jordon's plans are."

CHAPTER SEVEN

MONDAY MORNING WAS an early start for John and he couldn't deny there was something about waking up in Templeton Cove rather than in the inner city that instantly cleared the senses. He breathed in the sea air as he walked through the empty fair and into the office. It was barely eight and everything was eerily quiet.

The quietness, the faraway sound of seagulls and the roll of the ocean should have felt alien to him. It was far too soon for him to be feeling the appeal of life in this small seaside town, yet still it inched over his shoulders.

Had his father felt the same thing when he first came to Templeton years before?

God, he didn't want to even have *that* in common with the man. He wanted to continue to hate him as much as he always had. Time and again, he kicked himself for not ripping up Kyle's letter asking him to come here. Yet, here he was. Still in Templeton.

More than once, John had left Kyle's Templeton Cove mansion over the weekend, suitcase in hand, and headed for his car. He'd gotten as far as sitting in the driver's seat before getting out and going back inside.

He unlocked the office door and entered, tossing his jacket onto the back of his chair and sitting down. He slid the file box he carried onto the desk before lifting his feet onto the desk to rest next to the box, crossing his legs at the ankles. John leaned back and closed his eyes.

Somehow, he had to find the tenacity to stay and see his intentions through. He had to know who his father was now, and who he'd been when he shot and killed the man who murdered his wife—John's mother—nineteen years before. Once he found whatever the hell it was he was searching for to release the bitter resentment eating him from the inside out, he'd leave Templeton and never again have to think about the man who had abandoned him.

He opened his eyes and looked toward Sasha's desk at the opposite side of the room. His stomach instantly knotted. If he frittered away or gave away Kyle's earnings, would that extinguish the fire in his belly? Make John happier than he was now? Or did the annihilation lie *within* someone else…or maybe within himself? He'd be a liar if he said his draw to stay longer in the Cove hadn't been perpetuated by the exotic-looking and passionate Sasha Todd.

Time and again, he'd pondered how it would be to make love to her.

Yet, it wasn't just his attraction to her that drove his desire. It was how she made him look at himself through her eyes. It was unnerving. He thought he could do this. Thought his anger would keep his drive to ruin Kyle alive and strong throughout his mission…but she'd barely left his mind all weekend and with that, she made him think about how ugly a person this mission made him. The openness of her dark and beautiful gaze was more telling than that of any woman he'd ever met. Her thinly disguised emotions ripped at his heart and he hated it. One minute angry, the next sad, he felt as though he knew her and it entirely confused him.

His mother's soft, knowing laughter whispered in his ear. Her comforting presence seemed stronger than ever when Sasha smiled at him and unleashed a whirlwind of terrifying emotions. What the hell was he supposed to do with this new and sudden need to hold Sasha's hand? Ask her where she grew up and what her parents were like? What was that? A life alone was his destiny. He'd almost, but not quite, been comfortable with it. He didn't ever want to take the risk of letting his children down as his father had him.

Snatching his legs from the desk, John shook his head to rid his mind of Sasha and yanked Kyle's file box closer. The majority of his weekend had been spent studying the documents. Paper after paper provided the names of Kyle's friends and foes, business associates, paid police officers and tax bureau contacts, plus at least twenty people Kyle had guaranteed John he could rely on for support should he decide to keep the "businesses" going.

John scowled. Like he'd have anything to do with Kyle's illegal activities. The man wasn't going to know what hit him when his only son was done.

The click of the office door opening shook him from his intense contemplation. He snapped his head up as Sasha came in. He stared at her and when she met his eyes, his heart kicked.

Their eyes locked for a lingering moment before her cheeks flushed, and she headed for the coat stand. She shrugged out of her lightweight jacket and when she reached up to hang it, he tried and failed to drag his eyes from the inch of bare back that flashed into view. She turned and he feigned interest in the fairground rides outside the window.

She cleared her throat. "So, what's the plan for today?"

He faced her. "To continue where we left off on Friday."

"You want to go back to Marian's?" She stuck out her bottom lip. "You must be a lot less intelligent than you look."

He smiled. "Not Marian's. The Cove. I want to know Templeton. I want to know why Kyle decided to live here."

She came toward him and stopped a few feet away. She crossed her arms, her gaze curious. "You don't know that?"

"Why? Do you?"

She shook her head. "Not a clue, but considering you're his family, I thought—"

"I know very little about Kyle's decision making but intend to learn a lot." His gaze dropped to her full and ridiculously sensual mouth. "Will you show me around?"

"That depends."

Fighting his smile, he quirked an eyebrow. "On what?"

"Whether you've given any more thought to my offer over the weekend."

"Ah."

"What does *ah* mean?"

"It means I have, yes."

"And?"

"And we'll talk while you show me around."

The atmosphere chilled as the soft appraisal in her gaze turned steely. She waved toward the window. "Well, it's a nice day for sightseeing. Shall we go now before the fair opens this afternoon?"

"Why not?" He picked up the file box from his desk. "Ready?"

She glanced at the box before heading for the door. "As I'll ever be. How about I take you to the place where you'll see the best view of the entire town?"

"Sounds good."

She tossed him a smile over her shoulder, grabbed her jacket and led the way out the door.

His gaze fixed firmly on her tanned and shapely legs showing beneath the hem of her short black skirt. He sucked in a breath through his teeth. He couldn't help thinking she'd be hard-pushed to find him a better view than his current one.

TWENTY MINUTES LATER, Sasha drew in a long breath as Clover Point came into view. It was the highest point above Templeton and, ironically, where Inspector Garrett and her millionaire husband lived. They owned the cabin at its apex, but smaller cabins littered its circumference with strategically placed benches at optimum vantage points. Sasha had escaped here for years whenever she needed to get away to think…or brood…or cry.

They'd left the car in the designated parking area farther down the hill and now as they climbed its incline, the tension in her shoulders eased a little. She smiled, drawing satisfaction from John's heavy breathing behind her. The gradient wasn't particularly bad, but apparently enough for even six-foot men with shoulders the width of Goliath's to catch a breath or two.

"How're you doing back there?" She couldn't resist teasing him. The man deserved it. He shouldn't have touched her face outside Marian's last week. The heat of his fingers still lingered, no matter how much she wanted it to disappear.

He blew out a breath. "I'm doing just fine and dandy. How about you?"

Her smile stretched to a grin. "Almost there."

"Where? Heaven?"

She laughed. She couldn't deny in another world, another place and under entirely different circumstances, she would've made her attraction known to John. Extraordinarily good-looking, exceptionally built with a sense of humor that kept up easily with hers, he seemed like the nicest man she'd met in a *long* time. If ever.

Her smile slipped. The circumstances weren't different, so there was little point of dwelling on something that would never happen. The pressure surrounding them, pressing down and practically squeezing her heart from her body, meant she'd keep her attraction hidden beneath a steel plate. She had to keep her head—and heart—intact if she stood any chance of getting Funland flying under the Todd flag again.

Her granddad's memorial bench came into view, and she headed straight for it. "Let's take a seat here."

The vista was breathtaking. The clouds felt within touching distance. In one direction, the cliff face sank hundreds of feet toward the beach and in the other, a huge mass of blackened forest dominated the view. Sasha pointedly faced the sea as the memory of the murdered woman found in the forest two years before skittered over her skin. She shivered.

"Are you cold?"

She turned and squinted at him. He stood beside the bench, his face shadowed by the sun burning brightly behind him. He shrugged out of his jacket and held it open. "Here."

Her heart stuttered at yet another act of old-fashioned gallantry. She faced the beach, silently urging him to sit down. How did he manage to keep hiding his eyes from her? "I'm fine. Whenever I look at the forest over there, it reminds me Templeton has flaws the same as any other place."

John glanced toward the forest. "Did something happen?"

"A woman's body was found there a while ago. She'd been strangled. The whole town was shaken to its core by it."

His jaw tightened. "Did they find who killed her?"

"Yes." She drew in a long breath. "Can we talk about something else?"

He glanced again toward the forest before he sat beside her. The smell of him, the vicinity of his body next to hers caused attraction to pull at her insides, blurring her thoughts and skewing her rationale. How was her sexual pull to this man supposed to be sated when he possessed rugged good looks, combined with the age-old fantasy of a handsome, young and virile British prince?

He turned. She sensed his gaze on the small gold plaque on the seat behind them and held her breath.

"Your grandfather liked this spot, too." His voice was soft, careful.

Drawing a breath, Sasha shimmied forward and drew the folded letter to Kyle from her back pocket. No personal stuff. Business only. She stared at the paper in her hand and swallowed hard. "We need to talk about my offer."

Silence.

The seconds passed but Sasha refused to look at him. This was the way he wanted things to be, too. Hadn't he said they were to talk business and nothing else? He sat beside her and from the corner of her eye, she watched him lift his ankle to the knee of his other leg. Another second, and she was aware of his arm across the back of the seat behind her—the same as she'd been aware of it on the fairground ride a few days before.

Nerves leaped in her belly, and she breathed deep, letting her granddad's spirit bolster the determination John had managed to crack. Only a little, but still far too much. "I'm convinced Kyle took advantage of my granddad's age, increasing memory loss and emotional state to get the fair from him at a rock-bottom price."

She forced her eyes to his. The intense blue of his gaze bored into hers yet told her nothing of what he thought. She lifted her chin. "His once-agile mind was weakening. The fair was slipping into disrepair. It's likely he had no choice but to sell, especially when Kyle put on the pressure. He even signed the contract with a clause to say Kyle was never to resell it back to one of my family." She shook her head, sadness squeezing at her heart. "He would never have agreed to such a thing. Someone or something forced his hand, and I want Funland back. I was hoping with Kyle in prison for the next few years, he might be open to some reasonable negotiation.... Now I have to turn to you instead."

He continued to stare, his eyes roaming steadily over her face and hair.

Frustration simmered in her stomach, and Sasha thrust the paper toward him. "This is the best I can do."

With his eyes still on hers, he drew the paper from her fingers and finally broke eye contact. He opened the letter, and Sasha's nerves stretched as he read her words. Eventually, he slowly refolded the paper and stared out toward the ocean. "It's a fair offer."

She stiffened as a flicker of hope twisted inside her. "You're not going to dismiss it out of hand?"

"No."

Relief pushed the air from her lungs. "Good." She fell back against the seat. "That's a start, I suppose."

"But I won't consider it until you tell me everything you know about Kyle's dealings."

She snapped her head around. His jaw was sharp enough to cut diamonds and his lips were drawn into such a tight line, they were barely visible. "I told you. I don't know anything."

"I don't believe you."

She opened her mouth to respond; to tell him to go to hell. Yet, how could she when what he implied was true? Shame seared hot at her cheeks and she fisted her hands in her lap. "Why did you have to turn up here?"

"What do you know about my father's businesses, Sasha?"

Self-hatred smeared the inside of her mouth with a bitter tang. "Nothing. Why don't you ask Freddy? He's your father's confidant, not me."

"You've never left the place. Even when you believe Kyle practically stole it from your family. Why?"

"I told you—"

"Funland is your heart and soul. I'm starting to see that. Freddy is my father's lapdog, nothing more. You care about the fair. It clearly runs through your blood, and I won't dismiss that, as Kyle's done, but I need you to tell me the truth. About everything."

She trembled as her heart filled with a sense of intense validation. No one but her granddad had ever understood her passion for the fair and now this man, this *stranger,* seemed to understand. Part of her wanted to scream at him not to toy with her emotions, but how could she when nothing but sincerity showed in his eyes? She dragged her gaze from his to stare at the ocean. "If I knew anything, I'd tell you, but I don't."

Sasha's heart beat out the silent seconds.

Eventually, he blew out a heavy breath. "It must have been agony knowing my father was using the place for drugs and God knows what else."

She swallowed. "It was."

"So, why would you turn a blind eye to it? How *could* you turn a blind eye to it?"

The snappish tone of his voice ignited her anger and split her wide open. She turned. "Are you accusing me of not caring after saying you understand my feelings about the place?"

Color darkened his cheeks and his eyes flashed with irritation. "Help me out here. What else am I supposed to think if none of this makes sense to me?"

"I *had* to turn a blind eye. I *had* to stay here. I couldn't leave and let Kyle poison it from the ground up, otherwise what the hell would be left for me to build on when it finally became mine?"

He said nothing. It infuriated her to see his faint skepticism was blended with a supposedly genuine yearning to understand. "I'm not a fool and I'm not blind. Of course I saw the money exchanging hands and knew drugs were involved, but I kept out of it. I promised my..." She lowered her voice and slowly swiveled around. She ran her finger over granddad's plaque. "I promised him I'd be careful and I was. I had to stay, no matter what. If Kyle forced me out of Funland, there was hell's chance of me getting back in."

"So you're saying you acted ignorant, but if you really wanted to, you could tell me things I need to know?" He met her eyes. "Like who bought his drugs. Who sold him the drugs? Who the faces and names were that came through Funland before Kyle was sent down? I need to know who he really was. I need that as much as you need the fair. I can't move on until I understand Kyle and the kind of man he was when he lived here."

She frowned. "Can't move on from Templeton?"

He tightened his jaw. "Can't move on period."

Empathy rose and nestled like a ball behind her chest. She considered what he said and fear rippled through her. Was he here seeking closure to something she knew nothing about? Was he asking her to join forces with him? Asking her to be a part of whatever it was Kyle wanted him to do? She turned toward the forest as nausea rose in her throat. Why did she get the feeling she'd gone from paddling in the fairly safe arena of Templeton's lapping shoreline, to the acute danger of scuba diving in the Atlantic's deep, dark waters?

CHAPTER EIGHT

JOHN DRAGGED HIS gaze from her profile to the ocean. The water glinted under the glare of the sunshine as seagulls dove and soared above the waves, searching for lunch. He exhaled. “This could be a new beginning for both of us.”

“It could also be the beginning of the end.”

He turned, and her jet-black eyes caught and tugged at his chest once again. Her gaze held a whisper of something different he couldn’t ignore. Who was she? Where was she from? “Kyle told me your family were immigrants. Is that true?”

She raised her eyebrows before huffing out a breath of dry laughter. She shook her head. “Only Kyle.”

“What?”

“My family is Romany. My grandparents and mother are Spanish, thus the dark hair and eyes.” She smiled. “We’ve lived in the U.K. forever. I was born here, and I’ve no idea why Kyle thought otherwise. Unless, of course, you take into account the man is steeped in so much ignorance and contempt for his fellow man, he wouldn’t know if someone were English, Irish, Bohemian or African. The man's an asshole." She grimaced. "Sorry."

He smiled. "No need to apologize. We've just stumbled across another thing we agree on. Things are looking up."

She laughed. "Maybe they are."

Their eyes locked for a brief moment before she stared into the distance, a blush staining her cheeks.

John tightened his grip on the back of the bench as the urge to take her hand raced through him. "So…where do you suggest we go from here?"

"Do you mean as far as the fair and us is concerned? Or the next destination of this Magical Mystery Tour you've got going on?"

He smiled. The soft, ultrasexy huskiness in her voice washed over him and ran its caress across his groin. He shifted uncomfortably. "The fair and us for starters. We need to find a way to deal with this situation." He inhaled. "I need to figure out what to do about Kyle's demands, and I can't do that without you. You want to get the fair back into your family, and you can't do that without me. Surely we can work toward getting what we both want?"

"And what are his demands exactly?"

John drew in a shaky breath, released it. "I think ideally, he'd like me to carry things on as they have been."

"And is that likely to happen?" She shifted a little away from him.

He shook his head and looked ahead once more.

"I don't owe my father anything. I'll do what I want…once I've figured out what that is."

"Right." She cleared her throat. "So what do you think I know about Kyle's businesses?"

"I think you know his suppliers, his customers and maybe his contacts." He met her eyes. "On the other side of the coin, I hope you don't know any of the people who've ended up dead through his actions."

The seconds beat out like minutes. She pulled her mouth into a tight line as though trapping her words inside. He turned away. He didn't want to look into her eyes and see she knew everything; that she was a part of all the bad Kyle was involved with. If he did, he was scared it would turn her astounding beauty ugly.

Scared his gut was wrong and she was party to *everything* that went on at Funland. Scared he'd see her desire to make the place her own was really imbedded in financial greed and power rather than loyalty to her ancestry.

"I know *some* people."

He squeezed his eyes shut. "Who?"

"Well, I know faces, not names. I could recognize a few people in a lineup, I suppose. I also know from Kyle's sentencing that the cops only confiscated a tiny part of the drugs that have passed through the fair over the past six years."

He faced her. "Kyle's been dealing through the fair for that long?"

Sadness mixed with anger in her gaze. "Maybe longer. He bought the fair from my granddad over seven years ago. Eventually, the same faces started showing up and with them, Funland slowly changed from a place full of families and laughing children to a place of lost teenagers and men who had no place being there."

"I see."

"I knew what was happening, but you have to understand my position. I was powerless to stop it. I couldn't risk Kyle kicking me out. I had to stay."

He nodded. He liked her. He understood her. He'd not stopped thinking about her yesterday and her absence had only strengthened his fondness. He looked to the sky and concentrated on the birds soaring past the pure white clouds. He'd only known her for a matter of days, yet the overwhelming urge to kiss her, touch her face and smell her hair encompassed him.

They sat in silence. If she was part of Kyle's circle and he let her see his growing attraction toward her, he risked leaving himself wide open to manipulation. He had zero reason to trust his father or her. He'd yet to uncover why his father—or Sasha's grandfather—included the clause that Funland wasn't to be sold back to anyone in the Todd family. Would that still hold now he held ownership?

Kyle's limited instructions reeked of sabotage and spite.

Pushing abruptly to his feet, John turned his back to her and paced a few feet away, creating some much needed space. "It's going to take more than your say so for me to believe you had no involvement in the drugs. I'm sorry." He drew in the cleansing sea air, hating his inability to trust anything or anyone in the place where Kyle had settled for longer than anywhere else.

A long moment passed before he heard her soft footsteps. She stood so close, the breeze whipped her scent to him.

"I understand you've no reason to believe me. Just as I've no reason to believe you'll do the right thing in the end, but I'm telling the truth. That's all I know." She sighed. "I'm sure Freddy knows a wholc lot morc than I do."

He turned to face her. "I *will* do the right thing in the end, you know."

"Will you?" She raised her eyebrows, her gaze dark. "Then I guess we need to trust each other. Because as it stands now, neither of us has anyone else we can turn to with this problem."

He stared at her mouth; he couldn't help it. "What do you know about Freddy's background?"

"Nothing. Why?"

He curled his hands into fists inside his pockets. "He met my father in prison."

"Freddy was in prison, too?" She laughed drily. "My God, I work in one of the best places ever, don't I?"

"What was he in there for? That's the question." John scowled. "For all I know, the man could be a psycho."

Her cheeks darkened. She looked rattled by his blunt revelation. Guilt he'd blurted out Freddy's history so insensitively rolled through him. "You honestly didn't know?"

She shook her head. "No."

"Does it change the way you feel about him?"

She shrugged. "I don't really feel anything about Freddy. We work together and then go home in opposite directions. I'd say his bark is a whole lot worse than his bite and he's never given me reason to be afraid of him." She smiled. "In fact, the first time I saw him have an emotional reaction to anything was when you turned up."

"And that makes you smile?"

"Sure. It does me good to see Freddy teetering on his imaginary pedestal."

John smiled but his mind raced with questions. Why had Freddy served time? Just how dangerous was he? If he had been locked up in the same high-security prison as Kyle, it made sense Freddy had also been there for murder. Or maybe armed robbery. What had Freddy done to get along so well with Kyle?

Sasha coughed, breaking into his thoughts. "So what happens next?"

She was so much shorter than him, yet strength came from her in waves. He curled his fingers tighter as the overwhelming urge to cup her jaw in his hands rocketed through him. He stared at her mouth…again. “I don’t know.”

Her gaze wandered over his face, her dark lids falling to half-mast. A look so sexy and confident, it sent his arousal soaring. She lifted her eyes to his and they sparked with mischief. “Why not just sell Funland to me and to hell with everyone else? I’ll be happy to take the burden from you. No problem at all.”

He laughed and shook his head. “Why couldn’t you have been a bullheaded adversary who looked like a witch with warts and stringy hair?”

She stepped back and jauntily planted her hands on her hips. “As opposed to looking like Pocahontas in a skirt and low-cut top?”

“Exactly.”

She punched him playfully on the arm. “The Pocahontas reference was a joke. As my older sister likes telling me I look more like a miniature long-haired terrier. She says I’m always snarling and foaming at the mouth about something.” She lifted her shoulders. “Which is probably true.”

“With everything you’ve told me that’s gone on over the past seven years, I think you’ve had good reason.”

She looked toward the forest, her smile dissolving. “I can’t let the fair go. It’s all I want. It’s all I’ll *ever* want.”

Regret yanked at his chest and guilt clawed at

his conscience. He didn't want to hear those words from her. He hated that the fair appeared to be her only source of happiness and it was Kyle who had taken it away.

Kyle's letter to him reverberated in his mind....

I need you, son. I need you take care of things in Templeton Cove. I've worked too hard to lose it all. Everything is now yours. People want me dead. I can't trust anyone. I did what I had to as far as your mother is concerned—and I've done everything I can for you since she died. You have to understand what people are capable of when they're in love. I'm not the bad man you think I am. I promise you. Sell the other businesses, do what you will, but the fairground is not to go to the Todds. Not under any circumstances.

I need to know things are okay between us. That I've done the right thing by you come the end.

Heat simmered in John's gut as his resentment caught and burned. *Done the right thing by me?* Christ, his father had no clue. No idea what he'd done to his only child. John clenched his jaw as he tried to get a handle on his rising temper. Once again, Kyle had put him in an impossible situation and sent him off to sink or swim. The only difference? This time he was an adult and not an eleven-year-old boy desperately flailing for an anchor.

The one thing that remained clear was he couldn't start to look into overturning the contract clause until he knew for sure Sasha wasn't involved in the illegalities of Kyle's business. What evidence did he have that he could trust her? His gut wasn't enough. He had to protect his control over Kyle. For the first time in almost twenty years, he could break his father. Make him pay for what he'd done—or hadn't done.

He glowered at the beach below. "Whatever happens, just bear in mind I'm considering your offer… and I'm nothing like Kyle." He turned.

She studied him. "What happens if I do everything you ask of me only to have you keep the fair and throw my generosity back in my face?"

John tightened his jaw. He wouldn't make her any promises he wasn't sure he could keep. Kyle had owned Funland for almost seven and a half years and this woman had always been there. Had played a part, no matter how small, in supplying drugs to men, women and undoubtedly, children. She'd admitted she turned a blind eye to a lot of what was going on at the fair. Who did that? He scowled. Who could be that irresponsible at a place where children came to have fun? He cleared his throat. "You're going to have to trust me."

She huffed out a laugh. "Trust you?"

"That's the best I can say right now."

Tears glinted in her phenomenal eyes, sending his negative thoughts about her into a tailspin. She shook her head. "Well, I feel a million times better now we've had this chat."

"I'm sorry, but until I know more about your role in the whole sordid deal Kyle clearly had going on here, I can't give anyone, including you, an inch." He tilted his head toward the direction of the parking lot. "We should go."

Disappointment flashed in her dark eyes and then her shoulder brushed his chest as she stormed past him and down the hill. John's hatred of Kyle seeped ever deeper. No father put his son in the position of having the monopoly on what did and didn't happen with regards to other people's lives. Then again, Kyle wasn't a true father.

SASHA SWIPED AT her tears as she marched across the parking lot toward John's car. Who the hell did he think he was, practically accusing her of being involved in Kyle's illegalities? Surely her dislike of the man showed on her face and in her words? Yet, a horrible sense of shame blended with her anger because what John accused her of wasn't entirely unwarranted. She'd known what Kyle was doing to some degree. She'd seen money exchange hands. Seen packets of white and brown powder being loaded into trunks after nightfall.

She tipped her head back as further tears threatened. "God damn you, Kyle."

The locks of John's car shunted open, and she jumped. The crunch of his footsteps on the gravel sent her heartbeat into overdrive. She yanked open the door and slid into the passenger seat. The tension between them would only grow worse as time went on. Not to mention the sexual tension heating up faster than a flint on a line of paraffin.

He got into the car and as she was unable to trust her body's reaction whenever she looked into his solemn gaze, Sasha belted up and faced the side window. He had eyes bluer than the ocean. A jaw so defined, it was as though it was chiseled from marble. God, she even loved the way he towered above her when, before John, she'd hated feeling small and delicate in front of anyone. With him, it felt right....

"Sasha?"

She briefly closed her eyes before turning to face him. "What?"

"We have to be honest with each other if we stand any chance of coming to a mutually satisfying arrangement."

"A mutually satisfying agreement?" She shook her head. "Why do you have to speak like that? This isn't a civil conversation across a conference table. We're talking about my life. The entirety of what I want to do with it." She angrily swiped her hand at the hair that dared to fall in her eyes. "God damn it. I don't want you here."

His eyes flashed with anger and distrust. His

cheeks were red and his jaw tight. He faced front and turned the ignition. The powerful engine roared to life and he reversed.

Sasha cursed the trembling in her body and the twist of self-hate in her stomach. He hadn't dismissed her offer out of hand...but she wasn't convinced his intentions were honorable, either.

She swallowed. An inexplicable sense of integrity rolled off the man in waves.

They traveled the rest of the descent from Clover Point in silence and, twenty minutes later, arrived on the main road, High Street, that ran through Templeton Cove. The midday sun was high in the sky and the locals were out in droves, meandering along the promenade and peering in shop windows running along Cowden Beach. Sasha drew in a shaky breath. God, she loved this town and she loved Funland. There had to be a way to get it back.

John cleared his throat. "How do we get to Marchenton?"

Now what? She turned. "Why?"

"There's something I need to see there."

"It's out of town. Marchenton's not exactly... nice."

He smiled wryly. "I didn't expect it to be. Kyle wants me to go see something there that used to be his."

Sasha frowned. "Used to be?"

"It's a house. He's given me an address." He

glanced at her, his blue eyes dark and somber. “A crack house.”

“A…” Trepidation raised the hairs at her nape. “I’m not going to a crack house.”

“It’s not one anymore. Kyle’s adamant he was clearing things up before he was arrested.”

“I don’t understand. Kyle’s turned over a new leaf? Found God?” She sniffed. “I’ll believe that when I see it.”

He smiled. “Exactly, but it’s one of the places on his list that he deems important I see.”

Sasha stared at him, disbelief bringing her shoulders up around her earlobes. “He has a list? Like a brochure on what’s hot, what’s not as far as Templeton’s concerned? What’s the tagline? Places to Befriend a Druggie? Sit Back and Borrow a Needle?”

He smiled as he pressed on the accelerator, racing toward the far end of town. “Something like that.”

“Does Kyle know I’m tagging along on your little discovery trip?”

His smile vanished. “No.”

“Then why take me? I’m pretty sure he’d have a hissy fit if he thought for one minute I was learning any more about him and his illegal activities.”

“That’s exactly why I’d like you to come. If he wants me to take care of things, I’ll take care of them my way. Not his.”

“So, I’m a pawn in some sort of Mafia game?”

He glanced at her. “None of this is a game. As

much as Kyle likes to deem himself the town's hard man, he's not as far as I'm concerned."

Sasha glared at him before snapping her head around to stare at the passing scenery. As they made each turn, she gave him another direction. Eventually, any remaining picturesque and colorful parts of Templeton diminished and they edged their way into the gloomy gray and beige of Marchenton.

Once a well-to-do residential area, the suburb had taken a steep decline over the past few decades and now played host to families struggling to get on the employment ladder or others who'd succumbed to alcohol and drug abuse.

She glanced at John as they drove deeper into the estate. "What was the address?"

He nodded toward the glove box. "Grab my wallet. It's written on a piece of paper inside."

Opening the compartment, she extracted his black leather wallet. One side showed credit cards and a piece of paper…the other a faded photograph of a young woman cradling a small boy of four or five in her arms. Sasha smiled. "Is this you?"

"Address, Sasha."

Her smile dissolved, and she rolled her eyes before yanking out the scrap of paper. "Osworth Street, number twenty-one. Don't even ask me where that is. Thankfully, I've never had reason to come to Marchenton before, let alone roam the streets."

"What's the post code?" He pulled the car to a

stop at the curb and pushed a button on the dash. The radio screen flickered and changed to an inbuilt navigation system.

She wrinkled her nose. "Show off."

He flashed her a smile. "Post code."

"T-E-9-7-R-J."

After he'd input the code, an automated voice of an American woman with the teasing lilt of a 1970s porn star told him to take the next left in a hundred yards. He checked the mirrors and pulled back onto the road. As they drove, Sasha tried and failed to ignore the way his undoubtedly strong and incredibly masculine hands looked holding the steering wheel. The cuffs of his jacket and shirt lifted as he maneuvered left and right, and she swiftly looked away. She had a thing about men's hands and forearms. But she really, really didn't want to develop a thing about John's.

He pulled the car to a stop a second time. Sasha leaned over and peered out his side of the car. His breath tickled her ear, and she pretended not to notice how he stared at her rather than the house beside them. "So, this is what a crack house looks like. Nice."

Silence.

She turned and her heart did a little stumble. His eyes were so close. They really were the most amazing shade of blue. More navy than azure—shinier and clearer than the damn Pacific. She blinked and pulled back. "Are we getting out?"

He ran his gaze over her face and hair before yanking on the door handle. He climbed out of the car, and Sasha concentrated on leveling her breathing. Once again, he came to her side of the car and once again he opened her door. Her stomach knotted. Stupid, girly behavior on her part. Stupid, eighteenth-century nonsense on his. Still, she couldn't deny his gallantry was something she could get used to.

She alighted from the car, and his fingers touched the small of her back as they walked to the pavement. She pretended not to notice that, either. They stopped in front of the gate and stood side by side, staring at the house. His hand had yet to leave her spine and the spot where it lingered heated.

She swallowed. Hard. "Well, this is nice."

The house's gray-white walls were cracked and peeling; the garden was strewn with garbage and the customary supermarket trolley. Thick wooden boards covered the windows and a plank had been nailed horizontally across the door—hopefully to stop people from getting in rather than keeping anyone trapped inside forever.

Sasha tipped her head back to look at his profile. "Now what?"

He narrowed his eyes as his gaze wandered over the facade of the house, from its roof to the front stoop. "I don't know. Kyle wanted me to see it like this. To show me that things are different now, but

God knows what he thinks the boarding up of a onetime crack house proves to me."

"I suppose the real question is whether he boarded it up or someone else did. Didn't he tell you anything about it?"

"Nothing. I've been here less than a week and the man is getting to me more than I ever thought he would." He faced her. "I can't let that happen."

Before Sasha had time to respond, he frowned and lifted his hand from her back, pointing at what looked to be a Realtor's board in the corner of the front garden. "Looks like it's for sale."

He stepped closer to investigate. Sasha bit back a groan. She immediately missed the weight of his hand on her—missed the entirely misplaced feeling of security. What the hell was happening to her? John was the worst person she could possibly have this level of attraction toward. She grimaced. She might as well be fancying Kyle, for all the good it would do her. At least that thought dampened her yearning.

She walked to where he stood with his hands stuffed in his pockets. He studied the board in front of him. "Who's Jay Garrett?"

She looked at the board. "This place is Jay Garrett's now?"

"Do you know him?"

"Kind of, but I've no idea what he could possibly want with this dump."

"Who is he?"

His eyes were dark with demand, and Sasha stepped back. "He's our local entrepreneur and token millionaire. Owns a lot of the businesses in Templeton, including Marian's." She lifted an eyebrow. "Don't you recognize the surname?"

He frowned. "Should I?"

"He's married to none other than Detective Inspector Red Hair."

"The cop?" His eyes widened in disbelief. "He's married to the town's cop and this place is his?"

She lifted her shoulders. "It certainly looks that way."

He stared at the house. "What the hell would a millionaire want with a place once owned by Kyle that used to house addicts?"

Sasha brushed past him and leaned closer to the board. No details were given. Just that Garrett Holdings now owned it. "If you want to know that, maybe you should get yourself better acquainted with DI Garrett." She faced him. "I'm sure she'd welcome a visit from you anytime."

"What makes you say that?"

"She's had more than a couple of run-ins with Kyle. She knows him. The inspector will be watching you, whether you intend to play things by the book or not."

"And did these run-ins take place at the fair? Were they *about* the fair?"

Sasha glanced at the house. "Not as far as I know."

"I find it hard to believe the cops have never taken an interest in what was going on there."

"The old inspector was there a lot. Not so much DI Garrett, but she didn't take over as the woman in charge until around the time Kyle was arrested."

He gave a slow nod, comprehension registering. "And that's when things started getting quieter as far as Kyle's businesses were concerned."

Sasha studied him. It was a statement rather than a question and from the way he scowled at the house, she sensed his brain cogs revolved at lightning speed. He abruptly turned. "Okay, I've seen enough. We'll head back to the fair. I want to show you something."

Her defenses immediately leaped to high alert. "What?"

"Kyle gave me minimal instructions when he asked me to come here." His dark blue eyes shot from her face to the house behind her and back again. "And I wasn't expecting you to be a part of any of it." He exhaled. "In fact, I wasn't expecting *you,* period."

She tensed. "What does that mean?"

He stared deep into her eyes. "Despite what you might think, I'm not here to hurt you or mess up your life. I'm here out of curiosity and…anger." A muscle leaped in his jaw. "I owe Kyle absolutely no favors and the fact he seems to think I do irritates the hell out of me."

"I still don't understand what that has to do with me."

He closed his eyes. "I didn't expect to like anyone who worked for Kyle."

Her heart flipped, and she immediately resented that…and the smile at her lips. "You like me?"

"You're okay." He opened his eyes and smiled. "For a girl."

She grinned. "Funny."

"Let's go."

He headed for the car, leaving Sasha immobile as he opened the passenger door and waited. Inhaling, she approached and slid into the seat, her heart beating hard as he shut the door and walked around the hood. He got in and gunned the engine. Sasha's body quivered with apprehension as she pulled on her seat belt with a shaking hand. She wanted to kiss him. Touch him.

She faced the windshield. She needed to enforce some distance or God only knew how this thing would explode between them. Whatever scenario she imagined, someone got hurt.

"I won't be your ally against Kyle. I won't be dragged into his world when I've managed to survive this long at the fair without becoming involved. I want the fair and I'm willing to fight for it, but I don't deserve risking my reputation along the way."

"I know that."

"I've got my own issues and don't need to get in

the middle of any trouble you've got going on with Kyle. The one thing we both know about your dad is he's dangerous. Really dangerous." She faced him. "I stayed out of his way as best I could. In an ideal world, I'd like that to be an option with you, too."

His eyes bored into hers for such a length of time, her cheeks warmed. Never before had she been so conscious of every part of her body, of the power pulling her toward this unfathomable man.

His gaze dropped to her mouth. "Right now, neither of us has that option. No matter how much we both might want it."

He swiveled in his seat and snatched his sunglasses from the dash. Strange and unwanted regret wound tight inside her. They were on opposite sides of Kyle's playing field...and she had a horrible suspicion they were acting just as he had planned all along.

CHAPTER NINE

WHEN THEY RETURNED to Funland, the rides were in full swing and the music blared. Sasha immediately knew the meeting of minds John had planned for that afternoon would be promptly abandoned. Freddy had worn the expression of a bulldog chewing a wasp—and was about to burst a blood vessel—so Sasha shook off the stain of the morning's events and dove straight into work.

She hustled people to and from rides, sorted out a raving old woman shouting at the top of her lungs that a slot machine was "out to get her" and climbed under the boards of a flight simulator to check on an abnormal clanking noise.

The time now neared 9:00 p.m. Exhausted and ready to finish for the day, Sasha marched through the chaos of dating and screaming teenagers, parents trying to cajole younger kids toward the exit and the ride controllers trying their best to keep them there.

Despite the mania, Funland was where she belonged and always would. Her molestation was a moment in time that might take forever to fade, but if she won ownership of the fair, she'd be halfway back to gaining the life she wanted despite that. The thought that Matt Davidson's actions could've ruined her life but didn't went a long way to dispersing his power. She would never give up on that happening. Ever.

The sweet scent of cotton candy and toffee apples, and the bang and crash of blank pellets being shot and targets hit were all she'd ever need to keep her grounded and pushing forward. Her sense of safety had yet to return; her unending watching and protecting others yet to lessen…but it would, once Funland was hers to do with as she wanted.

She glanced around, looking for John. Every one of her plans moved like shifting sand beneath her feet and he was the catalyst who'd made it that way. She needed to get along with him until he accepted her offer. The more she thought about it, the more it made sense he'd want to leave Templeton as soon as possible. What was to keep him there but the empire of a man she sensed he despised? He'd sell her the fair eventually. It was just a matter of biding her time.

When Kyle had been in residence, she'd surrendered to the fact the fair wouldn't be hers for a long time. When he was arrested, her had heart leaped for joy at the prospect of an accelerated opportunity. Back then, Freddy hadn't shown an ounce of interest in taking over where Kyle left off. Of course, now Freddy wanted Funland, too—and neither of them had a clue what John wanted.

Sasha frowned. Least of all did the man in question know what he wanted, it seemed.

"You off for home then?"

She turned at Freddy's curt inquiry behind her. "Sure. In a minute."

He looked over her head toward the bumper cars. "Where did you go for most of the day?"

An air of wariness immediately skittered along Sasha's nerves and joined the hefty dose of distrust emanating from Freddy. She turned to follow the direction of his gaze. John stood at the far end of the bumper cars, steadily watching them. Freddy had been in prison with Kyle. John's words echoed in her mind. Who was to say he wasn't equally as prone as Kyle to violence and debauchery? She swallowed and kept her gaze on John. "Nowhere important."

"Humph."

Sasha rocked back and forth on the balls of her feet.

"So that's it. No further information?" Freddy snorted. "You're going to keep this thing you've got going on with Mr. Boss Man over there to yourself?"

Sasha faced him. If Freddy thought he could intimidate her, he'd better think again. "Mr. Boss Man, as you call him, took me for a little tour around town. Not that it's any of your business."

"Like that now, is it?"

She glared. "You're the one who made it clear we're on opposite sides now John's here. What did you expect me to do? Roll over and play nice? I think you know me better than that."

Their eyes locked and colors from the revolving lights above slithered over Freddy's face and bald pate, making him look like a moody nightclub bodyguard.

He glanced toward John, his jaw set. "So, what did he want in town? He speak to anyone?"

Sasha frowned. "Are we on the same team or not?"

"There aren't any teams. Until we know what Kyle's boy is doing here, we're both on our own, don't you think?"

Sasha shifted uncomfortably as indecision battled inside. She and Freddy had worked side by side for a long time—albeit him working a damn sight more closely with Kyle. She'd always liked Freddy. Thought him a decent enough guy, but now everything had been tainted with distrust and accusations. She didn't really know Freddy any more than she'd known Kyle. Maybe she needed to give a little something to receive the same in return.

"As far as I can tell, it was a case of him getting a feel for the Cove. He doesn't know anyone." She shrugged. "He wanted me to introduce him to a few people."

He frowned. "Like who? Who'd he want to meet?"

The sharpness of his demand rankled, and Sasha crossed her arms. "I took him to Marian's. Are you going to cool down a little?"

"Why Marian's?"

"Jeez, Freddy. What's this about? You know as much, if not more, than me right now."

"I don't trust the guy."

She glanced toward John. "Nor do I. But right now, we're stuck with him and it might pay to ease off the aggression pedal for a while."

He sneered. "Clearly you're prepared to do whatever it takes, eh?"

"What's that supposed to mean?"

"You think I haven't noticed the way your tongue hangs out every time you look at the guy?" He gave a dry laugh, his white teeth glinting in the semidarkness. "First time I've seen evidence you aren't a lesbian."

Heat assaulted her cheeks, and she raised her hands. "Okay, I'm out. If you're going to be so bloody obnoxious about the situation, you're on your own." She moved to walk away when he gripped her arm.

"Hey."

She glared. "What?"

"You can't blame me for being like this. How the bloody hell did this happen without either of us knowing it was coming?"

"I don't know, but turning on each other isn't helping." She snatched her arm from his grasp, her heart pumping. She glanced toward John. He laughed with one of the guys operating the cars, and the same sense of defending him she'd felt in the bakery rose again. "He seems an okay kind of a guy. Cold as ice occasionally, but not Kyle…if that makes sense."

They lapsed into silence as they both studied the chatting, laughing enigma of John Jordon. Freddy cleared his throat. "So he didn't specify who he wanted to meet? He just said people?"

"Yes."

"I've spoken to Kyle."

Sasha's heart leaped into her throat but she concentrated on keeping an impassive expression. "When?"

"This afternoon. He reckons he's out."

"Out?" Sasha swallowed against the unease turning her mouth desert-dry as John threw them a final look before walking from the bumper cars and back toward the office. "Of the fair?"

Silence.

She snapped her gaze to Freddy, adrenaline pumping through her. "Freddy?"

He shook his head and glared at her. "That's all it is with you, ain't it? This bloody fair. Kyle's concern has never been the fair. Don't you get that? Now everything's going tits up and I'll end up with nothing."

The venom in his voice set the hairs on the back of her neck singing their warning. She frowned. "If you're talking about the other components of Kyle's immoral enterprise, I don't want to hear about it. That's between you and him."

"Ah, yes. Little Miss Goody Two Shoes."

Irritation swept a hot flush onto Sasha's face. "I am good, Freddy. Always have been, as you well know. There's every possibility we'll have a fight on our hands as far as John's concerned, but I want the fair, nothing else. Everything else is up to you to sort out with him and Kyle, not me."

She spun away, wanting to get away from Freddy and his spitting anger. His heavy footsteps came straight behind her, and she halted. "Leave me alone."

He glared, his eyes manic. "Kyle didn't just give me a job here. He took my money, my investment. I'm owed, Sasha."

"Not from me." She lifted her chin. "So take it up with his damn son."

"You haven't got a clue what you're dealing with, have you?"

She frowned. "What I'm dealing with? Or who?"

"What, Sasha. You've no bloody clue."

The infernal feeling of being out of the loop shivered over her skin, making goose bumps erupt. "I know plenty."

She stormed toward the offices, her heart beating with a fear she'd never known around Freddy before. The one thing she couldn't accuse Kyle of was intimidation or bullying—at least as far she was concerned. She wasn't naive enough not to know Kyle's reputation manifested the way it had because he'd inflicted a certain amount of terror and violence, but she'd never experienced this level of animosity from Freddy or Kyle before.

With tears burning like hot needles behind her eyes, Sasha pushed open the office door and made for the coatrack.

John emerged from the bathroom at the back of the room. "Sasha?"

"Not now. I'm going home." She snatched her jacket and bag from the rack and strode toward the door.

"Sasha. Wait. Kyle gave me a file I want you to look at."

She spun around and nearly knocked face-first into his stupidly broad chest. The man moved like a damn panther. He gripped her upper arms. The last thing she wanted to do was look at him. The last she wanted was for him to see her upset or unnerved. The last thing she wanted was to like him…want him.

She met his eyes. "I'm going home. Let go of me."

He immediately released her and planted his hands on his hips instead. His eyes darkened with concern. "Are you okay?"

She glared. "Have you spoken to your dad this afternoon?"

He flinched. "What? Why?"

"Yes or no?"

"No."

The tension between them grew. Only their harried breathing punctured the heavy silence. Questions stormed in his gaze as Sasha's heart picked up speed. She couldn't help staring at his lips. *Kiss me. God damn it. Kiss it all away.*

"Sasha? What's going on?"

She blinked. "Nothing."

"Then why ask—"

"Why do I need to know about Kyle's file? Why isn't Freddy involved with this, too?"

The concern vanished from his eyes, leaving only steely determination in its wake. "I don't want him involved."

"So why involve me? Why have you singled me out to know about Kyle's affairs? What is it you actually want?"

A muscle worked rhythmically in his jaw, but Sasha held his cold stare. She wouldn't bend or walk away. He owed her an explanation and she'd damn well have it. Right now. She hitched her bag onto her shoulder and crossed her arms. "Well?"

"We'll talk about this in the morning. Go home. Get some sleep." He turned to walk away.

"No."

He halted with his back to her. His shoulders were rigid. A hard plane beneath white cotton. Her gaze ran of its own accord over the muscular expanse of his back, down to his narrowed waist and perfect ass. She swallowed and dragged her eyes to the back of his short, dark, conservatively cut hair.

Slowly, he turned. “Kyle only told me what he wanted me to know. He only told me your grandfather hung on to this fair until the very end. He laughed about it. Told me loyalty like that was a waste of time and his granddaughter had been cursed with it, too.”

Sasha trembled with rage—or maybe grief for her grandfather. “He *laughed* at us?”

“Yes. I didn’t think about that one way or the other…until I saw you for the first time. Until I saw the genuine panic and sorrow in your eyes when you realized who I was. I don’t want you to hate me. I’m not the villain here. Kyle is.”

Struggling to keep a hold on her rising temper and not throttle John in Kyle’s absence, she glared. “Then give me the fair and walk away.”

Time stood still as their breathing fell into sync. Their whispered breaths filled the room, fueling the tension and stretching it like an invisible band around them. Her heart ached. Had she lost this fight before it had even begun?

He closed his eyes. “I have to deal with the estrangement between Kyle and me.” He shook his head. “Something happened a long time ago. He’s been out of my life for two decades. I need to know who he is. If you can’t understand that, then maybe it’s better you stop working here.”

She flinched. “What?”

He opened his eyes. "I need to do this. I need to deal with my stuff before I can think about yours."

Her shock gave way to a rush of unwanted sympathy. His defensiveness had eased and now the pain in his eyes pleaded with her to understand his situation. Empathy lingered when Sasha thought of the wedge of resentment between her and her mother. She knew more than most the desire to understand a parent's actions and motivations. Silence and hidden secrets were a cruel and affecting way to send children into the world. They ended up doing incredible and often stupid things as adults.

She sighed, her hands falling to her sides. "This isn't right. Your issues with Kyle shouldn't stop you from giving me back the fair. What can you possibly want with it? What good will keeping it do for Kyle or you?"

The softness in his gaze morphed into stubborn determination. "It's important we work together to uncover the truth. Why didn't Kyle, or even your grandfather, want your family to have the fair? We deserve to know exactly what Kyle was up to when he was here."

She frowned. "Why do you even care? If you haven't spoken for so long, why does it matter what he did or didn't do?"

He wiped his hand over his face before tipping his head back to stare at the ceiling. "It shouldn't matter. I know that. It's just..." He dropped his chin. "It does."

Everything cleared in that moment. She got him. She understood him and why he was here…which meant the journey had just got a whole lot bumpier. They were both dealing with stuff. Baggage. Trying to move forward through the mire of the pasts they'd endured at someone else's hand. She swallowed and dropped her shoulders. "This is all so unfair."

"I know, but I'm just doing the best I can with the information I have. I didn't come here to leave without answers or to do Kyle's bidding. Soon enough, I'll know what to do."

"In the meantime, I'm supposed to do what?"

"Work with me. Wait for me."

Wait for him? Why did her heart just skip a beat? Why did it sound so intimate every time he said anything like that? She swallowed and pursed her lips, trapping any response for the sake of her sanity.

He cleared his throat, his gaze wandering over her face. "What if I decide to stay? What if I move to Templeton and make my life here?"

She tensed. *No, no, no.* He couldn't stay. He couldn't. Not here. Working where she was every day. She was strong, but not that strong. "What do you do for a living?"

"I'm a teacher at an elementary school."

"A teacher?" Well, that was surprising. "You work with kids?"

He smiled. "Is that so hard to believe?"

She closed her eyes. “Why couldn’t you be a nerdy scientist or a lecturer in quantum physics? Why kids?”

He laughed. “You’d like a nerd more?”

“No, I’d like you less. At least it would mean we have nothing in common.” She opened her eyes. “You’re making it hard for me to keep fighting you, John Jordon.”

He grinned. “Good.”

A smile tugged. “I can’t believe this. I’d laugh if I had the energy.”

“I’m sorry.” His smile dissolved. “I’m sorry that what I’m dealing with isn’t your problem, but you’re stuck in the middle. So’s Freddy. And no doubt, tens of other people. I want to know exactly how many people Kyle has screwed over and then I’ll decide what to do. I promise.”

“I won’t lose another chance to get the fair back where it belongs.”

“In your family, right? All this passion, it’s all about family?”

The uncertainty in his tone was undeniable, and Sasha’s stomach knotted. Why was he looking at her in such a knowing way all of a sudden? Why did it feel as though he could see deep inside her? That he knew she had nothing but the fair. That her family was segregated and barely spoke. Did he realize she feared if she washed her hands of the fair, she’d have no clue where to go or who to be?

Dread rippled through her as she stared at him.

She opened her mouth to respond but couldn't think past the panic that he knew what had happened to her. That Matt Davidson's abuse made her find purpose in the one place she should hate more than any other. Did he think she was crazy to want to make Funland as it was before: good and wholesome, before that despicable excuse for a man came along and ruined it?

She raised her hands in surrender, fighting the terror rising like a rumbling volcano. "I need to go."

"Fine. We'll talk tomorrow." He wandered to his desk and picked up some papers.

She had to do something to make this nightmare go away. She couldn't let the fair slip through her fingers. Not after all this time. "It's my day off tomorrow. I won't be here."

He looked up and smiled wryly. "I was under the impression you worked seven days a week."

"I do…did. Until you came into my life and started a war you'll lose."

His smiled disappeared. "This isn't a war."

"No? That's what you think." She spun around and strolled out of the office, leaving the door wide open behind her.

JOHN WOKE THE next day with a banging headache. The partially full bottle of Scotch sitting on his dresser was a cruel reminder of why he felt as if a hatchet had been buried in his skull. Groaning, he hauled his ass from Kyle's bed and padded into the enormous en suite bathroom. He gripped the sink and stared into the mirror. He looked like crap. Felt like crap—and all too aware the majority of his misery wasn't caused by the Scotch. The defensive hurt in Sasha's eyes when she stared at him in the office had haunted him all night.

One minute anger, the next a lingering fondness shone in her gaze, making his breath catch and his arms yearn to pull her close. Time and again when they argued, he'd had the urge to hold her against his chest just to absorb some of her weakly veiled vulnerability. She tried to hide it behind the loaded glares and fiery retorts, but he'd been around enough kids—and adults—to recognize a painful past when he saw one. The vibrations coming from Sasha were more painful than most. He closed his eyes.

For the first time in a long time, he was aware of another person's potential to understand him. To reciprocate his need for comfort and validation. The notion was scary and unwanted—and happening under the worst circumstances possible. Intellectually, it was a sign to deal with the contract clause so he could hand over the papers to Sasha and get the hell back home to Bridgewater.

Emotionally, he wondered if Kyle might have kick-started so much more than he realized. John was eager to get to know a woman who attracted him, fascinated him, inspired him and made him falter from a path he'd thought would be simple and entirely fueled by vengeance. He'd come to Templeton for one reason and one reason only—to see what the hell his father had done with his godforsaken life. What had been so important to prevent him ever contacting his only living family?

John cursed and pushed away from the sink.

Kyle had shot and killed the man who'd murdered his wife and then forced an estrangement from their child. Why? What would have driven him to make such stark and final decisions?

John strode to the shower and turned it on.

What the hell was he going to do today? Tomorrow? Next week? Did he really think he'd ever understand Kyle or his motivations?

Sasha's pleas and fiery temper sparked something inside him that made John ponder the impossible. To stay for a while. To explore this new and exciting attraction for a woman so different than any he'd met. He longed to know more about her and the deep, dark passion that stormed in her eyes whenever the fair was mentioned. It was as if Funland was the source of her entire life's purpose.

He stepped into the shower and his mind whirled. A day apart from Sasha would do him good. He needed to take action and deal with his anger toward Kyle before he'd have anything to offer anyone. The last thing he wanted to do was upset a woman already suffering—but that's exactly what he was doing.

The shower woke him and washed any weakness down the drain. He stepped out and snatched a towel from the rack. Everything in Kyle's home was lavish. From the towels to the parquet flooring that swept the entire lower level of his huge five-bedroom house, to the huge kitchen, with its gleaming surfaces and gadgets. Everything screamed of money and success.

He tied the towel at his waist and grabbed a hand towel from the stack neatly folded on solid pine shelving beside him. Scrubbing his hair, he left the bathroom and walked to the floor-to-ceiling window in the master bedroom. He whipped back the drapes. It was obvious Kyle had chosen his abode carefully. Whereas John would've chosen to live close to Cowden Beach or maybe the town center, with its constant activity and warm sense of community, Kyle lived on the outskirts of Templeton. Close enough he could get to where he needed to be within a half hour's drive, but far enough away he had the isolation he clearly craved.

Away from unwanted attention, no doubt.

John stared at the enormity of his father's domain. The back of the house faced the ocean, but not the beach. Below spanned a huge back garden with a paved patio and furniture so luxurious, it belonged inside someone's living room. In one corner stood a barbecue large enough to cook for the entire street and in the other, a hot tub that could comfortably seat six people and their champagne. The gate at the very end of the green lawn led to a planked wooden pier, where Kyle's speedboat glinted in the hazy sunshine. A boat named after his mother. *Fiona Forever.*

John gritted his teeth. *And they say crime doesn't pay.*

The front of the house faced a tree-lined avenue that John had learned was fondly referred to as "millionaire's row." The houses were all unique. Some brick and traditional, others art deco or contemporarily stylish. It was a strange mishmash of the owners' personalities. The whitewashed magnificence of his father's five-bedroom, balconied and minimalistic home told him nothing of who Kyle was today any more than it would have nineteen years ago.

Fiona Forever.

As far as he was aware, Kyle hadn't remarried and, based on the bundle of papers John had received from him, his son was the only next of kin who could lay claim to Kyle's fortune.

He turned from the window and pulled out some of his clothes from atop Kyle's in the dresser. It irked him that everything his father touched John now touched, too, but the alternative was to stay in a bed-and-breakfast. A boardinghouse couldn't give him any clues into unraveling the enigma otherwise known as "Dad." There was a small chance his home would sooner or later.

Once dressed, John left the bedroom and headed downstairs. The kitchen matched everything else in the house, with its over-the-top opulence and blank, white walls. No aspect of Kyle marked the walls nor chrome fittings. Not as much as a splash of paint, print or photograph marred the blank canvas. Not a plant, vase or flower brightened the glass-topped dining table.

The house was as cold and impersonal as Kyle.

Flicking on the coffeemaker, John pulled his cell phone from the charger on the countertop and flicked through his emails. Nothing of any importance. Certainly no voice mail from Kyle, Sasha or anyone else. Was their silence a reflection on him or them? John couldn't be sure.

He pulled open the patio doors and walked outside. The view was phenomenal, but he remained determinedly aloof as he sank into one of the three heavily cushioned settees. Keying in the web address of a search engine, he found the number for the local police station. In a town the size of Templeton Cove, he was pretty confident trouble was rare. No doubt Inspector Garrett would welcome some interest to break up the monotony of her day.

He took a deep breath and waited for the duty sergeant to answer.

"Good morning, Templeton Police Station. How may I help you?"

John leaned his aching head back on the cushions. "Is it possible I can speak to Inspector Garrett, please?"

"Good morning, sir. Can I ask what this would be regarding?"

"My name is John Jordon. I'm sure my name will be enough for her to understand it's a good idea we meet whenever she deems convenient."

There was a momentary silence before the duty sergeant cleared his throat. "One moment please, sir."

If there was nothing else he'd gained from being Kyle's son, it seemed the mention of their surname opened doors in Templeton…although that didn't mean the people on the other side greeted him with open arms. Clicks were followed by a few bars of some classical music, then another click. "Mr. Jordon. Inspector Garrett. What can I do for you?"

Her no-nonsense, down-to-business tone made John open his eyes and sit upright. He cleared his throat. "Good morning, Inspector. I'm calling in the hopes I'll be able to infringe on a few minutes of your time today."

"May I ask why?"

Surprised she wasn't biting his hand off to get him into the station to be interrogated and then put on the first ferry out of there, John contemplated his next words while watching the white-foamed trail of a Jet Ski out on the water. "I thought after yesterday, it would be best if we speak privately."

"As opposed to Marian breathing fire down your neck, you mean?"

He smiled. "Exactly."

Her exhalation rasped down the line. “Well, good. I think that’s the intelligent way to move forward, considering who your father is and the fact you’re going to be running the fair. Start as we mean to go on.”

John narrowed his eyes. “Absolutely. What time shall I come in?”

“How about after lunch? Say one-thirty?”

“Great. See you then.” He ended the call and tapped the phone against his bottom lip.

The only way forward was to create a picture. Piece together the puzzle of Kyle and why he’d chosen Templeton Cove as his home. The file box of names he’d given John meant nothing on their own. Kyle hadn’t provided much information to work from or histories to learn. John glowered unseeingly ahead. Instead, the man had asked his son to make his acquaintance with each in case he should need them in Kyle’s absence.

His father insisted his wealth had been accumulated with only his son in mind. Claimed John’s paid education would now be put to better use outside a classroom. The only problem was, John didn’t want the lifestyle Kyle had so carefully orchestrated for him, and he couldn’t help but wonder if the bastard would be disappointed his son hadn’t hardened in the same way as the man who’d sired him.

Thankfully, the years had hardened Kyle only.

John loved his classroom full of kids; he loved his friends and associates. True, he'd yet to allow a woman into his life, but who knew what the future might hold?

Did Kyle really think the son he abandoned so many years before would stand by and allow him to ruin more people's lives? *Does he think I'll carry on his filthy, illegal work and then just walk away when I've had enough?*

He pushed to his feet as Sasha's face filled his mind's eye. *Over my dead body.*

John walked into the hallway with every intention of grabbing his keys and heading into town for breakfast, when a white envelope lying on the doormat caught his eye. He tightened his jaw. The printed crown in the upper center could only mean it was from Kyle.

John snatched it up and ripped it open. His eyes scanned the text…and the floor shifted. What was this? He dropped into the antique chair beside him and reread the letter. The words leaped and jumped in his vision….

Cancer...liver...bones...inoperable...

The paper slipped from his hands and fluttered to the stone floor. John stared at the staircase. Was Kyle telling the truth? What did he have to gain by lying that he was dying from terminal cancer? John waited for the grief, waited for the sense of loss to overpower him. It didn't come—only a strange pain stabbed deep in his gut. A pain he couldn't name as regret or revenge or anything else. Kyle had made himself a stranger—and soon John would be entirely alone.

CHAPTER TEN

SASHA PEDALED HER bike as fast as possible through the Templeton town center and out toward the cottages of Melonworth Drive. She zigzagged expertly between cars and other traffic, waving to the people who raised their hands in friendly greeting. She'd woken that morning more focused than ever to do something positive toward buying the fair before she had to face John the next day.

She scowled through her sunglasses. She needed more of a plan than her offer of money and relying on John's occasional good nature. The alluring combination of hurt and confusion he frequently had going on in those blue eyes wasn't even funny. He held far too much power in his gaze whenever he looked at her. She had to keep focused. Until he accepted her offer, or she came up with an alternative plan of action, he was the enemy.

Keep your friends close and your enemies closer. Just not as close as her nocturnal dreams had implied. She swallowed as her body tingled with desire.

The insecurity that erupted inside her during

their final moments in his office last night had been nothing short of terrifying. He'd suddenly stopped his ranting, and instead, his demeanor and soft study of her had turned intense with concern. His gaze bored into her as though she were an enigma…one there was every possibility he would figure out far too quickly.

He seemed to look past the exterior and deep into her soul.

So much so, it scared her that her childhood abuse was painted on her skin, entirely visible to those who cared enough to see it. That couldn't happen. She didn't want people to know. Didn't want her abuse to be who she was…only something that happened to her.

Memories assaulted Sasha as she fought to concentrate on the road ahead. Yet, she'd never deny the reality of those days. The thrill she'd felt having a man's attention at almost thirteen. The shiver of excitement at his smile. The knot in her stomach when he told her she was beautiful. She couldn't deny she'd felt any of those things, because she'd felt every one.

Then came the darkness.

The locked door of the warehouse and the lingering stench of oil on his hand when he clamped it over her mouth. The moment when the touching went from tender to terrifying…

She released a slow breath to steady the roar of remembered horror. Faster and faster she pedaled, purposefully banishing the terror of her past. She wouldn't go there. She wouldn't let John's arrival make her feel it all over again.

Today, she'd take action and set the preliminaries of her plan in motion. It was paramount she understood where she *and* John stood legally. So, for the first time, she'd arranged to consult a lawyer. Turning off a main road, Sasha entered the quieter part of town. When she passed the gates of the Good Time Holiday Park, her fortitude soared. After the effects of the devastating flash flood last year, the park was due to reopen this summer. The staff and people of Templeton had worked tirelessly to get the park back to its former glory and now it shone brighter than ever.

The clubhouse and restaurant had been refitted and renovated, and new caravans, donated from holiday home businesses across the country, dotted the park with their shiny newness. The people of Templeton Cove were rarely beaten. She wouldn't be, either.

She had no legal claim to Funland and the clause was the biggest obstacle to overcome, but she needed to be absolutely sure of her options. In her backpack was the original sale agreement between Kyle and her grandfather. She hoped something in it might provide the tiniest loophole she could utilize to put a stop to John's potentially destructive tour of her life.

Turning into a pretty avenue of cottages, she

rolled to a stop outside the third cottage on the right and alighted her bike. Pushing open the gate, Sasha steered her bike along the short pathway to the door and stowed it against the side of the house. The brightly colored daffodils and pansies in the small front garden did nothing to elevate her dark mood. She inhaled a shaky breath and removed her helmet. Her hand trembled when she smoothed her low ponytail and adjusted her jacket.

I can do this. I can show John he's messing with the wrong girl.

Lifting her chin, she approached the front door and lifted the iron knocker.

A cacophony of barking dogs ensued before a mumbled admonishment was uttered and the door swung open. Liam Browne, her older sister's one-time boyfriend, was a kind and handsome man, three years her senior. His face broke into a wide smile. "Hey, you."

Sasha relaxed her shoulders and smiled. She'd done the right thing in coming. Liam would help her...if he could. "Hey, yourself. Thanks for seeing me."

"Anytime. You know that." He stood back and, with a wave of his hand, gestured her inside.

She stepped into the cottage, and he closed the door. Sasha glanced around the dark wood hallway. Landscape prints and photographs dotted the walls and an antique bookcase filled with leather-bound books dominated one wall. Her gaze wandered toward the polished staircase, its banister gleaming under the sunlight streaming through the landing window. "This is beautiful, Liam."

He smiled. "Thanks. Sometimes I think I have too much crammed into this little space, but it works for me."

"It's great." She smiled. "Really welcoming."

She imagined Liam's home to be a complete antithesis of John's. The man probably lived next door to HRH Prince Charles's country estate.

Liam's dogs—a black Labrador, a Border collie and a tiny Jack Russell—pushed and brushed against her, their mouths stretched into welcoming grins, their tongues lolling and their eyes bright.

"Well, good morning to you, too." She petted each of their heads, laughing as they shoved each other out of the way, vying for her attention. She glanced at Liam. "Guess you've constantly got your hands full with this lot."

"Sure do." He grinned. "Do you want a coffee or something before we go through to my office?"

Sasha straightened and shook her head. "I'm fine. Just eager to get started."

He nodded and tilted his head toward the far end of the hallway. "In that case, follow me."

She followed him along the hallway to a room at the back of the house, the dogs panting at her legs. Once inside his office, Sasha wandered close to the window. "Wow, that's one beautiful garden. Your handiwork, by any chance?"

"I'll only say yes if you promise not to tell anyone. A man who spends most of his spare time gardening and planting coordinating flowers and bulbs isn't often considered a sexual catch by the female population."

She turned and smiled. "You, Liam Browne, are a catch and a half. Look at this place. As for you? You're thirty years old, one of the top criminal lawyers in the southwest and possess looks that would give some Hollywood stars a run for their money."

"Flatterer." His smile faltered. "Shame your sister didn't think so. How is Tanya, by the way?"

Silently cussing her too often snooty sister, Sasha stepped from the window and sat in one of the two chairs by his desk. She blew out a breath. "Living in Poole…alone with her high-flying banking career. Tanya's not a lot different than Mum. She thinks our Romany background is an embarrassment, rather than something to be proud of." She gave him a soft smile. "Her leaving wasn't about you."

He lifted his shoulders. "It doesn't matter."

Hating the uncomfortable silence that fractured the previously pleasant atmosphere, Sasha cleared her throat and glanced at the dogs as they each settled in one of three baskets by the window. "So, did you get a chance to read over the copy of Granddad's contract I emailed you?"

Liam sat in the leather chair behind his desk

and pulled some sheets of paper from his top tray. "I did."

She leaned forward, her stomach knotting in anticipation. "And?"

"It's not good news." He slid on a pair of dark-framed glasses and met her gaze. "It's all pretty much there in black and white. Unless I'd heard it from you, I wouldn't have believed Kyle Jordon and his lawyer had drawn up the contract. It's fair and it's clean. There's nothing untoward or out of the ordinary. Your grandfather wasn't swindled or coerced into anything beyond the reasonable. I'm sorry."

"Unless you consider the price Kyle paid for the place. That wasn't reasonable."

"Maybe not, but it was your grandfather's choice."

"And the clause? The one saying it can't be sold back to my family?"

He leaned back in his chair and steepled his fingers. "I'm a criminal lawyer and that's contractual. Do you want me to look into it? What are you thinking?"

She blew out a breath. "More hoping than thinking."

He lifted an eyebrow in question.

Sasha frowned. "I never understood why Granddad sold it for so little. He loved Funland, yet all of a sudden he sold it at a rock-bottom price to the town's criminal mastermind. Add that clause, and the whole thing stinks to high heaven. I'm hoping that now Funland is Kyle's son's in its entirety, the clause is invalid…and I just have to convince John it's my right to buy it back into my family."

"Hmm. It might not make sense, but everything in that contract is completely aboveboard." He plucked a pen from a leather-bound pot on his desk. "I'll make a note to look into it for you. I'm pretty sure you're right and it's up to Kyle's son what he does with it." He scribbled on a legal pad and met her eyes. "Just take into account, there will be some hefty tax payable at some point…whether by you or Kyle's son."

Her heart kicked. "I'll deal with that when I have to. I'm running out of options other than biding my time and waiting to see what John does next." She slapped her hand onto the armrest. "I can't stand this."

"I did a little research into the circumstances of Kyle's arrest."

Sasha stared at him as curiosity—and more than a little apprehension—shot through her. "He's been inside for about a year now. What did you find out?"

"You're not going to like it."

"Tell me."

He gave a sympathetic grimace. "His sole heir, and the current thorn in your side, is the named beneficiary and entitled to the entirety of Kyle's immoral fortune. Everything."

Sasha's eyes grew wide. *"Everything?"*

"Yep. If Kyle has handed over his estate to his son, I estimate John Jordon is now worth in excess of four-point-two million pounds. Plus the properties Kyle owns here, in London and abroad are his son's, as well."

"Oh, my God."

Liam stared, his gaze somber. "When Kyle was arrested, he was caught with a cache of class A drugs amounting to a street value of half a million. The rest, everything else that might or might not have gone on before then, was inadmissible in court and so Kyle couldn't be charged. Taking into account what he's worth, the criminal liability for the cache was soon recovered through his possessions…."

"And the rest was his to keep…or give to John."

"Exactly."

"When will Kyle be released? Do you know?"

"He was sentenced to sixteen years. If he behaves himself, he'll more than likely be out in eight."

"Eight years for that kind of offense?"

Liam lifted his shoulders and removed his glasses, a frown line spearing the space between his brows. "There's only so much that can be done with regards to drug seizing and the following arrests. It's frustrating, but the police and lawyers like me are doing the best we can. What's his son like? Do I need to come to the fair and start throwing my weight around?" He winked.

Sasha smiled as John's face—and huge, masculine stature—appeared in her mind's eye. "He's… all right, I suppose. That's half the problem."

"Oh?" He gave her a knowing look. "You don't like the guy, do you?"

She huffed out a laugh. "Of course not. He's a pompous pain in the ass."

Liam grinned. "Sure he is."

"Liam…"

He raised his hands in surrender. "Okay, okay. I'm just saying. It's not very often I see you blush. It's kind of nice."

She pushed to her feet. "One, I am not blushing and two, I need to get out of here and think of a plan B."

He stood, a soft smile still playing at his lips. "There's nothing wrong with a bit of play and a little less work every now and then, you know."

She hitched her backpack onto her shoulder and glared. "If I wanted to *play,* it wouldn't be with John Jordon." *Yeah, right.*

He laughed. "Fair enough. I'll believe you even if millions of others wouldn't."

"I'm going. Now. Before I'm forced to hurt you." She smiled and headed for the door.

He followed her along the hallway, and after she opened the front door, Sasha turned and hugged him. She held him firmly and spoke into his shirt. "You're too good for Tanya. Way too good. Get out there and find a woman who deserves you, okay?"

"I'm trying." He squeezed her before pulling back and holding her at arm's length. "So, what's plan B?"

"I'll figure something out because there's no way I'm losing the fair to a Jordon." She swallowed the abrupt threat of tears. "I don't know anything but Funland. I don't *want* to know anything else. The thought of leaving Templeton and doing a job sitting behind a desk or in a shop scares me half to death. It would chip away at my soul until I was nothing but a shell. The fair was meant to be mine and whatever has happened, or will happen, I'm not letting it go."

She eased from his grip and walked out of the cottage. Pulling her bike from the side of the house, she mounted it before she looked at Liam. "You take care."

"It might be a good thing to tell this John Jordon what you've just told me, you know."

Sasha frowned. "Tell him what?"

"That without the fair you wouldn't be you. Who knows, it might be that sort of honesty that tips the scales with this guy."

Nausea dipped and flowed through her stomach as Sasha secured her helmet in place. "John Jordon is in no state of mind to take anything I have to say into account."

"What do you mean?"

"He's determined to find out who his father is, despite the fact he can't stand the man. They're estranged and, from what I can tell, John is entirely pissed at Kyle."

Liam's eyes darkened with concern. "Kyle Jordon is dangerous. His son has his father's blood running through his veins. Be careful. Don't go risking your life over something that once belonged to your grandfather. It's not worth it."

Even kind, wonderful Liam couldn't possibly understand the firm ground the fair gave her to build upon. "It belongs in my family, Liam. I need it. My kids will need it. I have to do this."

She pushed away on her bike with the weight of Liam's gaze burning a hole in her back.

"WHY DON'T WE go to my office, Mr. Jordon?"

John smiled inwardly despite the shock of his father's illness still bouncing around his body at a hundred miles an hour. The inspector's emphasis on his surname didn't go unnoticed by him or the other three or four uniformed cops working at the station reception desk. The officers stared openly, eyebrows raised. He steadfastly kept his focus forward and followed the inspector through a side door into the main arena of the station. It was a whirl of activity as the inspector walked among her inferiors with silent and confident authority.

Phones rang and voices carried above the noise of printers and humming computers, elevating his second headache of the day. She led him to an office at the far end of the room. Encased within two windowed walls, she had as much a view of her colleagues as they did of her. John wondered if her decision to keep the blinds open gave insight into the woman. Was she approachable and honest? Or was she forced to leave herself exposed to their judgment under duress?

She pushed open the door and waved him inside. "Take a seat."

He did. When she made no move to close the blinds, but came around and sat behind the desk in full view of her staff, a spark of positivity caught inside him. Maybe today he'd get some answers about Kyle and the reputation he had in this seaside town. Inspector Garrett gave the undeniable impression that she was amenable and, secondly, that she listened.

He cleared his throat. "Thanks for agreeing to see me."

She ran her cool green gaze over his face before picking up a pen and leaning back in her chair. Her demeanor appeared relaxed as she expertly laced the pen back and forth between her fingers. "I can't say I wasn't surprised or intrigued by your phone call. As you can imagine, once you and Sasha left the bakery yesterday, Marian was keen to fill in the blanks as to why you're here." She offered him a small smile. "Exactly how much of her musings are fiction remains to be seen."

Immediately warming to this undeniably beautiful, enigmatic head of the Templeton police, John laid his hands loosely on the chair's armrests and forced his wandering mind to focus on the task at hand rather than the prospect of Kyle dying. "I'm not in Templeton to cause trouble, Inspector."

"So, why are you here?"

"Because Kyle requested it."

She stared. "That instills caution rather than ease in me, I'm afraid."

"Why?"

"Isn't that obvious? Kyle was by no means Templeton Resident of the Year."

"I'm not my father."

"That remains to be seen. So, it was you who wanted to see me. Why don't you get straight to the reason you're here?"

John inhaled a long breath and released it. "It's simple. I want to garner more detail to the very little I know about Kyle and his life in Templeton."

She frowned. "You think a police inspector is likely to tell you anything about a convicted drug dealer? Your father was far from hospitable to his fellow man and I, for one, am glad he's in prison."

John cursed inwardly. His decision to appeal to the inspector's better nature had come from his need to keep things aboveboard for as long as humanly possible. He didn't want to lose his sense of integrity during his mission to uncover who his father really was. He was really hoping to glean information from the people of Templeton in as open and straightforward a way as possible.

He'd relied on the theory Inspector Garrett would tell him the kind of man Kyle was personally, as well as morally, in exchange for John being honest with her about his future intentions—once he'd figured them out. Maybe that theory was 100 percent off the mark.

He leaned forward. "I'd hoped you tell me about the circumstances surrounding his arrest. What he was like prior to that. Who his friends were. His enemies."

She studied him as she bounced the pen gently against her jaw. Eventually, she tossed it onto the desk and stood. John forced himself to stay in his seat and not fidget as she rounded the desk and leaned against it, directly in front of him. She crossed her arms, her gaze unwavering. "Why don't you be a bit more specific about what it is you want to know? Or even better, *why* you want to know. I've got zero intention of giving you any information without knowing why you've come to the Cove."

Frustration simmered deep in his stomach. "Until a month ago, I hadn't heard from Kyle since I was boy. Then, out of the blue, I received a letter from him asking me to come here and oversee things."

"Oversee things?"

"It's up to me what I do with his businesses now."

"Businesses? Kyle wouldn't know what legit business was if it up and slapped him in the face."

"I agree."

She studied him a moment longer before her gaze softened—a little—and seemed to pique with interest. “If you were estranged, why would he give you everything?”

“He has no one else he can trust.”

“Can he trust you?”

“I don’t know yet. That depends on whether I understand why he chose to never contact me.”

She raised her eyebrow. “He never contacted you at Saint Mark’s?”

John stiffened. “You know where I went to school?”

“Of course. I care about this town, Mr. Jordon. When I found out you were here, I dug a little deeper into Kyle’s background. Added a lot more to what I already knew. Your mother was killed during an armed robbery. She was an innocent civilian caught up in a horrific event. Kyle avenged her murder and paid for his crime. However, during that time, his eleven-year-old son was shipped off to one of the most prestigious boarding schools in the country.” She stared. “What I didn’t know was Kyle didn’t stay connected to you during the ensuing years.”

Nausea and anger twisted like barbed wire in his gut. “Clearly I don’t need to waste time explaining my family history.”

“I’m a cop. What else did you expect?”

She was right. He was Kyle’s offspring and the man was currently serving a sixteen-year sentence for drug offenses. The townspeople were hardly going to welcome him with open arms—nor was Templeton's inspector going to roll out the red carpet. He swallowed and confidently held her gaze. "Kyle's dying, Inspector."

Silence descended.

The muted clang of activity and voices outside the inspector's office suddenly sounded louder than before. John's heart picked up speed. He'd said the words out loud; made it real. Two spots of color appeared high on her cheeks and she slowly closed her eyes. "I'm sorry to hear that."

That he hadn't expected. "You are?"

"Yes." She opened her eyes and moved away from the desk to stare out into the working station. "It was me who arrested your father, Mr. Jordon. I made sure he went away for a long time."

Inexplicable annoyance prickled the hairs at the nape of John's neck as he stared at her back. "You sound as though he didn't deserve that. From what I know—"

"I didn't say that. Kyle deserved everything he got." She pivoted and planted her hands on slender hips. "It doesn't mean I relish the prospect of him dying alone in prison. From what little time I spent with your father, he didn't strike me as entirely bad. He helped me to put a coldhearted killer away for the rest of his life."

Resistance rippled through John's blood. He didn't need to hear anything good about Kyle. He wanted his decision to do as he pleased, once he figured out what that would be, to be cut and dried. He owed the man nothing. Why should his father die with a clear conscience? He should die knowing the pain he'd inflicted on innocent people through the drugs he supplied. He should know his child never forgave him for leaving him alone after the violent death of his mother.

John wanted him to know that by making the decision to go after the man who killed her, he had left his son with an inert fear of abandonment. A son who made a conscious decision to live his life alone, yet help as many people as he could along the way. He never walked away and left anyone to deal with their hardships alone. He wouldn't do that to Sasha, either. His ability to support people and see things through without resorting to violence proved just how unlike Kyle he really was.

With his heart beating steadily, John leaned back. "I went to Marchenton."

A flicker of surprise shot through her gaze before she blinked and cool interest showed once more. "And?"

"And as per Kyle's instructions, I went to see a former crack house of his…a crack house now owned by your husband. Why would he buy a place like that?"

Her green eyes turned dark with suspicion. Once more the chatter and noise from outside the office filtered into the room. "My husband's affairs have nothing to do with you. Now, if there's nothing else..."

He raised his hand in supplication. "You're right. It's none of my business, but will you at least tell me one thing?"

She crossed her arms. "What?"

"Did Kyle sell the house to your husband before his incarceration? Or did your husband buy it afterward?"

"Why does it matter? The property is now my husband's." She narrowed her eyes. "What's your interest in it, Mr. Jordon? Whatever went on in there when it was Kyle's is something I don't want resurrected...there, or anywhere else in Templeton."

"And it won't be if I have anything to do with it. I need to know because Kyle wants me to believe the narcotics side of his business is over. I'm not going to let him paint himself as a changed man if it isn't true. Was the closing down of the house enforced?"

She pursed her lips, her brow furrowed. Eventually, she blew out a breath. "Yes. Once he was arrested, the house went into repossession. My husband bought it because..." She lifted her chin. "He wants to use it as a symbol to the people in Marchenton that they can turn things around if they really want to."

"In what way?"

"He's going to turn it into a drop-in center. Despite everything your father represented, we're hoping to utilize the place Kyle once used as a private hell for people dependent on him as a place for those same people to get help."

John's stomach churned. "I see."

She walked to the door. Recognizing his cue to leave, John stood and approached her.

When they faced each other, she stared directly into his eyes. "I stand by what I said about Kyle. He wasn't all bad. I think his reaction to your mother's murder flicked a switch that couldn't be turned off. Especially considering his time locked up with real killers...nasty killers. When he was released the first time around, I doubt any aspect of the man he was before he went in there remained."

John's battle to see his father as anything but a liar and drug pusher roared to life once again. "I really can't understand why you'd cheerlead him this way."

She glared. "Cheerlead him? I don't think so."

"Then why defend him?"

She pulled open the door. "Because I'm certain Kyle has some good in him. The question is, do you?"

CHAPTER ELEVEN

IT WAS ONE o'clock the following afternoon before Sasha saw John again. The hairs at her nape prickled and she levered up from the stack of stuffed animals she was helping one of the stallholders store in the fairground warehouse. The fact she was in the only part of Funland she hated when she sensed him watching her, set her defenses screeching to high alert. He stood in the doorway, his face in silhouette due to the bright July sunshine streaming in behind him.

Her stomach flip-flopped as she strolled toward him, casually slapping her hands against her legs to rid her jeans of dust. Mindful of her decision to keep her cool and bide her time over the next few days, she plastered on a cheery smile. "Hi."

He stiffened, and the quirk of his eyebrow proved her new tactic of being polite might just work better than she could've hoped. Maybe a little feminine compliance would be the secret to her success.

He cleared his throat. "Hi, yourself. I wonder if you might be able to spare me a few minutes. In the office."

"Sure. I'm just about finished here."

Nodding curtly, he turned and headed outside. She cast a glance over the satisfying sight of his back and butt before stifling the need to emit a particularly girlish sigh. She seemed to be continually battling her lust for the man. She inhaled a steadying breath and followed him, purposely slowing her pace to his quickening one. As much as she tried to make peace with what Liam had said to her about letting John know how deeply she needed the fair, she refused to utter any confessions or tell him about her history.

He knew enough already that any further words would only arm him in a potentially devastating way. From the moment they had met, her impassioned reaction to his arrival had set the tone and mood of their relationship. Did she really need to reiterate her desperation? From now on, she would play it cool and calm. No matter what he threw at her, she would react with grace and sanity.

Her secrets would remain secrets to everyone but Leah. During a telephone conversation with her best friend the night before, Sasha agreed Leah could meet John when the time was right. She was more than aware her friend's motivation for their meeting was more grounded in her need to protect Sasha than anything else.

John entered the office and stood at the door, waiting for her. His passive expression almost fooled Sasha into believing his detachment, until she had to squeeze past his broad chest to get inside. When her gaze briefly locked on his, she recognized the storm of angry emotion he clearly fought to keep under control. Her stomach knotted. Now what?

She frowned. "Are you okay?"

"Sure. You?"

She lifted her shoulders even as her heart beat a little faster. "Sure."

His eyes blazed with irritation, and his jaw turned to stone as he tilted his head in the direction of the desk. "Why don't you take a seat?"

Steadfastly ignoring the tremble in her legs, she slid past him into the office. Her temper simmered just beneath the surface as she hesitated at the seat. The impulse to turn around and demand he tell her what was coming next was more than she could stand. She closed her eyes. She'd barely been in his company more than a few minutes and already the instinct to attack ricocheted through her system.

"Are you going to sit down?" His voice came from close behind her, the masculine spice of his aftershave jolting her desire into overdrive.

She swallowed. "Sure."

He didn't move and his breath gently lifted the hairs at the back of her neck. She resisted the urge to shiver. Clearly her decision to knot her hair on top of her head that morning had been a mistake. At least with her hair down, it took a gust of wind to penetrate its thickness and reach her bare skin.

Opening her eyes, she lowered into the seat with the regality of a queen. "So, what's up?"

He sat in Kyle's huge leather chair and, with his eyes on hers, slid a file box from the far corner of the desk and set it in front of him. His chest rose as he inhaled and then pushed the box toward her. "Some homework for you."

She frowned as her burgeoning temper deflated and evolved into curiosity. "What's this?"

"I've been busy over the past twenty-four hours. I've spent some time reconsidering your offer, but I also think before either of us can work toward what we want, we need to face what we're dealing with."

"Which is?"

"Kyle."

She narrowed her eyes. This was nothing more than a delaying tactic. Kyle was gone. The decision lay with John whether or not to sell her the fair. "I'm dealing with you. Not Kyle." She hesitated. "Aren't I?"

"Yes."

Frustration stormed through her mind and hopelessness threatened her heart. "Then what's the problem?"

He spread his hands on top of the box. "These are papers on everyone Kyle considered of any importance in his life."

She met his eyes. "Are you in there?"

He flinched like she'd slapped him and Sasha sucked in a breath. *What's wrong with me? What happened to being nice?* She closed her eyes. "I didn't mean… I didn't mean that Kyle…" She opened her eyes.

His pallor had turned a strange hue of gray. If she bounced a coin off his jaw, Sasha didn't doubt it would buckle on impact.

"Look, I'm sorry." She pulled the box onto her lap and lifted the lid. "I assume whatever is in this file, Kyle wanted it kept private. Why are you showing this to me?"

"I want to know if you can shed any light on who these people are." He shifted forward, his cheeks darkening, returning his skin to its former color. "If you know these people and can tell me how they're perceived in the Cove, then it might give me a better idea of what Kyle was up to just prior to his arrest. The instructions he left me are sketchy at best. I don't want to go about my business and end up unwittingly coming face-to-face with someone happy to smash my kneecaps."

She smiled. "Does Templeton really seem like the kind of place you'd find that person?"

"No, but there was something that kept Kyle here."

Her smile faltered. "That's true."

"He pretty much left things for me to deal with as I see fit, but for some reason he thinks the people in that box will help or hinder whatever path I decide to take. It would be good if I had an idea of who I'm dealing with before they start turning up demanding answers in the same vein you and Freddy are."

She slowly closed the lid and folded her hands on top. "I think we need to start being honest with each other. I can't go on like this. Am I putting myself in danger by helping you?"

His gaze was steady. "I won't let anything happen to you."

"You can't promise that. You said you don't know these people, and we both know Kyle didn't associate with the nice people around town. You wouldn't find him at the summer fete handing out fliers or whipping up a blanket to sell at the knitting stall. We need to start being honest." She drew in a breath and exhaled. "Shall I go first or you?"

He studied her. His cool blue gaze languidly wandered over her face and hair.

Her heart beat hard and her mouth went dry, but enough was enough. This standoff between them couldn't go on. "We've been circling each other like caged animals ever since you got here. I don't know about you, but I'm tired of it. Having time away from here yesterday did me some good."

Amusement softened his dark blue gaze and he smiled softly. "You mean you actually enjoyed being away from the fair for a while? Or from me?"

"Only you." She met his smile. It was impossible not to.

Seconds ticked by as they sat smiling at each other and when Sasha's cheeks turned warm, she

the threat of her demons as they rose and hovered around her like a dark cloud. "I still don't understand why you need my help."

He leaned forward and placed his elbows on the desk, clasping his hands together. His knuckles turned white, and Sasha flicked her gaze to his eyes. They were somber. "I think you play a bigger part than either of us knows in Kyle working to get the fair from your grandfather."

She frowned. "Why would you think that?"

"When he wrote asking me to come to Templeton, he said he'd had enough of running the businesses, but also that he'd done some things he shouldn't have. Things he deemed worse than the lives he messed up by supplying cocaine for God knows how long."

"What can be worse than that?"

He closed his eyes and Sasha's trepidation soared.

"Before my father was sent to prison the first time—"

"The first time? He's been in prison before? For what?"

"I can't tell you that. Not yet."

"I thought we were going to start being honest here." *Just as you are, you mean?*

"Once upon a time my father held family as the one true thing in life. The one thing we should respect and cherish."

Anger shot through her blood in a hot, piercing stream. "You're lying."

He snapped his eyes open. “What?”

“How can you say that when Kyle willingly ripped the one thing my family had to call their own right out from underneath them?”

“Exactly.” He stood and came around the desk. When he gripped her hands in his and held tight, preventing her from fleeing as she wanted to, Sasha’s fear of entrapment crawled through her veins.

She glanced toward the door. “I need to get out of here. I need to work. I don’t want to listen to this.”

He squeezed her hands, his gaze darting over her face. “He mentioned your mother. Even said he regretted using her, whatever the hell that means.”

She stared. She couldn’t believe what she was hearing, couldn’t believe he would say those things. “Why are you doing this?”

“I’m convinced he used your mother’s derision of Funland to get it from your family. For better or worse, the fairground deals in loads of cash every day. It was the simplest way for him to launder money and build new drug contacts.”

Revulsion hurtled through her as the vile words tumbled from his mouth. Her heart raced and her mind filled with images of her mother’s face, twisted in disgust every time Sasha begged her to help keep Funland in their family and not let Kyle turn it into something so loathsome, mothers would stop bringing their children and fathers would want their families to avoid it at all costs.

She squeezed her eyes shut. “My mother wouldn’t

do that. Yes, she hated this place. Thought it made our family look like gypsies and felt that made us inferior to others in Templeton, but to let it go to Kyle when she knew what he was…"

"I'm not lying to you. God knows, it's harder to tell you the truth. It's you, Sasha. I'm convinced the whole thing with the clause, your grandfather, I think you're the key to unraveling everything about this place."

"Why?" She opened her eyes as raw hurt and panic rushed through her. Her heart beat fast. *Does he know? Does he know what happened to me here? Does Kyle?* "What are you talking about? Your father barely spoke to me."

"He knew you were likely to go after the fair once he was in prison. He knew and asked me not to sell it to you under any circumstances."

"Me, specifically?"

"Yes."

"This is crazy. Is my money not good enough for the great Kyle Jordon?"

His gaze darted over her face, her hair and her lips. "This isn't about money."

"Then what the hell is it about?"

"I can only assume he doesn't want to face what he's done. How low he sank for greed and money. If you gain full access to the fair, you'll eventually find out everything."

"What do you mean *everything?*"

"I don't know. Not yet. But I know there's more."

She shook her head, hating that tears burned her eyes. "This is madness." She drew her hands from his. "The Kyle I knew practically spat in the face of anyone who dared judge him. Why worry about my reaction to his misdemeanors?"

"The circumstances have changed forever for Kyle. He knows that and for the first time ever, he's scared."

"Why? What are you talking about?"

"He's dying."

She stiffened. "What?"

He shrugged. "It seems even the invincible Kyle Jordon quakes at the thought of facing his maker after everything he's done. Maybe he liked you more than you realize and the prospect of you finding out what he did to take the fair is more than he's prepared to face."

"He's dying?"

He nodded.

Sasha closed her eyes. How could she scream and shout when John was facing the loss of a parent—no matter how wrong or bad that parent was?

"Oh, God. What a mess. I'm sorry your dad—" She opened her eyes.

"Don't be. I'm not." He lifted his shoulders, looked above her head toward the door.

He said the words, but the flicker of sad confusion in his gaze belied the casual dismissal of Kyle's plight. She shook her head. "How will we work this out?" she whispered. "How can you possibly go against a dying man's wishes? I want the fair and you're the one with the power."

"None of this is about power."

Sadness enveloped her. "Of course it is."

"It's not."

"Then let me undo everything that has gone on here and make things good again. If Kyle cared about me at all, he'd understand giving me the fair is the right thing to do."

His gaze wandered over her face once more. "Once I'm sure—"

Anger caught behind her rib cage and burst into flame. She leaped to her feet, shoving her chair backward. "Stop saying that. You don't know me. You have no obligation to protect me. I can handle—"

"Why do you want Funland if your mother hated it so much? Was willing to sell it to the devil? Don't you wonder what was going on with her before and after she coerced your grandfather into signing it over to Kyle? Everything feels tainted. Maybe it would be better for both of us to forget this place ever existed and get on with our lives. Kyle wasn't a good man...despite Inspector Garrett saying she saw good in him."

Sasha stared, confusion marring her emotion. "She said that?"

"Yes."

Images of Kyle smiling in that disconcerting and friendly way of his floated through her mind; the times she caught him staring fondly at a child with dark hair and blue eyes—not unlike John's—when he thought no one was looking.

"You have to sell it to me." Her heart beat like a hammer as she looked into his handsome face. Into blue eyes darkened with concern and care. "You *have* to."

"Why?"

"John, please—"

"Talk to me." He lifted his hand and brushed his thumb across her cheek. "Let me in. What is it about this place that *really* has such a hold on you?"

He moved closer.

Sasha's heart picked up speed as his gaze intensely searched hers. She tried and failed to drag some words into her mouth. He moved a little closer and laid his hands at her waist. She knew what was coming but made no move to stop him and instead, leaned closer and smoothed her hands to his rock-hard biceps. He eased her mouth open with lips tender and soft against hers.

His tongue was pliant and enraptured her with the perfect assertion of masculine power she'd failed to accept in any man before. The contact was a spark to a smoldering fire and she met his provocation with ardent fervor as she hungrily kissed him back, a whimper escaping her. Lust that had been building since she set eyes on him fanned to a frenzy by the hurt confusion burning inside and the rightness of being in his arms.

He slipped one hand to the back of her neck and gently tugged her closer with the other. She slid her hands down his arms to grip his strong, sinewy forearms—the part of him she'd wanted to touch in what felt like forever. They didn't disappoint and all the horror of her memories slipped away. She'd embrace these moments of liberty for as long as they lasted.

Her breasts pressed deliciously against the flat plane of his chest as she and John kissed and tussled, discovered and devoured. Her arousal turned feral and lust ripped through every cell in her body. She didn't step back and she didn't slow down. She'd only think when he stopped taking her and they had to face the reality that the fair separated their individual needs, yet it was the catalyst that brought them together.

Control. She had to have control. This was her decision. Not his. She chose when to have sex and with whom. Not the man. Never the man.

So why, for the first time in forever, did she feel John Jordon was the one stripping her of the basic instinct to breathe? Why did the prospect of him taking her feel so exciting, instead of terrifying? Her heart raced with anticipation; her body screamed for his touch. She wanted to have sex with this man. Now. Feel him deep inside her…

Deeper and deeper he kissed her before easing back. She stared at him, silently begging for more. She'd surrender to this moment rather than regret it forever. She felt his pain and heard his plea. She knew this man and, God help her, she really wanted to trust him with all her heart.

“This is crazy, but I want to do this, John. I want to be with you. All of you.”

A low guttural moan escaped him before he whispered her name and dropped his lips to the side of her neck.

CHAPTER TWELVE

John's heart hammered as he sucked and nipped at her neck. Her hands moved silkily like brushed velvet over the exposed skin of his arms, driving him insane with the need to have her. He lifted his head. Her dark eyes bored into his, her mouth swollen red and ridiculously inviting. He swallowed. "Are you sure? This feels insane, but I want you. I care about you, Sasha. I care what happens to you."

Her body trembled in his grasp. "Let's go in the kitchen."

He froze, his body wired with tension.

Her cheeks flushed as she took his hand. Silently, she led him toward the office kitchen. Once inside, she dropped his hand and closed the door. The key clicked in the lock.

She turned and they faced each other. John's mind raced and his libido soared. He lifted an eyebrow at the sexy, fiery intention in her eyes. "You want to do this now? In here?"

She nodded.

Indecision battled inside him. Lust versus gallantry battered his conscience. He swallowed. "We don't have to—"

"Yes, we do." She lunged forward and gripped his jaw in her strong fingers, before pulling him forward and hungrily closing her mouth over his.

His mind emptied of consideration as he yanked her shirt from her jeans. Their lips separated for the briefest of seconds as he pulled the shirt over her head, and then she went for his T-shirt. He glanced at her breasts, encased in black satin. The sun-kissed orbs showed above their tantalizing constraint. Christ, he longed to touch her, kiss her and take one sweet nipple deep into his mouth.

He pulled her to him and the cushion of her full breasts pressed against his chest. He smoothed his hand over her back, lower to grip her butt and press her fully against his erection. She whispered his name into his mouth before clawing cruel fingernails over his biceps, higher into the hair at the nape of his neck. Lust, disbelief and yearning rushed and battled through him as they kissed harder and deeper.

This woman was a hot, passionate dynamo who made him feel like everything and nothing at the same time. The delight in her eyes when she laughed made him want her. The sadness, when it came, even more so. He wanted to protect her, lift her, make her laugh and scream and shout and cuss. Time after time, women had come into his life and he'd easily let them go. Sasha Todd was different. He was in the deepest shit possible, but no way could he turn away from her now.

She eased him backward until his butt hit something solid. Her black eyes roamed over his face, his shoulders and the expanse of his chest until he felt about seven feet tall. Pure hunger glinted in the dark depths of her gaze. He'd never seen a woman look more beautiful or sexy in his damn life.

"Christ, who are you?" The question slipped from between his clenched teeth, and he gripped the counter, lest he lunge for her and devour every inch of her golden skin.

She smiled and released her belt buckle and the buttons on her jeans. "I'm the woman you're going to make love to. Right here, right now."

With his gaze locked on hers, he followed suit. She kicked off her shoes and he toed off his boots. Their jeans simultaneously fell to the tiled kitchen floor. Dragging his gaze from hers, he took in the sight of her.

Her panties were little more than a scrap of satin. Pink with black polka dots and cut high on her petite hips. His mouth went dry. He couldn't wait any longer. He had to give her pleasure; had to know her inside and out. He reached for her and smoothed his hands to her waist, kissing her forehead, her nose, her cheeks and finally her lips. Her face was hot, her body even more so.

He lifted her into his arms and she locked her legs around his waist, her mouth dropping to his neck and shoulders as he carried her across the room to the counter. He eased her onto the surface and stepped between her legs—at last, he allowed himself to feel her breasts. With his mouth still on hers, he slowly pulled one cup away from her breast and thumbed the hard pebble of her nipple, their tongues fighting for supremacy.

Pulling back, he had to see her, had to be sure this was what she wanted. She leaned back on her hands wantonly and watched him from beneath heavy lids. The desire in her gaze was all the permission he needed.

"You are…" He shook his head and leaned down to take her coffee-colored nipple into his mouth.

She groaned above him, her legs sliding farther apart as her fingers wove into his hair. He sucked and fed as his cock ached with need. The euphoria of being with her this way drove him nearly mad with desire.

"Touch me, John."

He lifted his head and stared deep into her eyes. Passion and yearning shone back at him as she exhaled against his face, soft and sexy. Unable to take his eyes off her, he slid his hand across her thighs and down behind her knees. He jerked her closer. Her gasp ignited a burst of male pride and he grinned, scoring his fingers to her hip. He gripped the string of her panties and snapped them off, tossing them behind him in one fluid motion.

Another gasp.

Then she smiled so widely, his heart damn near left his chest.

She reached for his face and held his jaw, plunging her tongue deep into his mouth. His fingers moved down her body, inching toward her most intimate place. When he reached it, she was hot, wet and ready. John pressed his thumb firmly against her clitoris.

"Oh, God. Yes." She pulled her mouth from his and closed her eyes. She dropped her head back.

John savored the look of her throat as the skin shifted and jerked. She pulled her bottom lip between her teeth as he massaged her and coaxed her forward to slide his fingers inside. God, he had to have her. He couldn't wait. As if reading his thoughts, she snapped open her eyes. "I need my bag." She groaned and writhed against his hand, her breaths short. "It's in the office."

He swallowed. How had he not thought of protection? He squeezed his eyes shut. "I forgot." He eased his fingers from inside her and dropped his forehead to hers.

She laughed. "So did I. It doesn't matter. What matters is which of us is going to go out and get it."

He lifted his head. Her eyes twinkled and her mouth was stretched into a grin. He smiled. "I guess that would be me then."

"Uh-huh."

"Bugger."

She gave him a little shove. "Be quick."

He snatched up his boxers and, using them to cover his manhood, strode toward the door. He unlocked it and peered into the office. Not a sound came from within and he made a mad dash for Sasha's bag, slung over the back of her chair. Gripping it tightly, his entire body humming with tension and sexual need, he ran back into the kitchen. Relocking the door, he turned and froze. She'd removed her bra and now sat naked and wanting on the countertop. He drew in a breath. God, he didn't know if he deserved to make love to a woman so stunningly beautiful, but he had to. If Sasha wanted him, he'd take her.

She held out her hand. "Give it to me."

Relief shuddered through him that the moment apart hadn't brought her to her senses; he didn't know how he'd walk away now. As she opened the bag, he eased her legs apart and stood between them once more. He softly caressed her shoulders and upper arms as she fumbled in her bag. After far too long a moment, she produced a silver packet.

"Yes." She whispered and tore it open.

She kissed him, her tongue urgently seeking his. He met her need, his penis and balls aching with desire. She reached between them and slid her hand around his erection and moaned into his mouth. She massaged him, her fingers as smooth as silk, teasing as they inched lower to cup his balls. He slid his hands over her body and down between her legs. He pushed two fingers deep inside and she whimpered and trembled against him.

They touched and caressed a little longer until they were back to the frenzied heat they'd basked in before. Reluctantly, he slid his fingers from her soft, sexy warmth and plucked the condom from her hand. He smoothed on the protection and met her eyes. All humor had vanished, leaving only pure need in its wake.

Holding the back of her knees, John yanked her forward, and she opened her legs wide. He guided himself inside her, and her breath left her lungs on a rush of warm air against his ear. She clung to him, her nails digging into his shoulders. He thrust deep and groaned aloud as the sensation of finding the pleasure he sought crashed down around him.

He held her tiny frame against his body and drove into her. She met him thrust for thrust. Her whispered whimpers and pleas fueled his passion as he waited for her to chase her climax first. His balls ached and his heart raced as he willed her on. Deeper and deeper, higher and higher they climbed until she stiffened in his arms. Satisfaction burst like a fireball in his chest and he leaned back to watch her climax. Her mouth dropped open and her cheeks flushed deep red as she stared blindly into his eyes.

"God, Sasha." He drove into her again.

The world exploded as he came and, in that moment, John knew he'd never be the same again.

He wanted this woman. He needed her. Wanted to make her happy. The problem was…would she ever feel the same way about him? About Kyle Jordon's son?

SASHA STRUGGLED TO get her breathing back to normal. Her cheek lay on the hard ridge of his shoulder as he smoothed gentle circles over her spine. A stupid smile she couldn't fight played at her lips as she listened to his heart slow from its rapid hammer to a steady, strong beat. She didn't want to pull away, didn't want to look in his eyes and see embarrassment, or worse, regret, lingering in their deep-blue depths.

Any minute now he'd move. Any minute now Freddy could try the kitchen door and find it locked….

She jerked up straight. His mouth was curved into a smile, too. His was wide, his teeth shining bright under the overhead lights. Heat warmed her cheeks as he stared at her, his eyes dancing with almost boyish delight. She laughed and prodded a finger into his chest. "What?"

He shook his head and ran his hand over her shoulder and down her upper arm. "Nothing."

Her stomach executed an alien and worryingly girlish loop-the-loop. God, she liked him so much. But she had to keep her head in the game…and her heart under control. Feeling more than a little rattled, she pushed him back and smiled. "Stop looking at me like that. We have to get dressed and out of here before Freddy comes searching for one of us."

He groaned and tipped his head back. "Can't we hide in here awhile longer?"

She grinned. "No."

Sliding from the countertop, her body hummed with nerves as she walked around the small space and grabbed her clothes. She snatched up what was left of her panties and screwed them tightly into her hand. Her lingering smile dissolved. What had they done? What would happen next? Emotions were high and her lust even more so. She wouldn't regret their lovemaking because it was entirely what she wanted, but now what? What did they say to each other? Feel for one another?

His feet sounded against the tiles behind her, followed by the rustle and swish of clothes. She swallowed her nerves and dressed with her back to him, as self-consciousness skimmed her body.

Once she was fully clothed, she inhaled a strengthening breath and turned.

He quirked an eyebrow. "So…what now?"

She stared. That was the big question. "I don't know."

His smile faltered and his shoulders slumped. "No regrets?"

She forced a smile. "No regrets."

Yet, the enormity of what they'd just done crashed into her heart and mind. The fair still hovered between them like an unwavering and dangerous boulder. Nothing had changed. One premature shove from either of them could send the whole thing over the cliff, crushing her beneath its weight.

If he found out about her past, would he think sex was how she got her way? Would he believe her when she said she wanted him because of him and the way he made her feel? That she'd risen above her molestation and used her pain as strength? The world was hers for the taking. Life was there to be discovered, enjoyed and grasped at every opportunity.

She wasn't ignoring the fact that the sexy confidence and intelligence that lingered in his cool blue eyes had pricked at her heart from the first moment he looked at her. Her passion for him wasn't about insecurity or what she had to gain. It was something so primal it pulled at her, making her yearn for his hands to touch her, his lips to kiss her and his penis to push deep inside her until nothing else mattered but how he made her want to climb into the sky and pluck out the sun.

Her heart shuddered. Why would he believe that when she scarcely could?

She tilted her chin and dragged her strength up from her toes. "We'll put what happened here on the back burner for a while. We have to deal with the revelation you suspect my mum had dealings with Kyle. That's the most important thing right now."

He stared at her, and a flash of something—

maybe disbelief—or hurt—filled his gaze before he blinked and it was gone. He nodded, his face impassive. "Absolutely."

He brushed past her, and Sasha stood stock-still. She closed her eyes when the door clicked open behind her. She wanted to move, but her feet wouldn't cooperate. She wanted to chase after him and tell him she didn't do what they'd done for anything but the desire to be intimate with him… for a few blessed moments. She didn't lay herself wide open to anyone, and her every truth had been there for him to take or reject whenever she kissed or touched him.

Forcing herself to move, she stuffed her panties into her bag before hurrying to the sink. She quickly washed her hands, gratefully splashing cold water over her hot face and neck. Her body yearned for John's from the moment she saw him and her desire was as confusing as it was exhilarating. Did he feel their connection as she did? Or was she alone in the mess of her runaway emotions? She cursed. She didn't want to feel this way about him. She wanted him to stay in the safety of enemy camp and not blur the battle lines.

Turning off the faucet, she grabbed her bag, left the kitchen. She wouldn't hide or run away. She would face whatever they decided to do next. One thing was certain, whether either of them liked it or not, from now on they both had to work out the problem of what happened next. It was the only way they could move past the mistakes and selfishness of their parents.

The office was empty. She sucked in a breath as a pain assaulted her chest. Had he left? Turned his back on her? The toilet flushed in the bathroom, and she snapped her head toward the closed door. John strolled out and flashed her a strained smile before he walked toward his desk. Her held breath whispered from her mouth. "You okay?"

He rubbed his hand over his face before he met her eyes. "Sure."

She approached the desk.

He leaned forward on his elbows, his eyes dark with concern and his brow furrowed. "I won't let you get hurt, Sasha. Not anymore."

Her gaze lingered on his for a moment longer before she stepped away and paced a few steps back and forth in front of him. He cared. She could no longer deny that or paint him as the enemy. His concern for her was genuine and, if the truth be told, she didn't want him to hurt anymore, either. She stopped and met his eyes. "So what do we do?"

"We work together to find out the truth and then take it from there."

She nodded. "Okay. And I don't want us to fight anymore." She smiled softly. "You're an okay kind of guy…to a point."

He met her smile. "And you're pretty hot…to a point."

Heat pinched her cheeks as the sexual tension

between them soared once more. She shook her head. "Let's focus on the here and now, mister. No more… You know."

He closed his eyes, his smile dissolving. "You're right. Sorry."

She moved the visitor's chair in front of his desk and gripped its back. "Where did these suspicions about my mother come from? Or have you known about her involvement the entire time you've been here?"

He opened his eyes wide. "God, no. Is that what you think?"

Insecurity and distrust hurtled into her before she could stop it. She might really like him, but it would take more than a pair of deep blue eyes and a body as hard as a brick to break her habitual suspicion.

She blew out a breath. "Then what happened for you to believe Kyle doesn't want me to know something went on between him and my mother?"

He leaned back in his chair, his eyes locked on hers. "It was something Freddy said to me earlier."

The floor shifted beneath her, and she gripped the chair tighter. "Freddy knows about this?"

"No. Yes. I'm not sure."

"Which is it? Yes or no?" Now she was angry.

"Sasha—"

"Tell me."

When he stood and came around the desk, she stepped back and his outstretched hand dropped to his side. "Freddy took great pleasure in telling me he spoke to Kyle this afternoon." He pulled a folded piece of paper from his pocket and held it up. "I received this visiting permit from Kyle a few days ago. It turns out he sent one to Freddy, too, summoning us both to attendance."

She stared at the paper. "Freddy told me he spoke to Kyle the day before yesterday. You didn't go?"

John shook his head. "I don't want to see him until I'm ready. He clearly thinks he's still in control." He glared. "He's not."

"He is as far as Freddy's concerned."

"Maybe, but I couldn't care less about Freddy right now."

"You should. Freddy's pissed off and that cannot be good news for you…or me."

He shoved the permit back in his pocket and pushed his hand into his hair, holding it there. "Freddy said it didn't matter that I'm Kyle's son. Kyle would always need him and Freddy would always know the fair better than me."

She fisted her hands on her hips. "What's that got to do with my mother?"

"I don't know. We batted words back and forth for a while, not really getting any further before he stormed out." He held her gaze. "Not before saying once you found out how much your mother hates this place, you'd hate me as much as you hate her."

She flinched. "I don't hate my mother. We don't see eye to eye about this place. That's as far as it goes."

He frowned. “So you speak? You and your mum?”

“Yes.” She lifted her shoulders. “We’re not the type to go for tea and cake, but we talk.” She squeezed her eyes shut. “I can’t stand the thought of Freddy knowing more about my family than I do. What would make him say that?” Frustration hummed inside her. *If Freddy knows things about my mother, what else does he know? Does he know about my past, too? Does Kyle?*

Nausea rose in her throat. *Does John?*

The threat of humiliation swarmed inside her. She liked John so much, had given herself to him with passion and need, but she couldn’t afford to be blinded by her feelings for him. It would lead to mistakes. Huge mistakes. Both emotionally and intellectually. She didn’t doubt for a moment that if John knew about her molestation, his need to take care of her would be grounded in that, rather than any romantic feelings he might have for her.

She lifted her chin against the pain lingering in her chest. “I’ve made you an offer for the fair, yet nothing’s changed, and I only have your word that it ever will. How do I really know you’ll give me what I want in the end?”

A flush darkened his cheeks and his eyes turned to steel. “I’m not Kyle. I don’t deal in business with a hidden agenda. I’m not a man who goes back on his word. If, at the end of this, I see no reason for you not to have the fair, I’ll do everything possible to damn well *give* it to you. I don’t want your money. What just happened…" He shook his head. "Meant something to me. That wasn't a hit-and-run. I admit, when I first came to Templeton, everything was about Kyle and how I could screw him over, but now I've met you…now I know he's dying…"

She swallowed, as sympathy whispered across her heart. "Now what?"

He stared into her eyes. "Now my head's more of a mess than it was before."

Her heart picked up speed. He must be grieving, despite his determination to believe the opposite. Is that what was making him reach for her? What was making this thing between them as irresistible to him as it was to her?

He stepped closer. "Everything is so much less about Kyle…and more about you."

Hope shot through her. She wanted more than anything to believe his care for her was genuine, but the man had to be reeling with confusion and grief. She would be a fool to believe John could really walk into her life and make it better. Make her feel less lonely; less afraid of ever trusting anyone but her best friend.

He continued forward and she stepped back. He kept coming until her butt hit another desk. He stood in front of her, his darkened gaze lingering at her lips. "I've already told you. I like you. I like you a lot. I won't let you hurt anymore."

Sasha tipped her head back to meet his eyes, her tears burning. "I'm not hurt. I don't hurt."

"You hurt, Sasha. You hurt bad, and now that hurts me, too."

He leaned his hands on the desk on either side of her. Trapping her in his cage, he lowered his mouth to hers. Her heart slammed against her rib cage as a raw need for him to protect her erupted. Her lips remained rigid beneath his for the briefest moment before softening. Her surrender kicked like a steel-capped boot into her gut. He drew his free hand over the crown of her head, lower to hold her jaw…

She couldn't do this. She'd given him her body—and maybe far too big a part of her heart—but she refused to entirely give him her trust. Not yet. Not until she was sure.

She eased her hands against his chest and pushed him backward. "No, John. I have to find out what Freddy knows. It's too important."

She stormed toward the door, chasing the habitual control of her life that had somehow vanished.

"Sasha, wait."

She moved like lightning, slamming the door behind her so hard, the glass rattled in its frame.

CHAPTER THIRTEEN

"SHIT." JOHN RUSHED to the door and yanked it open. Breaking into a sprint, he caught up with Sasha as she pivoted expertly between teenagers and the grown men towering above her. He gripped her arm. "Sasha, just hold on."

She pulled her arm from his grip. "If Freddy knows something about my mother's past relationship with Kyle, then I damn well want to know what it is. How dare he keep that from me? He had no right."

Her tears and the crack of her voice sliced through John's heart, revving his resolve to cause his father more pain than he'd ever inflicted on anyone. Why should he care Kyle was dying? Kyle had caused Sasha indisputable hurt, along with himself and possibly her mother.

He reached for Sasha's hand, not caring it might be the final straw that would earn him a slapped face. "You need to stop and think this through. Freddy's not on your side. If my suspicions are right, he's never been on your side and is working his own agenda. If that's true, the more knowledge you have and keep to yourself, the better. Right?"

She didn't slap him but stared, her eyes wide with the adrenaline undoubtedly ripping through her. Her breasts rose and fell with each harried breath. "This is so damn unfair. All of it. Why can't I trust the people around me? Just for once."

The whistling and screeching around them, the rumbling and thumping, pumping dance music and blowing horns, reverberated louder than ever. John ached to touch her, to pull her to him, to feel her skin beneath his lips again, inhale Sasha's scent and tell her he'd fix her pain and the situation.

Instead, he stood like a man trapped on a square of sand in the middle of a turbulent ocean—helpless and trying to think of the best way forward. The best way to make her dream come true without handing her the one thing she thought she wanted. His gut told him Funland hid more secrets, more destruction for her, than anything else.

He glanced around, part of him hoping to see Freddy before she did. The asshole was nowhere to be seen. He faced her. "Come back to the office. Let's talk some more. It'll do no good for you to run headlong into Freddy when you're this worked up."

She glared. "Worked up? You think this is me worked up?" She huffed out a laugh. "You've no idea what I'm like when I'm worked up. I suggest you get out of the firing line."

A smile pulled at his mouth, and he pursed his

lips. Was it perverted that the sudden vision of Sasha tossing him onto a king-size bed with the ease of a superstrong ninja turned him on?

"Are you laughing at me?" She fisted her hands on her hips.

John blinked and fought his smile into submission. "Of course not."

She closed her eyes and pressed a trembling hand to her abdomen. "I feel sick. My grandfather meant the world to me, and I promised him...*promised* him I'd get Funland back." She opened her eyes and a tear escaped as she jabbed her finger toward the sky. "He's up there looking down and knows his daughter, his *daughter,* John, had something to do with us losing what he treasured. Something my ancestors treasured until my mother deemed herself above tradition, above what generations of Romany people have kept sacred before us."

"Don't you know how messed up families are?"

"My family is nothing like yours."

"Why?"

Color rushed to her face. "Because my family isn't Kyle."

He deserved the jab. His demons had nothing to do with Sasha's. He pushed his hands into his hair. "You're right. I'm sorry."

They stood in silence as John grappled with what to do next. He wanted so much to take this pain away from her, but he couldn't. His gut instinct told him her anger went so much deeper than family tradition. Frustration and pride weighed heavy on his heart and soul. Neither felt good nor worthwhile. He needed to know he was strong enough to wipe his bitterness toward his father out of his life once and for all.

He came to Templeton to expose Kyle for the man he really was, to fix the wrongs that had tormented him ever since Kyle walked out of his life. He wouldn't leave until everything was out in the open, until Sasha and he himself accepted he was nothing like his father.

He faced her. "We'll get to the bottom of this."

She scowled, her shoulders coming up around her earlobes and her dark eyes flashing fire. "How?"

Their gazes locked. They were on the same side of the playing field, but their wants were so different a hard rock remained between them. From the raw and stormy frustration in her eyes, it was clear their lovemaking was forgotten. So far from her mind, a pain constricted his heart to see her look at him with such mistrust. The possibility she saw him as little more than the flesh-and-blood reason the entirety of what she had planned for her life was going wrong hurt more than it should. He wasn't Kyle and he wouldn't leave her to drown in a hole he'd inadvertently slashed wide open.

He shook his head. "I didn't ask for any of this, but here it is…for both of us. We can sort this out if we work together."

She raised her hands. "I've had enough."

"Enough of what?"

"Standing here doing nothing. I need to speak to Freddy, my mother and your father." Her cheeks flamed with anger. Her pulse beat fast in the hollow at the base of her neck. "It's pretty clear all three know something that I've got every damn right to know, too."

He gritted his teeth as fear struck through his blood. "There's no way you're talking to Kyle."

She fisted her hands on her hips. "Do you really think you can stop me?"

"He won't see you."

"I'll try anyway."

"There's no way I am letting you within ten feet—"

She spun away, and this time he let her go before he did something stupid like throw her over his shoulder and lock her in his bedroom for the rest of her damn life. The passion of their lovemaking couldn't be denied—but that didn't mean Sasha wouldn't ignore it had happened. He was already beginning to know her. His teaching had put him in good stead for dealing with the anger pumping through her right now. Spending day after day with kids, and their unrelenting honesty, gave him the insight and experience to recognize tenacity. Sasha had it in spades.

Her resolve was indisputable. She had a lightning fire inside that both attracted him and scared him senseless. She stirred an overpowering need to protect and help her. Thoughts and possible decisions raced around in his mind as the whirlwind he cared far too much for ran into the crowd. God help Freddy when she caught up with him.

If she caught up with him.

John whipped his head left and right, narrowing his eyes as he scanned the area above the heads of more and more people as they filled the fairground, looking for fun…and God only knew what else. He couldn't stand by and let her face Freddy alone. As for her confronting Kyle, that wasn't even an option.

He glared ahead. Feeling Sasha's heartbeat beneath his palm and her lips on his had brought his mission to a dangerous place. Freddy worked with Kyle, spent time in prison with him and, as far as John knew, could be equally as ruthless. He'd yet to find out what Freddy had done to get his ass thrown in jail, but he damn well would. Who knew what Freddy would do to Sasha if she unwittingly messed with whatever the hell he had planned?

Freddy had made it perfectly clear he felt used by Kyle. How would that manifest itself? He had to get to Freddy before Sasha did and shield her from more potentially painful revelations. He wanted her to know the truth but not be alone when she found it.

From now on, supporting her was his priority. Until he figured out what the hell Kyle wanted the fair for and what he'd done to get it, he would make sure Sasha knew he was on her side. Her frustration was burning her up from the inside out, and he wouldn't rest until he got to the bottom of what had taken place between Kyle and Sasha's mother.

He stormed forward, brushing past families and teenagers, his eyes darting manically as he searched for Freddy's bald head amidst the throng. The prison visitor's permit in John's front pocket scratched against his thigh as he jogged, reminding him of his refusal to see Kyle today as he'd requested.

His father clearly sent a permit to Freddy for the same day because Kyle wanted to see his second-in-command and his son together. No doubt wanted both of them in front of him for confessions…or manipulation. John gritted his teeth. What had he missed by refusing to see Kyle? Had his stubbornness meant Freddy now held a better hand of cards than him and Sasha?

He scowled. Kyle had once again played his son for an idiot, but this time John only had himself to blame.

SASHA FOUGHT HER tears as she slumped forward with her hands on her knees, a stitch mercilessly aching in her side. Freddy was nowhere to be found. She couldn't allow John's suggestion that her mother was involved in the selling of the fair to penetrate her head and heart. It was too devastating to contemplate. The result would be the claws of her mother's disregard being pushed deeper into Sasha's heart than ever before.

Images and recollections flashed through her mind. Snippets of conversations when her mother denied Funland being anything of importance. Her mother blushing or turning away from Sasha's scrutiny whenever she accused her of being able to help retain the fair in their family if she really wanted to.

Had her mother been dealing with Kyle behind her grandfather's back while her daughter implored her for help? Had she made money from the deal? Laughed at her daughter's ignorance?

Straightening, Sasha planted her hands on her hips and breathed deep. Where the hell was Freddy? The habitual lull between late afternoon and evening would soon arrive at the fair, and then he was bound to come out from wherever he was hiding and face her. Fewer people meant less madness, and often she and Freddy shared a cup of tea in the office before they braced themselves for the evening onslaught. He had to reveal himself sooner or later.

She narrowed her eyes and scanned the crowds once more.

Maybe Freddy had already seen her and guessed from the horror on her face that John had told her what Freddy inferred about her mother? She swallowed the ball of anger lodged in her throat. He clearly didn't give a damn about her or he would have told her before now what he knew.

Sasha snatched her cell phone from her back

pocket. Well, that was fine. She'd go straight to the source. Clutching her phone tightly, she strode for the fairground gates in the hope she could make herself heard above the screaming and music when she spoke to her mother. She stole into a nook between a wall and the public bathroom, punched in her mother's number and inhaled a strengthening breath.

"Hello?"

"Hi, Mum. It's me."

"Sasha." The surprise in her mother's voice couldn't be denied—neither could the warmth.

Sasha closed her eyes and leaned back against the wall. She couldn't let her mother's care for her lessen the fact she never once supported Sasha's need to make Funland hers one day. "I need to ask you something. I'd appreciate the truth."

A few seconds passed before her mother spoke. "How are you? How are things in Templeton?"

"I don't want to talk about Templeton."

"Why? What's wrong? Usually that's *all* you talk about. Are you finally getting out of there? Is that why you're calling me?"

Sasha squeezed her eyes tighter. "I'm not Tanya, Mum, and I'm not you. I'm happy here…at least I could be. I'll never leave."

"You know as well as I do, the only way you'll ever be happy is to put as much space as possible between you and Templeton. You could get a new job, new friends…. You're worth so, so much more.

Why do you insist on staying? The cove brings you nothing but misery."

Sasha snapped her eyes open. "I want the fair, Mum. I always will."

"Sasha…" Her mother's exhalation rasped down the line.

"Did you ever speak to Kyle Jordon about the fair? Before Granddad died?"

"What?"

"Did you?" Sasha tightened her grip on the phone.

Silence.

Anger hummed through her blood as Sasha waited. She would not be the one to fill the silence. God damn it, if her mother had anything to do with the selling of the fair to Kyle, she would never forgive her. Their relationship hung by a single thread and just one more act of disloyalty would snap it, never to be put back together again.

"I've no idea what you're talking about. Now, please, will you listen to me? For years, I've been begging you to leave that place. Why do you insist on putting yourself through—"

"I've found out there's a chance you were involved in the sale of the fair to Kyle Jordon. Is it true? Did you strike a deal with that man behind my back? Behind Granddad's back?"

Her mother laughed. "That's ridiculous."

A throb beat rhythmically at Sasha's temples. The sudden escalation in pitch of her mother's voice told Sasha she was lying. Her stomach knotted with revulsion as bitterness rose in a dry tang in her throat. "Tell me the truth."

"I've never made a secret of wanting the place gone from our lives, but I was not involved in the sale. That was between Kyle and your grandfather. It had nothing to do with me."

Doubt edged into the periphery of Sasha's mind. "Then why would someone say such a thing, huh? It makes no sense. As far as anyone was concerned, it was only me and Granddad fighting to hold on to Funland. Why would Freddy even mention your name?"

"I've no idea. Now, please, just let the fair go and move on. You're better off without it."

"That isn't your decision to make. Moreover, I don't believe you." Betrayal slashed across Sasha's heart, and she sucked in a breath as her grandfather's face filled her mind's eye. "I'm not leaving this, Mum. I'm going to find out what happened to make Granddad give up the way he did."

"That place will only make you miserable."

Sasha shook her head. "When I make Funland mine, I will make it good again. You've seen the photographs. The old videos. Our family was happy here, and now we're splintered, working on our own lives. We should be coming together to protect what was ours from being overrun with drugs and God knows what else." *Molesters. Predators. Groomers.*

"When are you going to stop this?" Her mother's

voice cracked. "People are in business to make money. The fair isn't something to get sentimental about. It's a place of business now. Why can't you see it for what it really is?"

Resentment burned and passion lit inside Sasha as she gripped the back of her neck. "I'll make the fair as it used to be and people will flock to see it. People love nostalgia. They want to be back when times were good, when a community was a community and the people in it fought for one another. Drugs, alcohol and nightly fights are not what people want in Templeton. It's not what people want to see when they come here on holiday."

"When times were good, Sasha? What about the bad times? How can you deny there haven't been bad times? Stop looking at that place through rose-tinted glasses and acknowledge the reality of it."

Sasha's heart beat fast. "I am."

"No, you're not. It's overrun with badness and has been for years. Get out of there, for goodness' sake."

"No." Tears burned as she trembled. "I'll make it good again." Her voice hitched. "I'll make it good again and prove you wrong."

"The fair is Kyle's now. He'll never give it back to you."

The certainty in her statement poured raw determination into Sasha's veins. "You seem very sure about that."

Seconds passed before her mother spoke again. "I am."

"Why?"

"Because you and I both know Kyle's reputation. He needs that place."

"Not anymore."

Her mother laughed. "You think because he's in prison, that will stop him making money?"

"Granddad and I were fighting Kyle. We were holding him at bay and then one morning, Granddad calls and says it's over. Funland is Kyle's. Why? Why did he give up like that? What happened to back him into a corner so he gave up and died?" She pushed away from the wall. "I'll never forgive you if I find out you went to Kyle behind Granddad's back and made it impossible for him not to give Kyle what he wanted."

"Sasha, please—"

"Only one thing would make Granddad give up. Family."

"What?"

"Granddad would not have let anything bad happen to you, me or Tanya. Ever. I know this has something to do with one of us, if not all of us, and when I find out the truth, you'd better hope to God you had nothing to do with it."

She snapped the phone closed and strode from the nook. She stopped short and stared at the bustling activity ahead of her, A few days of vile memories marred a childhood of happy ones, but she wouldn't let that terrifying time ruin it forever. If she did, her molester would have succeeded in taking away her dreams as well as her innocence and ability to trust.

The days she was violated came alive in vivid Technicolor, as though they had occurred yesterday rather than fifteen years before. Heat rushed to her face. Her paranoia that people might know what happened to her reared its ugly head once more. Again and again, she suspected it ever since the sale of the fair went through. If her mother knew and told her grandfather what happened that summer… Sasha shivered and shook her head. No. That was impossible. What mother would learn something like that and do nothing but take away the one thing her daughter loved more than anything else in the world?

She had to find a way to stop this endless doubt. Sasha stormed forward. There was only one other person with the same emotions pumping through his blood. Only one other person who cared about setting the story straight and starting again.

Jogging through the gates, she went in search of John.

CHAPTER FOURTEEN

JOHN SMILED AS he rounded the back of the bumper cars and followed Freddy toward the storage warehouse. Nothing could have been more perfect. Alone in there, they'd be far enough away from the fairground to avoid detection. He wanted answers and would get them any way necessary, before Sasha had a chance to ask questions and be exposed to the risk of repercussions.

Kyle and Freddy were involved in the kind of lifestyle that brought threats and violence. As far as John knew, neither of them would think twice about hurting Sasha should she get too close to uncovering something either of them wanted to remain secret.

Freddy tossed a glance over each shoulder before ducking inside, and John narrowed his eyes. Freddy was definitely up to no good. He picked up his pace and rushed forward just as Freddy moved to push the door closed. John shoved it open, sending Kyle's second-in-command stumbling backward, causing him to lose his grip on his cell phone. It dropped to the concrete floor and landed with an unhealthy clatter.

"How's it going, Freddy?" John locked his glare on Freddy as he kicked the door closed.

Freddy leaned his considerable weight forward to retrieve his phone. He wiped it over with his fingers before slipping it into his shirt pocket. "What do you want?"

"I want a lot of things. First and foremost, I want to know what my father and you talked about when you went to see him the other day."

Freddy sniffed and smiled, revealing more gum than teeth. "Oh, yeah?"

"Yeah." John strolled farther into the warehouse and stuffed his hands into his pockets, casually scuffing up the ground dust with the toe of his boot. "And you're going to tell me. You started something by mentioning Sasha's mum to me earlier. Something that makes my decision of what to do next pretty cut and dried, depending on the outcome of this conversation."

Freddy's smile stretched to a grin. "You really think you're something, don't you?"

"Not particularly, but I am a man who doesn't walk away from people who think they can intimidate or distract me from finding out what I want to know. Now, you either tell me what you talked about or I'll be forced to ask Kyle. As that option will royally piss me off, you'll leave me no choice but to fire you. So…what's it going to be?"

"You can't fire me."

John smiled. "You know that's not true. I'm not

putting up with any crap from my staff. Including you."

Freddy raised his eyebrows, his eyes dark with anger. "You really think your dad's going to let you push me out of here when I've been here as long as I have?"

"Funland's mine. I can do whatever the hell I want with it."

"That's not the impression Kyle gave me." He grinned. "Seems to me Kyle wants me here to keep my ear to the ground."

Frustration quivered over the surface of John's skin, making him want to slap the superior look off Freddy's face. He curled his hands into fists inside his pockets. "Well, Kyle should've thought about what he did and didn't want before he handed me the papers for everything he owned. Now I'll ask you again, what did you talk about? Why did you mention Sasha's mum and the fair in the same sentence?"

Freddy's gaze roamed over John's face as he blew out a theatrical breath. "This is interesting. You give the impression you don't give a crap what your dad has to say and you'll run things the way you want. Yet here you are, all fired up about him. I'm guessing this has a lot more to do with the way you feel about Sasha than anything else." He laughed. "Please tell me that girl hasn't gotten to you. Didn't your dad warn you about her the minute before you set foot in this place?"

John glowered as the niggling doubt that he was entirely out of the loop as far as his father's enterprises were concerned resurfaced. What if Sasha only thought about her own agenda when they made love? What if her mind had been on her goal rather than on him? Anger threatened, and he forced it aside. How could anyone fake the longing way she looked at him? How could anyone fake the trembling, which revealed a need as raw as his when he touched her?

Impatience was never a good thing, but it was especially bad when a man wanted to protect a woman and had come face-to-face with the asshole stopping him from doing just that. "Why don't you tell me what he said about Sasha's mother and drop the act? You and I both know any information Kyle shares with you will be for his own benefit. This isn't about him including you in the inner circle. This is about him pulling the strings from behind Her Majesty's concrete walls. Considering you're on very shaky ground right now, you'd do well to pledge your allegiance to me rather than a man who won't be much good to you as far as your future prospects are concerned."

Freddy's cheeks darkened. "Kyle and me are friends. The sooner you realize that, the better off you'll be around these parts. I keep telling you, Templeton don't like strangers."

John huffed out a laugh. "As opposed to drug dealers, you mean."

Freddy shot him a sneer and pulled out a pack of cigarettes. He tapped one out and lit it with casual indifference to John. The smoke plumed on his exhalation, rising between them in a gray mist before evaporating. Freddy narrowed his eyes. "Considering you and your dad have been separated for years, it's interesting how well he knows you."

John stiffened. "What does that mean?"

Freddy lifted his shoulders. "He knew you'd ask questions about what was said even though you didn't accept his invitation to join us." He took another drag on the cigarette. "He also knew you'd be taken in by Sasha and that fake, fragile 'woe is me' thing she likes to use whenever the mood strikes her."

"My father knows nothing about me. He's playing games. When will you learn the man is a piece of shit who likes to mess with people's minds and lives?"

Freddy smiled. "He knows you. He knows everything about you."

Anger simmered like a smoldering fire in John's gut, and he dragged every ounce of self-control he possessed to the surface. He had to think of Sasha's needs and not the urge to smash Freddy square in the face. "The hell he does."

"He's had people following you for years." Freddy sniffed and wandered toward a stack of boxes at the side of the room containing various bits of metal machinery. He sat atop one of them.

"No son of Kyle Jordon's was ever going to go without what he needed. Kyle's words, not mine."

"What I needed?" John laughed. "What I needed was a father who..." He pursed his lips. What the hell was he doing? The last thing he needed to blurt out was the height of his vulnerability. God only knew what Freddy would do with the knowledge the only thing John ever wanted from his father was his presence. He cleared his throat. "He's playing with the pair of us. He wants us to dance to his tune, and it looks as though his plan is working."

Freddy's eyes shone with malice in the shadowed darkness of the room. Weak afternoon light filtered through the gaps in the corrugated iron roof, sending sunny beams dancing across the dusty floor. There was nothing sunny about the rising hostility crackling like electricity between them.

John paced back and forth, tension rippling through him. "He doesn't want Sasha to have this place. Did he tell you that?" He stopped and faced Freddy.

The other man glowered, saying nothing.

John smiled. "Did he tell you he'd give you back the investments you've made with him? Maybe demand I give you Funland as recompense for your years of loyalty and service?"

Freddy's continued silence spoke volumes.

John grinned. "As I thought. He's giving you nothing but the runaround. Now, you have a choice here. You either work with me, which means telling me what Kyle told you about Sasha's mother, or you continue with this stupid hangdog thing you've got going and let Kyle carry on kicking you around like he has for the past ten years. Which is it going to be?"

John held Freddy's steady gaze as he tossed his cigarette butt to the floor and ground it out with the heel of his boot. "My loyalty stays with Kyle until I know what he's got in mind for this place and the business we've got going on here."

John lifted an eyebrow. "*We,* Freddy? Is any of it really yours? What does Kyle give you in return for your investment exactly? Cash? Women? Drugs? Or does he just toss you the odd promise of a stake in his fortune? One that never actually comes to fruition?"

Freddy glowered. "You haven't got a bloody clue about Kyle and me."

"Oh, I think I do. Now what did he say about Sasha's mother?"

The shrill ringing of Freddy's cell phone cut through the palpable tension, and John stiffened. Freddy glared at him a moment longer before pulling it from his pocket and glancing at the display. His cheeks instantly colored. When he flashed an anxious glance in John's direction, John immediately knew who was on the other end.

He gritted his teeth. "Answer it."

Freddy tilted his chin. "No."

"I said, answer it." John charged forward and

tried to wrench the phone from Freddy's hand before the big guy had the chance to push to his feet. John held the phone inches from Freddy's face. "Now."

Freddy's eyes bulged with rage and a vein pumped dangerously at his temple, but John didn't move. Years of unadulterated resentment toward his father coursed through his veins on a tidal wave.

Ring, ring.

Freddy grabbed the phone from John's fingers and stood. John stepped back and narrowed his eyes as Freddy lifted the cell to his ear, his eyes locked on John's. "Hello?" A few seconds passed before Freddy nodded. "He's with me right now."

John clenched his jaw, his pulse throbbing at his temple.

Another heartbeat passed before Freddy lowered the phone and held it out. "He wants to speak to you."

SASHA PUSHED HER key into the lock and stepped inside her apartment, her head nearly exploding with an impending migraine. After searching for John and Freddy for a full half hour with no luck, she'd drawn the conclusion the reason she couldn't find either of them was because they were together. No doubt to discuss her and her mother…with a hefty dose of Kyle and Funland thrown in for good measure. It was clear she still couldn't afford to trust anyone to be honest with her.

She wandered into the kitchen and tossed her keys onto the counter. Curling her fingers around its edge, she closed her eyes. Just as she'd given up looking for John and Freddy, a massive fight had broken out between two groups of teenagers by the Ferris wheel, bringing her quest to kick some ass upon a different target than originally intended. Chaos had broken out as families scattered, most likely never to return, while other teenage spectators chanted for further bloodshed.

It had been yet another incident to add substance to her mother's claim that Funland would never be as it once was.

Sasha had let her emotions get the better of her after her arguments with John and her mother. Her mind had slipped from the job—something that would've been unfathomable a few days ago—and her usually careful watch over the fairground had wavered, resulting in unnecessary violence.

The scuffle had escalated quickly and Freddy and John appeared from nowhere and she, Freddy, John and the other fair workers split the boys up before ejecting them from the grounds. She opened her eyes and stared ahead. The kids' nonsensical shouts, cursing and manic stares had made it clear at least two of the boys were on some kind of substance.

She pursed her lips. Had that been sold to them at Funland? Was drug dealing still going on right under her nose? Under John's?

Distrust caught and stuck in her throat. Was there a possibility he actually knew and was doing nothing about it? She shook her head. That notion was ridiculous. If there was one thing she wouldn't do, despite John's reluctance to start doing everything he could to give her the fair, it was doubt the instinct in her heart that told her John was a good man. Albeit a good man with bad breeding.

Pushing away from the counter, Sasha filled a glass with water and took some aspirin from a drawer. She swallowed the pills. The horrible thought that John might be continuing business as usual until he figured things out sent an involuntary shiver down her spine. She didn't want him to be that guy. She touched her lips, and memories of their lovemaking flowed. She couldn't afford to be ignorant to the possibility he could be more like Kyle than she wanted to believe.

Exhaling a long breath, she refilled her glass and carried it into the living room. She kicked off her ballet flats and slumped onto the couch. Photographs of her grandfather that lined the mantel above her open fireplace taunted her, fuelling the simmering anger the conversation with her mother had ignited.

The tension between her, Freddy and John had been palpable as they dealt with the teenagers and cleared the fair at closing. No further conversation had taken place and they'd all left the fairground at the same time.

Freddy hadn't as much as tossed her a smile all afternoon and slid into his car without a backward glance or a "see you tomorrow." When she pushed her bike through the fairground gates, John was loitering at his car and she purposely strode past him, her head high. Oh, she'd heard him call her name—twice—but couldn't find the strength to listen to what he had to say.

Her emotions had been wrung and stretched, pulled and tightened to such an extent in the past twenty-four hours, she was afraid of making a wrong and irreparable decision. Her feelings for John were gathering momentum at a frightening speed, and that left her doubting her sanity, let alone the ability to think rationally and calmly.

She raised her glass to her lips and shivered. He'd looked worried, confused and more than a little riled up. Maybe she should have stopped and spoken with him….

Tired and frustrated, she pushed to her feet and strolled into the bathroom. She placed her glass by the sink and grabbed some lavender oil from a shelf above her. A long soak in the tub was what she needed before she collapsed into bed. She had some serious thinking to do, and the tension running through her system was nothing but a detrimental hindrance. The heat of John's caresses and the smell of his aftershave still lingered on her skin, leaving her wanting more of him. Maybe if she washed them away, it would be easier to face the reality that sex between them might never happen again.

She longed to pursue their growing care for each other. She wanted to push her rationale and fear away and be free in her feelings, to give herself over to someone else to take care of her for a while. Yet, couldn't, despite the way she reveled in the thrill of intimate and loving human contact, of his skin beneath her fingers and his lips on hers.

Her body quivered as tears threatened.

Had their lovemaking been something never to be repeated? Had they made a hungry, passionate mistake? Did she now have to vanquish the belief they were meant to repeat their intimacy over and over until neither of them could breathe without the other?

Her heart thundered with the overwhelming possibility her nemesis's son was her destiny. The man to make her feel loved and keep her safe. She swiped at her face. The prospect she was wrong about John hurt as much as anything else in her life.

She turned on the faucets over the tub and poured some oil into the water. She'd been stupid today. She'd had sex with a man she barely knew, attacked her mother without knowing the facts and gone after Freddy with absolutely no idea what to say to him. She hadn't held her place at Funland by making emotionally driven mistakes. Kyle had given every indication he wanted her out of the fair without actually saying it, so she'd never given him a reason that would stick should he try to fire her. He knew that and so did she.

She stripped off her clothes and padded into her bedroom to turn on the digital radio, hoping to find something to banish her desperate need to call John.

The abrupt knocking at her front door ground her to a halt in the corridor. She hurried into the bathroom and turned off the running water before whipping her robe from a hook on the back of the door.

She yanked it on, tying the sash at her waist before she crept to the front door. When she peered through the peephole, her heart shot into her throat. What was he doing here at this time of night? Her hand flew to her hair, her lips, her waist. She grimaced as she struggled to decide what to do next.

Another knock.

She swallowed. "Who is it?"

John leaned close to the peephole and wiggled his eyebrows. "If you're not looking at me right now, I'm James Bond."

Damn it. She bit back her smile and forced a scowl instead, steadfastly planting her hand on her hip. "What do you want?"

He stepped back and lifted his hands to reveal a paper bag of take-out food and a bottle of red wine. "Provisions. We need to talk." His smile dissolved and he dropped his arms. "This can't wait until the morning. I'm sorry to turn up like this—"

"Okay, okay. Just…just stay there. I'll be two seconds."

He nodded and glanced along the corridor of her apartment floor.

Pushing away from the door, Sasha hurried into her bedroom, discarded her robe and quickly pulled on a bra and panties, her heart hammering. God, why did she have to find him so attractive? She squeezed her eyes shut and took a deep breath. Her headache had miraculously disappeared the moment she'd lain eyes on him…

Damn, she was so happy to see him.

She straightened and stared through her open bedroom door. She had to be coolness personified. She couldn't allow him to see how much he rattled or weakened her. She was angry. Angry he'd suggested—and was probably right—that her mother had been in cahoots with Kyle years before. She had to keep that feeling at the forefront at all times if her weakening heart had any chance of staying intact.

She put her robe back on before hurrying to her dressing table. She fluffed her hair and licked her finger before drawing it across her unruly eyebrows in an attempt to coerce them into a more acceptable shape.

"Why is he here?" She stared at her reflection. *Why didn't I just talk to him at the fairground?*

Her legs shook as she left the bedroom and approached the front door. The sexual tension between them had been palpable and unnerving before they'd released it on the kitchen countertop. Lord only knew how it would be once she let him in her apartment and they were alone again.

Clearing her throat, she fought her frown into submission, unlocked the door and swung it open. "Sorry about that."

Silence.

His gaze instantaneously left her face and wandered lower. She stood stock-still as his study languidly passed over her breasts and abdomen to her legs, revealed beneath the short length of her robe. His eyes widened and when he lifted them to hers, Sasha swallowed and thanked God a gaze didn't have the power to untie a sash. His stare was feral—and sexy as hell.

"Are you coming in?" She lifted an eyebrow, battling the pull high between her legs. "Or just going to stand there staring?"

He coughed. "I'm coming in."

She flung out her arm and gestured him inside. He brushed past her and the distinct smell of his rich, musky aftershave assaulted her senses. She inhaled and then silently admonished herself. *No. None of that, thank you very much.*

Closing the door, she turned. He lifted the bag and wine. "I didn't know what you like, so I went for a Chinese banquet. Hope that's okay?"

She smiled. If she didn't know better, the nervousness in his eyes gave her the impression he was eager to please. Anxious John Jordon was a new—and kind of cute—development. "Chinese is great." She took the bag. "Although, I'm not sure I can manage a banquet at eleven-thirty."

He smiled. "We can try."

"Take a seat. I'll grab some plates."

Sasha went to the kitchen and busied herself plating up half the enormous amount of food. He'd be eating leftovers for the rest of the week. Battling the tension that quivered over her skin, she concentrated on slowing her racing pulse.

As cute as John had looked a moment before, the fact he had news that couldn't wait set warning bells screaming. Their last conversation had been tense and then he and Freddy had disappeared.

Yes, they'd had sex…but that didn't mean he'd give her an ounce of commitment as far as the fair or anything else was concerned. It didn't mean he was more likely to accept her offer, either. He'd already admitted they'd be wise to take steps together to uncover the truth about their parents instead of squabbling. Maybe he was there to reiterate that point after she left without talking to him…in that mature, kick-ass way of hers.

Swallowing against the dryness in her throat, she returned to the living room. He sat on her sofa, the bottle of wine in his hands, staring at the label as though it held the secret to world peace. She had no idea whether his expression was due to the low lighting or the tense atmosphere, but he suddenly looked so drawn and pale. Her stomach knotted tighter as the urge to slide onto his lap and offer comfort seeped into her heart.

"Here you go." She smiled, forcing buoyancy. "Do you want me to open that wine?"

"Sure." He blinked as though forgetting he held it and passed her the bottle, his eyes lingering on hers. "Thanks."

She took the wine and walked back into the kitchen. Her hands shook as she drew a corkscrew out of a drawer. Twice she tried and failed to open the wine before the cork popped free. Releasing her held breath, she grabbed two glasses and some cutlery before reentering the living room. She lowered onto the sofa and placed everything next to the plates on the low table in front of them.

Taking a deep breath, she jumped straight in. "Why are you here?"

He met her eyes. They stormed with an emotion she couldn't name. Dark and so beautifully blue, his gaze bored into hers as though searching for answers. "I've spoken to Kyle."

For a long moment, words failed her. She held his gaze, trying to think of a suitable response. "I see."

"Do you?"

Her shoulders slumped. "No, not really."

He sighed. "Me, neither. I think I'm still in some sort of delayed shock. He rang Freddy when I happened to be with him. Once Kyle knew I was there, he wanted to talk to me."

"And you agreed?"

"He caught me in a weak moment." His jaw tightened.

Her gaze wandered over his handsome face. No anger showed. No resentment. Just confusion. She swallowed. "Is that the first time you've spoken since..."

"I was eleven. Yes."

"God." She put her hand over his closed fist at his thigh and squeezed. "Are you okay?"

A muscle worked rhythmically in his jaw. "I will be."

They didn't move. Their eyes locked, and her emotions went into free fall with sympathy for the little boy who'd never known his father—and the man who was now forced into a situation where nearly twenty years of absence was tainted with demand rather than devotion.

"My feelings aren't why I'm here." He exhaled. "I'm here because of what he told me. It was a lot more than he said in the letters he sent weeks ago. I'm more informed than when I got here."

Foreboding tripped over her skin. "About what?"

"About you, the fair...and your mother."

She slipped her hand from his and reached for the wine bottle. Its neck shook when she attempted to fill their glasses.

"Let me." He eased the bottle away, and she sat

motionless as he poured out a glass and handed it to her.

"Thanks." She took a hefty gulp. "You tried to talk to me at the fair earlier when you were waiting outside, didn't you? I ignored you. I'm sorry."

"Don't be. It's probably better that I've had time to calm down."

She nodded and looked to the cooling food in front of them. "I've lost my appetite."

He huffed a laugh. "Me, too." He took a sip and lowered his wine to the table, drawing his hands tightly together between his knees as though steeling himself. Sasha stiffened, waiting for the inevitable blow.

He turned. "Kyle was definitely approached by your mother."

She stared as her stomach filled with dread. "When?"

"Once she learned from your grandfather that Kyle wanted to buy the fair."

"You mean, before I knew?"

"I think so." He blew out a long breath. "Your mother told him she had information Kyle could use to convince her father to sell. Information that would guarantee he'd want to be rid of Funland and, more important, it would make your grandfather want you away from there forever."

She frowned. "But that can't be right."

"Why?"

"I promised Granddad on his deathbed I'd get the

fair back. Why wouldn't he have told me what Kyle said? Why wouldn't he…" She froze. *Unless… No. No. No.* Tears sprang into her eyes and she squeezed them shut. "Oh, God."

His hand slid onto her thigh. "What is it?"

She opened her eyes. "He didn't want me there, not really." Memories of her and her grandfather heatedly discussing the pros and cons of keeping the fair charged her mind. More often than not, her grandfather came up with a hell of a lot more cons than she did. She swept the fallen hair from her face. "He said I was too good for the place. Said it would suck the life out of me. That I was meant for bigger and better things. I thought he was feeling guilty because of the years my mother told him he was selfish keeping me there, holding on to a bygone age." She shook her head. "Granddad said the words, but the conviction he wanted me to turn my back on the fair and walk away was always lacking." She met his eyes. "No. He loved that place. We spent so many nights tossing words back and forth, but deep down, I know he dreamed of me running it. I know he did."

He took her hand. "If what Kyle is saying is true, that your grandfather didn't want you there, you running Funland was the last thing he wanted."

"I don't understand. He could speak to me about anything. Why wouldn't he tell me what was going on?"

"Your mother told Kyle she wanted money for

her information. Money to move you and your sister out of Templeton. She knew your grandfather would leave the money from the sale of the fair to you and you only. She wanted you away from Templeton and making a different life for yourself before that happened."

Anger burned deep inside her. "The woman is forever trying to run my life, as well as my sister's. Her influence might have worked with Tanya, but it will never work with me."

His concerned gaze wandered over her face to settle on her lips. "What do you want to do next?"

Her eyes narrowed. "Not once did Granddad tell me to leave Templeton. The fair, yes, but not the town." Realization seeped into her veins and she slumped. "He did beg me not to put every ounce of my happiness into one thing. Clearly, he meant Funland." She picked up her glass and took another mouthful.

"Sasha, your mother told Kyle something happened to you at the fair. Something that changed you overnight. Do you know what she was referring to?"

She stared at him as her breath caught like a jagged blade in her throat and her glass slipped from her hand.

Red wine splashed across her lap like spilled blood from an open wound.

CHAPTER FIFTEEN

JOHN LEAPED TO his feet and rushed to the kitchen, leaving Sasha frozen on the sofa. "It's all right. I've got it." He ripped sheet after sheet of paper towel from the roll on the counter. "Have you got any club soda? I heard something about club soda and red wine…Sasha?"

She hadn't moved an inch. He strode from the kitchen and shoved the table to the side, sinking to his knees. He mopped at the wine on her legs and the hem of her satin robe. She trembled beneath his fingers. He looked up. She stared at him, her eyes wide with fear.

He cupped his hand to her jaw. "Sasha, talk to me. What is it?"

"She knew and didn't do anything about it."

Her trembling grew worse, and John tossed the sodden kitchen towel onto the coffee table and took her hands. He pulled her rigid body from the sofa and held her.

After a moment, she collapsed her weight against him. "I can't believe she would do this to me."

He dropped his lips to her hair and closed his eyes.

What the hell had his words done to her? Had Kyle made this cryptic reference, knowing it would have this effect? Anger burned as his heart yearned to take back his words. God damn it. He should've kept his mouth shut. Investigated the root of Kyle's claims himself before saying a single word to her.

"I'm sorry, Sasha. If I would've known asking that question would upset you like this, I wouldn't—"

"I'm glad you did."

"You're shaking."

She pulled back. "Nothing my mother or your father has done in the past is going to stop me from wanting to make Funland mine, John." Fire raged in her jet eyes, her olive skin pale and her jaw tight. "I will help you in any way I can to heal whatever it is you need to heal, and then you can help me to do the same. After that, we go our separate ways as winners. You'll have what you need to move on, and so will I. Now, what is it you need? Because I need Funland."

You. I need you. John swallowed and stepped back for his own protection, as much as hers. He rubbed his hand over the back of his neck and turned away from her. He planted his hands on his hips and looked to the ceiling. "I need to know my life has been better for not having Kyle around while I was growing up. I need proof he did me a favor by staying away."

"Aren't you getting that by learning what he

did? What he was involved in? The drugs? The money laundering?"

He turned.

Her gaze wandered over his face as she clasped his hand. "What more do you need to convince you what kind of a man he is now? Surely you know you were better off without him?"

He shook his head. "He couldn't have been out-and-out bad. The inspector doesn't exactly despise him. Plus, I've spoken to other people who even smile when I say I'm Kyle's son." He sighed as conflicting emotions continued to twist and turn. "It's like he did them a good turn or something. Even you don't entirely dislike him."

She opened her mouth to disagree and then her shoulders slumped. "You're right. I don't."

Frustration burned and John shoved his hand into his hair. "I need to know who Kyle is…really. Then maybe I can start to move on from all the pain and supposition I've built up in my head over the years. I can't stand not knowing the truth."

She nodded. "Right. So that's what we'll deal with first."

She marched past him, toward the kitchen, and snatched a bottle of soda and a cloth from a cupboard before returning to the living area. She attacked the spilled wine with a gusto that had him thanking God he wasn't the carpet.

Leaving her to her cleaning, he cleared their cold food from the table and carried their plates into the kitchen. His mind whirled and his gut churned as he scraped the untouched food back into containers.

After that, we go our separate ways as winners.

Her words taunted him. What the hell happened from here on out? Had their lovemaking meant nothing to her? Did she take him the way she did because she knew she could? Would she do whatever it took to get the fair and to hell with the consequences? He snapped on the container lids as pride swelled in his gut.

Nobody used him. Nobody. He'd made love to her because he'd never wanted a woman with the ferocity he wanted Sasha. He had come to her tonight rather than in the morning because after her reaction to Freddy possibly knowing something from her past, he didn't want to hold back any information from her. Yet, it seemed she had no problem holding back from him.

What had she been referring to when she said her mother knew something and didn't do anything about it? Her entire demeanor had changed from frozen mummy to whirlwind in a matter of seconds once she said that.

Frowning, he stacked the take-out boxes in her fridge and ran his hands under the faucet. He turned to grab the towel that hung from a hook beneath the counter and watched her. She scrubbed mercilessly at the sofa, her stunning face flushed and her cheeks streaked with tracks of dried tears.

He tossed the towel onto the counter and strode

from the kitchen. Just as he was about to touch her back, she abruptly stood.

Her determined, dark and beautiful gaze bored into his. “You might as well go. I’ll see you at work in the morning.”

Her words cut through his weakening heart and he shook his head. “I’m not leaving you like this.” He drew his thumb over her cheek. “You’ve been crying.”

She stepped back. “And now I’m done. We’ll talk more tomorrow.”

“And you’ll tell me what you meant by your mother knowing something and not doing anything about it?”

The skin at her neck shifted as she swallowed. “I will…when I can find the words.” She lifted onto her toes and gently pressed her lips to his. “Give me a little time to absorb what you’ve told me, okay?”

What else could he say to that request? He couldn’t harangue her or beg to sleep on her sofa so that she wouldn’t be entirely alone in the sadness that lingered in her gaze. He closed his eyes and drew in a long breath. “If you really want me to go, I’ll go. But—”

“I want you to go, John. Please.”

He opened his eyes and stared at her a moment longer before raising his hands in surrender. “Okay.”

She lifted her chin. “I need to see my mother.”

He nodded. “I understand that.”

"The sooner, the better."

"Okay. Do you want tomorrow off?"

"Can you can manage without me? I don't want to leave you understaffed."

"I'll be fine." He cleared his throat. "If nothing else, it'll give me some time alone with Freddy while he packs up his desk."

She flinched. "What? You're firing him?"

He straightened his shoulders. "Yes."

"Do you think that's wise?" Her eyes were wide. "Kyle will go mad if you get rid of Freddy like that. He's…he's Kyle's."

"This decision has nothing to do with Kyle. I asked Freddy what was said when he saw Kyle at the prison. He wasn't forthcoming, so he's going. His nose is so far up Kyle's ass, I can only see his damn chin when I look at him."

Her mouth lifted at the corner. "Nice imagery."

He shrugged. "He's made it clear he'll never accept me being in charge and resents every second I'm here. I don't need his skulking and scowling. I've got enough on my plate. He's out of here. As far as I can ascertain, he's easily replaceable. He's nothing but a bloody henchman who thinks the world owes him a favor."

Her gaze turned wary. "Have you thought what he might do when you deliver the news he's fired?"

"I don't care."

She shook her head. "Freddy wants Funland as much as I do, albeit for very different reasons. If you kick him out now, I'm worried you'll be looking over your shoulder every damn minute in case the man sticks a knife in your back."

Sasha had worked with Freddy a long time and almost certainly knew more than John what the man was capable of, but he refused to be intimidated by anyone—least of all Freddy Campton. "I appreciate your concern but, as time goes on, I'm starting to realize who *I* am. I might have had a privileged life, Sasha, but whether I like it or not, the longer I'm here, the more I realize Kyle's blood runs through my veins as much as my mother's. Up until now, her genes have been the strongest. From now on, it might just be Kyle's that take over until I'm done."

He could have sworn she shivered, but her gaze confidently held his. "Well, rightly or wrongly, I've got a feeling I'll never be the target of your anger, so be who you have to be to deal with this."

He dropped his gaze to her mouth. "You're right. You won't." He raised his eyes to hers and they stood that way, neither moving, for a long moment before she crossed her arms.

The softness in her dark eyes glinted with challenge. "So…if I'm seeing my mum tomorrow, when are you seeing Kyle? You should see him face-to-face. No phone calls or letters. You need to go to the prison."

His stomach wound tight. He exhaled. "I will."

"When?"

"I'll ring the prison tomorrow and see about getting a visitor's permit. I've no idea how these things work."

"Me neither, but I'm pretty sure he'll see you."

He nodded and winked. "I'll see you soon."

He turned and strode to her front door. Once he'd pulled it shut behind him, he stopped. How the hell had his coming to her apartment to help her ended up with him agreeing to see Kyle? That was the last thing he intended on doing when he came to Templeton.

By now, he expected to be halfway home, having pissed every penny of Kyle's drug money up the wall. Now he was going to meet the man who abandoned him years before for the very first time in almost two decades. John straightened his spine. This time he was an adult and a man. He was Kyle's equal. No…his better.

John marched along the corridor. He'd slept with a beautiful woman, spent day after day with her and, what's more, wanted to spend the coming days and weeks with her. Whichever way he looked at it, he was up shit alley with only one direction left to take.

THE NEXT MORNING, Sasha warily watched Marian from the corner of her eye as she served the couple holding hands like inseparable lovebirds at the bakery counter. Sasha resisted the urge to roll her eyes. Since when was a couple ever that happy?

Sex was sex. Men came and went. Women trusted then got hurt. Love was no more than a carousel of people running around in endless circles of disappointment.

She scowled and pushed her sunglasses onto the top of her head. Sooner or later, the frisson of lust she felt every time she remembered the warmth of John's hands on her skin would abate. Sooner or later, the stupid dip she got in her stomach and the hammer in her heart when he looked at her would give way to friendship.

That was her cycle. Lover then friend. She was proud of her "friendships." They meant she wasn't really the ice queen people assumed she was, just because she wasn't married or in a relationship at the grand old age of twenty-seven. No one knew she chose to keep men at arm's length. They didn't need to know. She had to be the one in control… not the man. Never the man.

But John had arrived like a tornado and turned her life on a different path—shooting her off on an emotional rocket with him in the pilot's seat. He was a good man. A good man whom she liked way too much…

"Sasha, my darlin'!" Marian's voice rang out from across the counter.

Sasha's smile sprang into place and she reached over the counter for a clumsy hug. "Hi. How are you?"

Marian grinned. "Just fine. All the better for

seeing you. Can you stop for a chinwag or do you need to get to work?" Her smile faltered and her gaze turned suspicious. "All okay at the fair? That Jordon upstart behaving himself?"

Sasha waved her hand dismissively. "Him? He's a pussycat, honestly."

Marian narrowed her gaze. Sasha's mouth trembled with the effort it took to keep smiling under the older woman's scrutiny. Time stood still. After what felt like an eternity, Marian emitted an inelegant snort. "Hmm, I'm sure he is." She tilted her head toward the tables at the back of the shop. "Grab a seat. Looks as though we need to have us a little chat."

Sasha exhaled. "We do."

"Good. I'll be right over."

When Marian turned toward the coffee machine, Sasha moved between the tables to a vacant booth. She slid along one of the seats and stared out the window at the passing morning traffic. Thoughts of the conversation she was about to have with Marian had kept her awake all night.

Before she saw her mother, she was determined to arm herself with as much information as possible. If anyone wanted to know anything about what had gone on in the Cove in the past, they went to Marian. She had only been a Templeton resident for about seven years, but thanks to her often nosy conversations with the regular customers who had come to be reliant on her cakes and pastries,

Marian knew the good, the bad and the ugly about everyone. *Except me. Please, God, except me.*

The aroma of freshly ground coffee wafted over her, and Sasha plastered on a smile and turned. Her stomach seemed to remain facing the other way. "Ooh, fabulous. A chocolate croissant, too? You spoil me."

Marian's eyes glinted with wisdom as she stared at Sasha and slid her ample behind into the opposite seat. "I bring food and drink because you're skinnier than a drainpipe. Don't you know Templeton men like something to grab ahold of? Look at me. Do you think these young men come in here after my food? Don't you believe it."

Sasha grinned and relaxed her shoulders. "Thanks. I'll bear that in mind."

"Make sure you do. Right..." She lifted her cup of tea from its saucer and sipped. "What's going on?"

Taking the pastry from the plate, Sasha took a deep breath. "My mother."

"Ah." Marian slowly returned her cup to its saucer.

Sasha chewed with difficulty, due to the saliva suddenly disappearing from her mouth.

Marian's brown eyes darkened as she pulled her mouth into a thin line. "What about her?"

The hunk of pastry finally descended Sasha's throat. "I need to know everything you know about what went on between her and Granddad..." She inhaled and exhaled the next words in a rush. "And between her and Kyle."

Marian raised her eyebrows. "Her and Kyle? Don't talk daft. Even your mother didn't consort with the likes of him." She frowned. "Did she?"

A burst of relief blended with a rush of frustration. If Marian wasn't aware of her mother's dealings with Kyle, there was a good chance she didn't know about Sasha's molestation, either. She slumped back. It also meant she couldn't throw any more light on what her mother might tell her.

Forewarned was forearmed, and now she'd have to face her mother as though blindfolded. "Damn it."

"You're disappointed?" Marian stared wide-eyed. "Why would you want her to have anything to do with Kyle Jordon? What's going on?"

"She's denying it, but there's some…speculation she might have had a hand in getting Granddad to sell the fair. When I leave here, I'm going to see her but wanted to have all the facts beforehand." She smiled wryly. "It was worth running things past the Cove's oracle first."

Marian frowned. "Who told you she had something to do with Kyle? Not that son of his…"

Sasha nodded. "And I believe him. First it came from Freddy and then John spoke directly with his dad." She swallowed. "Kyle has no reason to make anything up. He's dying."

"He's…" She closed her eyes. "Oh."

Sasha couldn't ignore the hint of disappointment that coated Marian's tone. "John's under the impression people in the Cove didn't hate Kyle as much as he originally thought. From your reaction to him dying, and mine, I think he's right."

Marian opened her eyes. "Kyle Jordon is a complicated man, sweetheart. My George says he always has been. If he's dying and called his son to Templeton, maybe this means worse things aren't to come. It could mean better things instead. Kyle has his nasty side, yes, but he was also a man who stood up for people he felt were wrongly treated. I've seen him help old people across the street and play five minutes of impromptu soccer with kids on the beach. It's confusing as can be, and his split personality left us treading on eggshells, but you couldn't deny Kyle was a man with a heart…even if it was entirely unpredictable."

Sasha blew out a breath. "Choosing when to be good or bad doesn't make Kyle Jordon a nice person."

"Of course not. He had zero integrity. There was a payoff for him, no matter what he did."

"So, you think he could be making this up about my mother then?"

Marian locked her kindly gaze on Sasha. "All I know is your mother wanted out of here and away from that fair. She wanted you and Tanya as far away as possible. Everyone knew it, but not why.

Then, bam, one day she comes into some money and she's leaving."

Sasha froze. "What money? When she and Tanya left, Mum told me she'd rather live in a pigsty than stay in Templeton and be branded a Gypsy. She didn't have any money. She lives in a tiny flat."

"With your father dead and leaving nothing behind, how could she up and move like that? It takes money to move and start again elsewhere. She must have had something."

Sasha closed her eyes. *So she did give Kyle information he was willing to pay for.* "You're right." Revulsion curdled like sour milk in Sasha's stomach, and she pressed a hand there. She opened her eyes and studied Marian for a reaction. "This is speculation, right? You'd tell me if you knew anything for sure?"

"Of course I would." Marian squeezed Sasha's hand on the table. "You know what you young ones mean to me. You're our future. I don't want you leaving the Cove any more than anyone else, but I do want you to live here happily. You haven't been truly happy since you were a young girl, from what I've heard."

Heat pinched Sasha's cheeks, and she slid her hand gently from Marian's and into her lap. She swallowed. "Who said that?"

Two spots of color darkened Marian's cheeks and she shrugged. "No one in particular, but you're a pretty girl. People are watching you all the time."

She smiled softly. “Especially the men hankering for a second of your attention.”

Sasha shook her head. “I’ve pushed John to go and see Kyle. I told him to ask Kyle everything he wants to know. The trouble is, if John is prepared to do that, it’s only right I keep up my end of the bargain and get to the truth of the sale between Kyle and Granddad.” She stared into Marian’s eyes. “So, it wasn’t my mother who said anything to you about me changing?”

Marian frowned. “No. Why? Did something happen?”

Sasha shook her head and gulped a mouthful of coffee. “It doesn’t matter. I’d better go before I change my mind about seeing her.”

She pushed to her feet, and Marian slid from the booth. She opened her arms and Sasha tried not to collapse into the older woman’s embrace. In that moment, she would’ve given the world for Marian to be her mother…and to not have to face her real one.

CHAPTER SIXTEEN

"JUST LEAVE, FREDDY. Just get your stuff and get out of here." John feigned interest in his laptop, grappling to suppress the overwhelming urge to grab Freddy's wide neck and throttle him.

"You can't do this. When Kyle finds out—"

John snapped his head up. "That I fired your ass because I don't need you he'll come after me? I don't think so. When will you listen to me? He doesn't care. He used you and you're not worth anything to him now. He won't give a crap you're gone. Trust me."

Freddy's eyes bulged as his chest rose and fell. "I'm not walking away with nothing after years of working for Kyle."

"I've paid you fair and square." He nodded toward the brown envelope in Freddy's hand. "There's a wad of extra cash in there because I figured you deserve some compensation for the risks you've undoubtedly taken for Kyle over the years, but that's where it ends. I don't owe you anything. If you think Kyle does, take it up with him."

He slid his gaze back to the laptop, his heart

pumping. If Freddy wanted to fight him, he could bring it on. A morning spent going over Kyle's file box of names had left John in a murderous mood. If Freddy wanted to feel the brunt of his anger, that was fine and dandy. One by one, John intended on going through Kyle's list and paying off the people he'd manipulated for his benefit. It was the quickest and easiest way to get rid of the tainted money he didn't want.

What was left, John had saved for DI Garrett's husband and his plans for a new drop-in center in Marchenton. The thought of Kyle's immoral proceeds being used to help the people he'd hurt held no end of ironic appeal.

"You'll regret this, Jordon."

John shook his head. "The hell I will."

With a grunt and a curse, Freddy left the office, leaving the door wide open behind him. John shoved back his chair and strode to the door, slamming it succinctly. He fisted his hands on his hips as the need to get out of the office, the fair—God damn it, Templeton—rose like a tsunami inside him. He glanced at the wall clock. Sasha was most likely with her mother by now and thoughts of her hurting sent his brain pulsing with helplessness. How was he supposed to sit and do nothing? Worse, wait until tomorrow until he saw her again?

He marched to his desk and forced his ass into the chair. He had plenty to get on with. He glanced at the computer screen once more. He could get in the car and start distributing Kyle's money. Damn, he could get in the car and go see Jay Garrett and hand over a big fat check right now. He could think of nothing else to bring him more satisfaction....

How would Sasha get to her mother's? He didn't even know where she lived. John frowned and stared at his cell phone on the desk. It had been tauntingly silent all morning. As far as he knew, Sasha didn't own a car. He'd only seen her on her bike. Maybe she'd appreciate a lift there. Save her having to pay for the train.

"You sad sap," he muttered. *Leave her be. She's managed well enough without you so far.*

He didn't want her to *manage;* he wanted to take care of her. He wanted to atone for some of the pain that Kyle, and maybe her mother, had caused her. He reached for his cell and tapped it against his bottom lip. He'd called the prison and put in a request for a visiting permit. The official there had said if Kyle agreed to the visit, the permit would then take a couple of days to produce. That couple of days fell on the weekend, so now John faced four days of waiting. He ground his teeth together and hissed out a breath.

He hated waiting.

Waiting was for people who had time to sit around doing nothing. People who liked to have time to linger and think. That wasn't him.

He snatched up his phone before he could change his mind and dialed Sasha's number.

"John?" Surprise, followed by a hint of apprehension, laced her tone. "Everything okay?"

He grimaced, wishing he felt more like a gentleman wanting to help a woman than a stalker hassling a Spanish princess. "Sure. Everything's fine."

Her exhalation sounded down the line. "Good. For a moment there, I thought Freddy might have you strung up on the Ferris wheel by your pants." She laughed.

"Funny." He smiled, his shoulders relaxing. "Where are you?"

"I'm just waiting for a taxi to take me to the station, then it's on to visit with Mummy Dearest. Have you spoken to Freddy?"

"Yes. And yes, he's gone. And yes, he's pissed."

"He's not going to go quietly. I hope you're prepared for the fallout."

"I am. Don't worry." He inhaled a long breath. "Listen, I want to get out of here. How about I keep you company and drive you to your mum's?"

Silence.

John stared ahead, ignoring the voice in his head telling him he'd taken a step too far, was pushing into her personal life at a rate of forty knots. Getting personal was never the deal, but they obliterated the business boundary the moment his lips hungrily touched hers.

"You don't have to do that."

"I'd like to. We're in this together now. And that

means more than the fair. We're in it together with regards to your mother and Kyle, too."

"Did you call the prison?"

"Yes. It looks as though I'll be seeing him Monday or Tuesday next week."

"Right."

"So? Can I drive you?"

"Okay."

He stiffened as surprise rippled through him. "Okay?"

"Sure. It beats getting the train, but you don't get to come in my mother's house. You'll have to grab a coffee somewhere while I talk to her. Agreed?"

He smiled, relief pumping through him. "Agreed."

"What about leaving the fair unattended?"

"I'll lock the office and leave the others to it. It'll be fine for a few hours."

"What if Freddy comes back? The stallholders can't be held responsible for having to deal with trouble. Each stall is a separate franchise, but the fair itself is mine...I mean, yours, to take care of."

John squeezed his eyes shut, willing the pang of guilt that struck his gut into submission. Keeping the fair from her for the time being was an indisputable decision. Kyle couldn't be trusted. Sooner or later, she'd realize John was doing what he thought best for her right now. He opened his eyes. "The stallholders and the people who run the rides will handle it. I trust them to do the right thing while

I'm gone. Don't you? I thought you knew the people here."

"I do."

"Do you trust them?"

"Yes. But if—"

"I don't deal in ifs and maybes. I don't want to be here today…I want to be with you."

"That's nice, but—"

"Nice?" He pulled the phone from his ear and stared at it. *Nice?* He put it back to his ear.

She laughed. "What's wrong with nice?"

He scowled, his male pride well and truly dented. "Sasha, when a man has taken a woman on a kitchen counter and had her whisper her pleasure in his ear, he doesn't appreciate being called *nice*."

"I can't believe you just said that." She laughed. "My God, you'd better be alone right now."

"I am." He grinned. "Where are you?"

"Outside Marian's."

"Cancel the taxi. I'll be there in fifteen minutes." He snapped the phone shut and strode to his desk. Whistling, he yanked his jacket from the back of his chair and his keys from the desktop.

Walking outside, he locked the office and made his way through the fair, talking to as many employees as possible, telling him they were on their own for the afternoon and making sure they had his cell number. Nerves leaped through him. Sasha's words of warning about Freddy pummeled at his conscience no matter how hard he tried to fight them.

He couldn't stay here day in and day out, waiting for Freddy's next move. When or if it came, he'd deal with it. Deep inside, the right thing was for Sasha to have Funland and make it hers. Once he found out the real reason she wanted it so badly and that it wouldn't bring her more pain—or that Kyle hadn't done anything to make someone else want it more and potentially threaten her—he'd find out for sure if his suspicion that the contract clause would be invalid now Funland was his. If he was right, John would hand it over and didn't want a penny in return.

Until then, he'd watch her back and hope she came to care for him as much as he cared for her. He'd yet to find a way to break through the barrier of distrust that lingered like a black shield in her eyes. He yearned to explore the feeling that Sasha was his destiny. A destiny he would never acknowledge Kyle had unwittingly—or wittingly—brought about.

He strode toward his car and slid onto the seat. Turning the ignition, the engine roared to life and John left the parking lot.

IT HAD TAKEN ducking into Marian's for a can of diet soda to cool the fire burning in every feminine pore from Sasha's lips to her panties after John's referral to her ear whispering. Hardly an hour had passed since their kitchen *thing* without her quivering as she reminisced over a snatched moment or two. Her memories were driving her insane. Once John had left her apartment the night before, she'd bounced from being relieved he was gone and knowing it was for the best, to wanting to yank open her apartment door and slam him against the elevator wall for some more wild sex.

Like an itch she couldn't resist scratching, he provided a tantalizing combination of pleasure versus pain every time she looked into his sea-blue eyes. His humor, his protectiveness and even his anger toward Kyle resonated through her, making her want John more and more.

At the sound of an approaching engine, Sasha snapped her gaze to the right. His car moved slowly through traffic, indicator flashing. She straightened her shoulders and ignored the knot that yanked tight in her lower regions when he pulled his stupid fancy car to a stop at the curb.

The warm temperature was the perfect excuse to lower the roof. Why did the sight of his car with the top down fill her with such girlish excitement? Clearly, her lack of interest in boys and their first cars when she'd been a teenager had left behind a residual need to play passenger in a hot car with a hot man.

He moved to get out of the car and she quickly yanked on the passenger door handle. "Stay where you are. I've got it."

He slumped back and smiled. "You really don't like me opening doors for you, do you?"

"Among other things. I'm sure by the end of the day you will have managed to add a few more to the list."

She flashed him a smile and slid into the luxury of butter-soft leather, instantly reminded of Liam's revelation that John was a multimillionaire, albeit from his father's less-than-moral earnings. If John came away with a different feeling about Kyle after being reunited with him, he had the money to do whatever—and go wherever—he wanted. For her, the entirety of her money would be used in getting the fair back, if he agreed to sell it back to her, of course. She'd have the fair and she'd be in Templeton, just like she always wanted.

So, why did that scenario suddenly make her feel trapped instead of free?

A shiver whispered up her spine, and she snapped on her seat belt. She glanced toward John.

He frowned. "Are you okay?"

"I'm fine." She forced a smile. "It might be best we move away from the bakery, though."

He glanced past her toward the shop window, and she followed his gaze. Marian stood at the other side of the glass, scowling at them, her hands fisted on her hips. Sasha waved, and Marian promptly shook her head. Sasha turned to John and quirked her eyebrow. "Do you think?"

He checked the mirrors before pulling into traffic. They sped from Templeton with only the radio breaking the silence. Yet the atmosphere didn't feel awkward or tense, and Sasha slipped deeper into the seat, her head falling back against the headrest. It felt comfortable and right. Her gaze danced over his hands as they maneuvered the steering wheel, down to his biteable forearms with their sinewy tendons and muscles, up to his biceps encased in black cotton…

"You're staring."

She started and flicked her gaze to his smiling profile. "So?"

Without hesitation, he reached for her hand and lifted it onto his denim-clad thigh and held it there. Her heart stuttered, but she didn't pull away. She'd allow herself to enjoy this drive and be thankful she wasn't alone on a train, going through each anticipated second of her visit with her mother.

This was better, *much* better.

"Shall I program the GPS? Or will you direct me?" His voice broke through her happy reverie.

"I'll direct you. It's about an hour's drive. I hope that's okay? I did warn you about leaving the fair too long."

He glanced at her, his gaze meeting hers. "I'm glad. It gives us a chance to talk."

"About what?" She stiffened, knowing it was only a matter of time before he mentioned what happened at her apartment.

He smiled. "Anything we want."

Relief that he wasn't pushing her softened her rigid spine, and she shifted back into the comfort of her seat. Maybe he would let her outburst about her mother go. She lifted her finger toward the windshield and a sign directing them from Templeton toward the neighboring town. "Follow the signs to Abbeyfield. Once we get there, I can direct you again."

The next few minutes lapsed into silence, and Sasha pondered the prospect of seeing her mother again after three months of non-face-to-face contact. She tapped her fingers to the music from the radio and tried to think of a way to bring up the subject of Kyle talking with her mother without simply demanding answers from her.

Her mother would most likely withhold the information Sasha wanted if she sensed her desperation. Her best strategy would be to keep ahold of her temper and play it as cool as possible.

Sasha pressed her hand to the trembling in her stomach. If she learned her mother had betrayed her, it would be another blow to her already wafer-thin sense of trust. It was one thing to deal with her mother not helping to get the fair back, but quite another if she'd had a hand in taking it from her and her granddad in the first place.

"Do you want to talk about last night?" John's voice broke into her thoughts.

Damn it. Her body tensed. "Which part?"

"The part where you mentioned your mother

knowing something and not doing anything about it." He glanced at her, his blue eyes apologetic. "I know it's none of my business, but I care about you. I want to help you even if I can't give you Funland just yet."

She eased her hand from his and laced her fingers tightly together in her lap. Her knuckles ached. "It happened a long time ago. It's not important."

"Yet you threw a glass of wine all over the place and cried." He glanced at her. "If you don't want to tell me, I'll have to accept that, but don't expect me to believe it's not important."

She turned to stare at the passing view of cottages and green fields, her heart a lump in her throat. Liam's words about appealing to John's softer side filtered through her heart and mind, sending her emotions into a tailspin. How could she trust John as she trusted Leah? Resistance to surrender even a small amount of control over what happened to her in the past rippled through her.

"I can't tell you."

Her heart beat loudly as the longing to share with this man ebbed and flowed. She turned and stared at his profile. His expression was unreadable. He concentrated on the road ahead, a muscle moving in his jaw. The seconds beat with her heart until he reached out and lowered the volume on the radio. She held her breath and waited.

He cleared his throat. "I don't want you to do or say anything you don't want to. Maybe I shouldn't have asked." He met her eyes. "But I'm not going anywhere for a while if you want to talk about it, okay?"

Not going anywhere for a while, but you will eventually.

A huge, unwanted sense of loss enveloped her. She stared at him. It was now or never. If she didn't leap now, she never would. It felt right. *He* felt right. She took a deep breath.

"I was twelve." The words slipped out and a strange sense of release washed over her. "I thought I was in love."

He smiled as he stared ahead. "Don't we all at that age?"

She swallowed. "He was older than me…a lot older."

His smile vanished and Sasha noticed the way he gripped the steering wheel a little harder until his knuckles showed white. "Right."

Stop talking. Stop talking now. "It was a Saturday afternoon when I first saw him. I was working at the fair, as always. Helping out, but mostly getting under the stallholders' feet. He was new there. I'd never seen him before." She huffed out a wry laugh. "I'd never noticed anyone *look* at me the way he did that first time. It made me feel…" She inhaled a shaky breath. "Grown-up, I guess."

He continued to stare through the windshield, his lips pursed tightly together.

Sasha blew out a steadying breath. The floodgates to her heart had burst wide open. Confessions and admissions danced on her tongue, scalding it. The only way to stop them was to get them out. Get them out of her body and into the open. She prayed they would be caught on the wind, never to return.

"Now I'm older, I see so clearly it was his fault what happened and how easily I walked straight into the scenario he had planned. The years of blaming myself, of hating myself, lasted a long time, but I've learned to live with them."

"Where is he now?"

The tight, strained and incredibly unnerving tone of his voice sent a shiver down her spine.

She swallowed as her mouth went dry. "I don't know. He disappeared. As far I know, no one saw him again after those three days."

"Did he…?" The skin at his neck shifted.

"He didn't rape me, but he did make me do things I didn't want to do. I was terrified, strangled by inexperience and fear…but I said yes anyway."

"You didn't know how to deal with that situation. How could you have?"

"I was young, but it was still me that let him—"

"You didn't know, Sasha." He reached across and took her hand, tightly holding it in his lap, and she welcomed the pain of his grip. "Do you get that? You didn't know."

"I know I didn't. But I still find it hard to believe it happened to me. That it still happens to kids every day, all over the world."

He maneuvered the car to the side of the country road and killed the engine.

Panic gripped her. It was easier to talk and confess when he wasn't looking at her, when his soft, blue eyes were focused on the road and not her. She didn't want to see pity in his gaze. Didn't want to witness his caring when she was over her ordeal—over it in spades and all the stronger for it.

She swallowed. "What are you doing?"

His gaze wandered over her face, lingered at her mouth and then tentatively, gently, he leaned closer and took her jaw in his hands. He stared deep into her eyes. "Thank you."

"For what?"

He gently wiped his thumb across her cheek. "For trusting me. Finally. It means a lot you shared that with me."

A traitorous tear broke and trickled over her cheek. She smiled. "You're welcome…and I do trust you."

His lips touched hers, warm and in control. So comforting, so trusting, so loving that she never ever wanted to have to say she let John Jordon go. She reached up and gripped his shoulders, pulling him closer and kissing him deeper. Her heart left her body and moved under his skin, beneath the shield of his ribs to merge with his. There would be no going back. Only forward. *God, please take me forward.*

CHAPTER SEVENTEEN

AWARE OF JOHN'S gaze on her back, Sasha walked around the street corner from where he sat in his parked car. Once she was certain she was out of his view, she exhaled a shaky breath and leaned against someone's garden wall. She needed a moment before she saw her mother and asked her questions she wasn't sure she wanted to know the answers to. Her heart beat erratically and her hands shook.

She had to get this done. Had to remember the real or imagined promise in John's kiss. He would be there for her—even temporarily—after her mother's revelations. Just knowing that, she could get through whatever happened in the next few minutes.

Pushing away from the wall, Sasha lifted her chin and smoothed her hands over the legs of her jeans. *Here goes nothing.*

She strode forward, past the houses of people she didn't know, toward a block of apartments where her mother had lived since she left Templeton. Sasha gritted her teeth. How could her mother have insisted the fair made her aware—no, ashamed—of her Romany roots? It hadn't rung true with Sasha and now she knew why…her mother had been talking complete rubbish. Spewing excuses rather than reasons.

Pressing the buzzer to apartment 410, Sasha drew in a long breath. The intercom crackled and her mother's voice came through. "Hello, darling. Come on up."

The buzzer sounded and Sasha pulled open the door.

Throughout the brief elevator journey to the fourth floor, Sasha's mind whirled and her confidence wavered. She met her eyes in the mirrored wall of the elevator and pulled back her shoulders. She had come here for the truth. Once she had it, she could move on, let go of her family's reluctance to help her secure Funland for her own and deal with her only option. To overturn Kyle's clause and to convince John no further harm would come to her if he sold it to her.

Her heart twisted. His hesitation to pass her the fair had very little to do with his anger toward Kyle now and a hell of a lot to do with his feelings for her. Feelings that were wholly—and scarily—reciprocated.

"He's going home, stupid. He's going home."

She whispered the words that had kept her awake half the night, and echoed in her head while they kissed in his car. Sooner rather than later, John would return home to his own life and career.

The doors pinged and slid open.

Pushing John to the back of her mind for the time being, Sasha strode forward and stopped outside her mother's closed apartment door. Swallowing against her desert-dry throat, she rapped her knuckles against the door. Barely two seconds later, it swung open and she came face-to-face with her mother after a three-month separation.

Sasha forced a wide smile. "Hi, Mum."

"Darling." Her mother grinned and opened her arms. "It's so lovely to see you."

Stepping into her embrace, Sasha closed her eyes as they hugged. Her mother might have done something Sasha would be hard-pressed to forgive, but they did love each other. They slowly parted and, with hands joined, the door was closed and together they entered the apartment.

It was modestly decorated in shades of pale green and cream. The three-piece sofa suite was black leather and invitingly adorned with cushions of varying sizes. The windows were open and the soft July breeze lifted the gauzy, floor-length curtains. Feeling the tension in her mother's grip, Sasha turned and smiled.

"This is lovely, Mum. You must be happy here."

She sighed. "I'd be happier if you were here with me."

"That's not going to happen." Sasha eased her hand from her mother's and walked farther into the room.

Snapshots of Sasha and Tanya adorned nearly every available surface, occasionally interrupted with pictures of her dead father and their childhood family Labrador, Beau. She picked up the picture of her father. “I wonder what Dad would make of you moving away from Templeton and my wanting to stay.”

“He’d understand.”

Irritation rippled across the surface of her forearms as Sasha replaced the photo. “Would he?” She met her mother’s gaze and their identically dark eyes locked.

“Why don’t we sit? Do you want coffee? A cold drink?”

Sasha moved to the sofa and sat, crossing her legs. “No, thanks. I want you to tell me what happened between you and Kyle and then I’ll go.”

Her mother hesitated, her face a closed mask. “I’m glad you came. I’m glad you want answers. It’s time.”

Biting back the urge to shout that she’d always had the right to know what happened with regard to Funland, Sasha leaned back into the cushions and waited.

Her mother sat beside her. “I had no choice, Sasha. I did what I thought best to protect you.”

“From what?”

“From…from what happened to you.”

Sasha breath caught painfully in her throat.

"You knew. You really knew. My God, does Tanya know, too?"

"Of course not, I would never have—"

"Never have what? Kept my molestation from her? Or the fact you struck a deal with Kyle? A fact you've kept from me?"

Color rushed into her mother's cheeks and tears suddenly filled her eyes. She looked down to her hands clenched tightly together in her lap and nodded. "I didn't know what else to do." She looked up, her gaze pleading. "Tanya doesn't know anything. I promise."

"I really don't know what to say, Mum." Sasha's face burned with hurt and disappointment. "How could you—"

Her mother snapped her head up and stared deep into Sasha's eyes. "You have to understand…and when you have children of your own one day, I hope you will. I was never sure that man did anything to you until I was talking to a few of the mums at the supermarket one day. You were in school and doing well, but there was something different about you after the summer. You seemed… older, more mature. Funland became a mission to you rather than a place you enjoyed. It consumed you, and while your grandfather was excited about your determination to make it yours, I was scared by it."

Sasha stared as memories crashed and burned inside her. How could she deny the shift from childhood excitement to unadulterated hunger hadn't ignited inside her once Matt Davidson disappeared? How could she lie and say the place hadn't felt tainted and dirty after those three short days? That it became her entire life's purpose to make Funland clean again. To make it hers so she could repaint and replenish it to its former glory…before *him?*

She swallowed. "So what happened? Did you know Matt Davidson?"

Her mother clutched Sasha's hand, making her flinch. Her gaze darted over Sasha's face, her face a mask of fury. "My God, do you think if I knew the man, knew where he was, I wouldn't have tracked him down and made him pay for what he did to you and those other young girls? By the time I knew the truth, it was too late. I found out what had happened years after. I just wanted to move away, take you and your sister far away, where you could be safe and forget Funland ever existed." A lone tear slipped down her cheek, and she lifted her hand to cup Sasha's jaw. "But how could I do that when you were so determined to stay? To work with Granddad every day as though your entire life depended on it?"

"Did you give Kyle Matt Davidson's name?"

Her mother nodded.

Tears clogged Sasha's throat and pain mixed with anger…for him…for her mother. "But you weren't sure and you told Kyle anyway. Worse…" Sasha trembled and lifted her mother's hand from her face. "You thought telling Granddad was the right thing to do. How could you do that?"

"I had to." Her mother's eyes darkened with determination. "Once I found out Kyle wanted the fair, I was prepared to do anything to ensure he had it. The place reeked with filth so why not let Kyle run it into the ground where it belonged?"

Sasha's heart picked up speed. "I love Funland. So did Granddad. It wasn't Funland that molested me, it was one animal. One man among a million good. You had no right to tell Granddad. How do you know it wasn't that knowledge that broke his damn heart?" She pushed to her feet and whirled away from the sofa—from her mother. She glared through the open window at the deserted street below. "This is all your fault. Everything that I've worked so hard to call my own could now be out of reach forever." She turned around. "If Kyle's son doesn't sell me Funland, I'll never forgive you."

Her mother stood and came toward her, her hand outstretched. Sasha stiffened and her mother pushed her hand into her hair and held it there. "I did what I thought was best. It was hard for me, too, Sasha. Hard for me to see you lose weight and buckle under so much determination to learn the fair from the ground up, to see you work for Kyle when he knew..." Her mother closed her eyes. "It was hard and I couldn't watch anymore. I had to leave even if you didn't come with me."

Sasha fought the burn in her eyes and crossed

her arms. "So you told Kyle the information he needed to ensure Granddad never wanted me to have anything to do with the place. You told Kyle and accepted money."

Her mother opened her eyes. "Money I could use to set us up somewhere new. Why can't you see I did this for—"

"For you, Mum. You did this for you."

Unable to stand another minute looking into her mother's pleading eyes, Sasha stormed toward the door and yanked it open. With a final glance at her mother, she marched from the apartment and jogged to the elevator. She punched the call button, praying for its speedy arrival.

Her mother's apartment door clicked open behind her. "Sasha, please. Come back in, we have to talk about this."

The elevator doors slid open, and Sasha rushed inside, her finger shaking as she pressed the button for the ground floor.

"Sasha, wait. Please."

The doors slid closed and her mother's desperate face disappeared. Sasha slumped against the back wall, covered her face with her hands and cried.

THE PAST FORTY-FIVE minutes and thirty-two seconds would go down as the longest of John's life. He'd drank one painfully inadequate espresso and scanned enough of a tabloid newspaper to keep him up on celebrity nonsense for the next twelve months. Who gave a crap who was marrying whom or sleeping with whom when the woman you were falling in love with was about to confront her mother about a fifteen-year-old hurt that lingered on her heart like a bruise?

He stared out his windshield. He was falling in love. The notion was unexpected…yet entirely welcome. A lonely life waited for him back in Bridgewater, and he wasn't sure he wanted to return. Meeting Sasha had taught him all the years he'd thought he'd been avoiding getting involved with a woman hadn't been that at all.

He'd simply been waiting for the right woman to come along. The beat of his heart and the roar of love in his veins told him Sasha could be "The One." The one to provide good times and laughter in his life. What if together they could have a future full of promise rather than carrying the endless weight of resentment toward parents who'd made dire mistakes?

At last, he realized his anger toward Kyle served no purpose. John exhaled a breath. Whereas being with Sasha served every purpose he could think of. They understood each other and cared for one another. The heat between them was undeniable, and the need to learn more about her likes and loves, dreams and wishes, burned hot inside him.

He glanced at his watch and hissed out a breath from between clenched teeth. He'd promised her he'd wait for her call and not come looking for her.

He closed his eyes. God, it was killing him not to get out of the car and make sure she was okay.

The moment she opened up to him about her past, everything changed. An avalanche of emotion consumed him and burst into his blood on a tidal wave.

What happened to her had made her fight to hold on to the possibility of turning something ugly into something pretty for the future hordes of kids who came to Funland looking for a good time. His past made him bitter and full of hatred toward Kyle, a man who hadn't given his son a second thought until he needed him for his own means. To make his narcissistic choices seem worthwhile.

The seconds passed like minutes as John tapped out his impatience on the steering wheel. He'd promised Sasha he wouldn't even enter her mother's street, let alone knock on her door. His foot bounced against the car mat as he waited in the street around the corner, fighting every instinct to seek out his lover.

Who was the faceless piece of shit who hurt her? Who stole a young girl's innocence and then disappeared? The heavy, throbbing weight of revenge flowed through his veins. For the first time in forever, John's vengeance was concentrated on a man who might still roam the streets, preying on other innocent young girls, rather than for a man who would soon lose his life to cancer.

He drew in a shaky breath.

Deep inside, he sensed it was important to be what Sasha needed right now and not take the yearned-for steps toward tracking the bastard who'd hurt her and make him pay. At least not yet. He couldn't leave her so he could scour the country and exact justice when there was such pain in her eyes, or a tremble in her lips when he kissed her.

He would have to bide his time.

He tightened his jaw. What would his father do in this moment? Hadn't Kyle taken a gun and shot the man who'd killed his mother?

John shook his head. He wouldn't do that. He wouldn't kill Sasha's abuser and leave her alone to deal with the aftermath. Together, they'd find him. They'd make DI Garrett and the police help them every step of the way…and then John would be with her as Sasha's pain was put to rest forever.

Memories flowed, and John closed his eyes. Images of his father lifting his mother from her feet to swing her around in circles during a rain shower, while his six-year-old self laughed until he cried in the shelter of their garden porch. Another time, John had climbed from his bed and crept downstairs…only to peer into the living room and see his father massaging his mother's feet, the light of flickering candles dancing across her smiling face….

John swallowed back the sting of tears and angrily swiped his hand over his face. No. He wouldn't do this. He wouldn't justify a moment of Kyle's existence. Especially when it was Kyle's actions that brought a pile of pain between him and Sasha.

She came around the corner, her frame rigid and strong as she jogged toward the car. He yanked on the door handle and got out of the car. He hurried toward her, and when she fell into his arms, he held her tight. She fit in the circle of his arms like a child. Her sobs were harsh and raw, racking her body.

"Shh, it's all right," he murmured against her hair. "I've got you. It's all right."

"She did it, John. She took Kyle's money."

His mind raced as he glared over her head toward the street from where she'd emerged. "Did she tell you what she told him?"

She pulled back from his arms, her fingers clinging tightly to his biceps. "She told him who hurt me."

He frowned. "I thought you never told her what happened to you."

"I didn't. She guessed. She even guessed who was responsible." She closed her eyes. "She said when I was a mother, I'd understand."

"So why the hell didn't she ask you about it?"

"She tried." She opened her eyes. "I realize now the times she attempted to get me to open up about it. I can see what she tried to do. You have to understand how I shut down. I didn't want anyone to know. I pushed her away and I held it all in. It was the only way I could get through it. I wanted to pretend it didn't happen."

The pain in her eyes tore at John's heart, and he pulled her to him, kissing her forehead.

She shook her head. "She knew who he was."

He glanced toward her mother's street once more, his pulse thumping in his temple. "Did she confront him?"

"No."

"I don't believe this."

"John, look at me." She swiped the tears from her cheeks. "My family… We've never been close. Mum, Dad and Tanya wanted so much more than Templeton could ever give them." She shook her head. "Whereas Granddad and I had everything we needed right here. I've never felt connected to my mum, not ever. This was a wall so thick neither of us stood a chance of breaking it down."

His mind raced with thoughts of a mother who'd been there but in reality abandoned her daughter in no different way than Kyle had done to him. Revulsion crawled over his skin. "How in God's name did this lead her to take money from Kyle years later? I don't understand how anyone could do that."

Her hand trembled as she pushed the hair back from her face. "About eight or nine years ago, she spoke to some friends who had girls the same age and younger than me. One of them told her she needed to move away from Templeton so her daughter could get over what happened to her at

Funland one summer." Her eyes shone with unshed tears. "The same summer it happened to me. Mum figured too many years had gone by for her or the police to have any chance of tracking him down."

John clenched his jaw but said nothing.

She exhaled. "She was desperate to get me out of there, but with Dad gone, she didn't have the money."

"Then she discovered Kyle wanted Funland."

She nodded. "She was confident if Kyle told Granddad what happened and that she suspected it was part of the reason I was obsessed with staying and making Funland good again, Granddad would want to get rid of it."

"For whatever price he could get."

"Exactly."

John's heart thundered. "My father used your pain and your mother's fears to stick the knife in your grandfather. My God, the man is scum."

Tears slipped over her cheeks. "I'm struggling to see the good in him, despite what Inspector Garrett or anyone else thinks."

"What do you want to do now?" He curled his hands into fists and stuffed them deep into his pockets, fighting to get control of himself and not jump in the car and drive to Her Majesty's prison right there and then.

She inhaled a long breath. "I don't know. I need to think. To reconsider. I'm so mad at her. At Kyle...at *him*. The man who made all this happen." She looked deep into his eyes, confusion and hurt storming in her gaze. "I really don't know what to do."

He cupped her elbow, pain scratching harshly at his heart as his mind whirled with violent intention. He stole his arm around her shoulders and gently steered her to his car. "Let's get you home."

She stood firm, her fingers clutching his forearm and her eyes wide with panic. "I don't want to go home. I don't want to be alone tonight."

"You won't be. You're staying with me."

Her gaze darted over his face. "What about the fair? With Freddy gone—"

"I'll drop you at Kyle's house. You can have a bath and try to relax. I'll make sure everything is taken care of at the fair and come straight back as soon as I can." He brushed the fallen hair from her eyes. "Let me take care of you, Sasha. Please."

Her eyes locked with his. They stormed with apprehension, fear and doubt. "I can't… I don't know…"

He stepped closer and dipped his head to brush his lips across hers. "Please."

She closed her eyes and nodded, her shoulders slumping. "I'd like that. I'd like that very much."

Slipping his fingers into hers, John threw a final glance over his shoulder toward her mother's street and led Sasha to his car.

CHAPTER EIGHTEEN

SASHA LET JOHN take her hurriedly packed bag from her fingers as she stood stock-still in the enormous lobby area of Kyle Jordon's mansion. Hysterical laughter bubbled in her throat as she stared at the majestic, marbled opulence of it.

A huge ebony staircase lay ahead of her, leading to God only knew how many rooms on the second floor. She looked left and right toward the rooms on either side of her. Her strong and often troublesome curiosity battled with decorum as she resisted the need to explore them. Who would've ever believed she would one day be standing in Kyle's Jordon's hallway—her stomach knotted—and maybe even sleeping in his bed?

She glanced at John.

He stared down at her, his blue eyes intense as he studied her. "Are you okay?"

"Yes."

A soft smile played at his lips. "This place feels less cold already. Just having you standing inside these four walls dispels the blandness of it."

Heat pinched at her cheeks, and she dragged her gaze from his. "It's not that bad."

"Liar."

She smiled and stared at the blank walls and complete lack of decor surrounding them. "Well, maybe it is."

"Do you want a glass of wine? A cup of coffee? I can get you whatever you want."

She met his eyes and her heart turned over. "How did this happen?"

He frowned. "What?"

"How did you manage to get me here? Like this? With you? And have me be so damn happy about it?" She grinned.

He dropped her bag and the bag of provisions they'd picked up from the store onto the floor. Smiling that soft, sexy smile of his, he closed the foot of space between them in one easy stride. He curled his fingertips into the front pockets of her jeans and tugged her forward in the way she was starting to love. Her breasts pressed deliciously against the broad expanse of his rock-hard chest.

"I want you to be happy." His gaze wandered over her face before he dropped his lips to her neck. "I want you to be happy to be with me."

She tilted her head to the side, giving him greater access to her sensitized skin as she smoothed her hands over his biceps and up to his shoulders. "Things like this don't happen to me. I don't let them. I don't let men get too close…and if I do, it's always by my rules and not theirs."

"There are no rules. We're on neutral ground." He slowly pulled back, and his hungry gaze locked on hers. "If you want me to back off, I will. I want you to relax. I didn't ask you here to do anything but relax."

She smiled. "We'll see how that goes, shall we?"

He brought his mouth to hers and kissed her, his tongue softly touching hers, and she leaned into him, her heart blending with the gathering strength of her need for this most unlikely man who had somehow come to matter so much more than she'd thought possible. No longer an adversary, John was her confidant, her savior and more than anything, her lover.

Could she really allow herself to trust him as much as her heart wanted her to? Could she let him take care of her? Make everything feel so good when really her world had taken a tumble into the very, very bad.

She opened her heavy lids when he gently eased back and lifted her bag from the floor. "I'll put this upstairs. You go into the living room and get comfortable. I'll be just a minute." He waved toward the room on her left before moving to walk away. He stopped at the bottom stair. "Do you want me to run you a bath?"

She smiled. "Sounds perfect."

He winked before bounding up the huge staircase

two steps at a time and disappearing out of view. Pulling back her shoulders, Sasha walked slowly through the archway leading into Kyle's living room. A gasp caught in her throat and she put her hand to her chest. Everything was pristine. Shades of cream and the palest beige made the room feel enormous. It was only the flashes of deep red from the cushions, vases and dried flower arrangements that broke the blank canvas.

It was clear Kyle had added nothing to his home since the day the interior decorator left. Not that it mattered. To Sasha, there was nothing worth seeing once you stepped into the room because it was impossible to avoid the breathtaking view through the floor-to-ceiling windows and centered patio doors covering the entire breadth of the far wall.

She slowly approached, her feet sinking into the plush cream carpet as she trailed her fingertips along the back of one of the enormous fabric sofas. She turned the key in the lock of the doors and suppressed a laugh as she flung them open and stepped outside.

"My God." The words whispered from her lips as she walked across the flagstones toward the enormous hot tub, past a barbecue and luxurious sitting area.

She tried and failed to stop gawking as she wandered farther still. Strolling along a pier that stretched out over the shore and beyond to an enormous white yacht. She shook her head and planted her hands on her hips.

Seagulls dove and bobbed on the water's surface. Soft white clouds scudded lazily across a perfect blue sky. The fading sun lingered in its downward descent as though not wanting to leave a place so pretty and peaceful. She drew in a long breath and took it all in because God only knew what tomorrow would bring.

Time ticked by and she let it. Suddenly, she wanted this moment to last forever, without having to deal with the things going wrong in her life. She didn't regret telling John what happened to her, but she did regret putting the flash of anger in his beautiful blue eyes. Eyes that told her so much.

The yacht beside her clanked gently against the pier as a rush of water from a passing Jet Ski rippled its surface. She stared at the exterior of the boat. *Fiona Forever.* Her heart beat with sorrow. Was Fiona John's mother?

A plank creaked a few feet behind her, and she spun around.

John strolled toward her, his face inscrutable behind the cover of his dark sunglasses. "Now you see what evil can pay for."

She forced a laugh. "I can't believe this place."

He turned toward the yacht and stared at it for a moment before lifting his shoulders. "It reeks of criminality. I hate it. As soon as I leave here, this is the first place I'll sell."

Sasha's stomach knotted, and she turned her back to him, preferring to watch the ripple of the ocean than acknowledge the ripple of regret that ebbed through her blood. "You could put your own stamp on it if you wanted to stay. This is a shell. It could be made into anything you want it to be."

His hands came to rest on her shoulders, and when he rubbed his thumbs at the knot at the base of her neck, her knees trembled.

"I don't think I could ever live here." His breath whispered against her ear. "Not knowing this is where Kyle made his home…where he ruined so many people's lives."

"You're not him, John. You're your own person."

"I know that, but I've also accepted there's little hope of the people in Templeton not looking at me without thinking of him."

"You don't know that. You'll just have to bide your time." She turned, and his hands slipped to her waist. She smiled. "I look at you and I see so much more than Kyle."

"I need to go."

Her stomach knotted, and her heart stuck like a rock in her throat. "You're really going to leave Templeton? Just like that?" She stepped back from his grip and crossed her arms across her stomach.

"What? No. I mean I need to go from here. Now." He pulled one hand away from her stomach and lifted it to his lips. "Nothing is going to be simple about me leaving Templeton. Not anymore."

"Oh." His soft insinuation and her misinterpretation of his leaving town forever brought embarrassed heat to her face.

He smiled. "I'd better make sure everything is locked up at the fair. Kyle's files are there and I'm sure they're locked in my desk, but I want to make sure." He wiggled his eyebrows. "Especially as I intend to take a long weekend."

The glint in his eyes chased her insecurity away and she smiled. "A long weekend? What's that?"

He winked. "You'll see. I'll be back as soon as I can."

Her breath escaped on a laugh. "Then I'll see you soon."

He smiled and kissed her knuckles again. "The bathroom is upstairs, third door along the corridor."

"Thanks." She glanced past him toward the house. "There's nothing I want more than to wash some of this day off me."

He kissed her gently. "Enjoy. I'll see you later."

Her smile trembled as he walked away and into the house. No matter how much she wanted to enjoy this moment, she was afraid of what it meant. He'd just said he couldn't stay here, so what did that mean for them? She shouldn't have let her desperation to have him near her, now and possibly forever, to show so openly through her words and reactions. He'd know how she needed him. Know he held her heart in the palm of his hand to use and abuse as he saw fit.

Nausea churned and whirled and no matter how much she told herself John wouldn't do that, that he wasn't there to hurt her, the feeling wouldn't abate. *I have to go. This is too soon. I can't need him this way.*

She ran for the house and into the living room, yanking the patio doors closed behind her. She raced to the front door and stopped. Her hand trembled on the handle as her heart hammered.

She looked over her shoulder to the stairs.

To stay or go. Fight or flee.

Her feelings for John were terrifying and stripped her of her need to control and categorize every aspect of her life. Was that such a bad thing? Her hand slipped from the door. She could do this. She could see where her feelings took her. Didn't John make her happier than anyone had in years?

Possibility tugged hard at her heart, and Sasha lifted her chin. She wouldn't run. Nor would she hide. She never had before and she wasn't about to start now.

She breathed deep and wandered toward the stairs. With her hand on the ebony banister, Sasha headed toward Kyle's bathroom. She pushed open the door, and her heart melted.

My God, have I found the perfect man?

Fifteen minutes later, she lounged deeper into the mammoth tub and her tension drifted away, leaving her limbs weak. Sasha smiled. She felt like Cleopatra. John had filled the tub with the most delicious, jasmine-scented bubbles and lined its edges and every other available surface with flickering candles.

Never before had she indulged in such luxury, nor felt so cared for or romanced. Where had the bubble bath and candles come from? He must have bought them along with the wine and food when they stopped in the supermarket because there was no way someone as masculine and built as John would take a damn bubble bath.

She grinned.

Her mind should be filled with her conversation with her mother, the known truth that she'd dealt with Kyle and instigated a way for him to get the fair from Granddad. Yet, all Sasha wanted to do was linger a little longer in the enjoyment of being cared for by someone else, of letting someone behind the armor she'd erected years before. Finally a man had found a way inside her heart. Finally he'd come into her life and she already felt stronger and more capable with John than she did alone.

She couldn't remember a time when she'd been happier…or more afraid her happiness could be snatched from her in a heartbeat.

Turning her thoughts from losing John before anything had really begun between them, she focused on her mother. Confusion and fear of what happened next reigned supreme. She couldn't deny her mother had mistakenly done what she thought best for her youngest daughter. Her baby. Tears had streaked her mother's cheeks earlier that afternoon as she implored Sasha to understand.

Sasha stared unseeingly ahead. Having never experienced abuse, how was her mother to truly understand that wherever a victim of abuse went, the memories followed?

The biggest saving grace was Tanya didn't know what happened that summer, which meant from that moment on, only her mother, Leah, Kyle and now John would know what she went through. Maybe, finally, that chapter of her life could close.

A shrill ringing of her cell phone on a table beside the tub shot Sasha's heart into her throat. She bolted upright and swiped at the tears she didn't know she'd cried. With her hand trembling, she snatched up the phone and looked at the display. Leah. Sasha released her held breath and pressed the talk button. "Hey, you."

"At last. Don't you check your phone anymore?"

Sasha grimaced. "I know you've been calling, but I've been…"

"Avoiding me? Running from criminals? Going after Kyle with a shotgun? What?" Leah groaned. "I've been going out of my head today wondering why you aren't picking up or calling me back."

"I'm sorry." Guilt she'd caused Leah distress pushed Sasha from her unexpected cocoon of comfort. She abruptly stood and stepped out of the bath. "Things have gone crazy." She reached for one of John's, or likely Kyle's, huge white towels and wrapped it around herself, the phone balanced in the crook of her neck.

"Crazy how? I was hoping you had some good news by now. Better still, you'd be up for a bit of fun this weekend and we can talk things out over a cocktail or two at the Oceanside."

Sasha slumped into an armchair in the corner of the enormous bathroom. An armchair that would fit nicely in her apartment it was so big, soft and comfy. "That sounds good, but I don't think it will be happening anytime soon."

"Why not?"

Because all I want to do is hide out here in my nemesis's house and maybe get to know his son a little better....

Sasha grimaced. "Things aren't so good right now."

"Tell me."

"I don't even know how to do that."

A couple of seconds ticked by before Leah sighed. "The beginning is as good a place as any. Come on, love. You can tell me anything. You know that."

Sasha's body dried where she sat. The next fifteen minutes passed as she took Leah from her conversation with John at Clover Point to her realization he carried equally as many family hang-ups as she did, to Freddy being a second, unexpected adversary, to…

"You had sex with him on the kitchen counter?

Jesus, Sasha." Leah emitted a high-pitched shriek. "I frigging love it. You go, girlfriend. You've got this. You're in control so don't worry about it. Mark my words, he'll be handing you that fair on a plate."

Sasha squeezed her eyes shut and dropped her head into her hand. "It's not about that. I had sex with him because I really, really like him."

"I was joking! I know you, remember?"

Sasha closed her eyes. "Sorry. I just…if there was any chance John might think—"

"He won't. You've already said he's nothing like Kyle and he hates everything that has gone on at Funland. Take a chance. He's handsome, rich and clearly gotten right under your skin. It's time. It's time to trust someone."

"I don't know…."

"I do. Look, why don't I meet him? Maybe it will make you feel better knowing what I think of him after I've actually spoken to the guy. We could set something up this weekend. I'll find a man for a double date. It'll be fun."

"Maybe."

"Maybe? Don't you want me to meet him?"

"Of course. It's just finding out about Mum and what she did… It's sent me running and wanting to hide for a while. Socializing is the last thing on my mind."

"Where are you now? Shall I come over with a bottle of wine?"

"Why don't you guess where I am?" Sasha rubbed

her head against her palm as though trying to scrub some sanity into her brain.

Now her best friend was on the other end of the line, the reality she was sitting in Kyle Jordon's towel, in Kyle Jordon's house, waiting for Kyle Jordon's son to come back, didn't feel quite so surreal as it did half an hour ago. Now it felt deranged.

Leah coughed. "Okay, I could say where I think you are, but that will mean part of your brain has fallen out."

"I think it has."

"You're at his house, aren't you? You're actually at Kyle Jordon's house. Oh. My. God."

Sasha laughed and pushed up from the chair. "I am, and it's amazing."

"That's it. I've got to see this for myself. Please, Sasha. Let me come over there."

"Now? No, you can't."

"Tomorrow then. Please. Run the dating idea past John. Maybe we could have a quiet night in…at Kyle's house."

Sasha grinned at the excitement and slyness in Leah's voice. "You're a bad girl, Leah Dixon."

"Is that a yes? You'll set something up?"

"I'll see. Now get off this phone before…" The slamming of a door downstairs brought her words to a halt and her heart beat erratically. He was home. John was back. "I've got to go."

"What is it? What's wrong?"

Sasha smiled and dropped her towel. "Nothing's

wrong. Everything's absolutely right. I'll call you tomorrow."

"Promise?"

"Promise." Sasha ended the call, hoping Leah understood the succinct ending of their conversation held the silent "do not disturb" signal and her friend wouldn't consider calling her again later.

For now, she didn't want to think, breathe or consider the mess of her life. She wanted to keep hold of the feeling of being loved and cared for. She wanted to be free. She wanted to be a woman exploring the discovery of a new relationship—no matter how futile the longing for something lasting might be.

More than anything, she wanted to be free.

Drawing in a long breath, Sasha strode from the bathroom, feigning sexual confidence despite the tangle of knots in her stomach. Her entire body hummed with the need for comfort, for the feel of John's hard muscled body beneath her hands and the thump of his pulse joining hers. Every moment with her mother had been washed from her skin and now it was time to eradicate it from her heart. For tonight, she wanted to think of nothing else but John. God only knew how long she had left with him before he left Templeton and her life.

Her heart ached with sadness at that thought, but she had no intention of wasting a single moment when John could be hers.

She padded from the bathroom and along the

pale cream opulence of the upper floor landing. Her ears strained for his movements and when she leaned her hands on the ebony banister and looked over, their eyes met.

She didn't smile. She didn't speak.

His darkly intense gaze wandered the entire length of her naked body. Her heart pounded and her body tingled with anticipation, yet she stood perfectly still as his gaze wandered over her. He slowly ascended the grand staircase, not taking his eyes from hers.

Second by unbearable second passed as he closed the space that separated them. He reached the landing and paused.

His jaw tightened and his midnight-blue gaze lit with a raw animal lust that shot sensation after sensation through her core and her entire body. He opened the buttons on his shirt, and it fell to the floor behind him. She swallowed and drank in the sight of his bronzed, muscular chest and washboard stomach. His feet whispered over the carpet as he strolled toward her, snapping open the top button of his jeans.

She wet her lips and resisted the urge to run at him. No more taking over. No more rushing to the end. He'd see her bare and vulnerable. He'd see her. She wanted him to make love to her. She wanted his love.

He stopped so close, she had to tip her head

back to meet his gaze. His eyes bore deep into hers before dropping lower to her lips. Without touching her, he kissed her. The soft gentle persuasion as he opened her mouth and slipped his tongue inside, was the most sensual moment of her life. She trembled for him, yearned for him, but the slow, concentrated feel of his mouth on hers was all she needed to understand the emotions that pumped through his blood equally matched the ferocity of hers.

Slowly, he eased back and slipped his hand around hers. Silently, she followed as he led her along the landing toward a bedroom. They stepped inside, and Sasha flicked her gaze to the setting sun in the distance. The entirety of the dove-gray room was bathed in pink from the lowering sunlight coming through the floor-to-ceiling French doors at the other end of the room. Together, they moved onto the gray satin sheets of the enormous four-poster bed.

The material slid across her naked body as she collapsed against the pillows. His lips caressed her collarbone and her breasts, teasing and licking at her hardened nipples.

Moaning softly, she slid her hands over the rigid planes of his shoulders as he kissed her skin. His eyes were closed and his dark lashes fanned his cheeks, Smiling, she smoothed her fingertips through his hair, and he opened his eyes.

"You're so beautiful, Sasha."

Tears burned. "When you look at me, I feel beautiful."

He smiled softly and eased from the bed, the mattress lifting with his weight. She didn't want him to leave her. Not for a single second. She wanted the moments to last until they truly had to end when he walked from the Cove.

With his eyes locked on hers, he removed his shoes and socks, jeans and boxers, before climbing back on the bed beside her. He leaned up on one elbow, his body pressed to the side of hers and his gaze roaming over her face and lower to her breasts. His erection firmly lay across her thigh, and she lifted her fingers to it. She smoothed them back and forth across the engorged and silken skin, circling the head and back down to run her nails through his thatch of pubic hair. His eyes closed as he inhaled a shaky breath through flared nostrils.

There was no power game here. No better or worse. She sensed his enthrallment as she embraced hers. With the front door locked and the world kept out, Sasha had never felt more at peace. This was the man she was meant to be with. This was the man whom fate had decided should share her life. Would it happen? Would they *make* it so?

She stared into his eyes. "Make love to me."

He leaned over her, and she closed her eyes as he stroked the back of his fingers down her side, from the curve of her breast to her rib cage, featherlight over her waist and thigh until her nerves screamed for him. He brushed his fingertips over her thigh and along the inside of her leg. She opened them instinctively, and he fingered her aching clitoris.

She opened her eyes. He smiled. She opened her mouth, but no words formed as he slid two fingers deep inside her. She clamped tightly around him, urging him deeper and harder. He complied, their eyes locked.

He caught her breath in a rough kiss that sent her desire rocketing. She reached for his penis as they kissed and sighed, moaned and explored. She clasped him firmly and moved her hand up and down the length of him, fast, then slow…fast again as he mirrored the action inside her.

"No more." She closed her eyes and moved her head to the side as he sucked and nipped at her breasts. "I have to have you. All of you."

He lifted away from her and reached toward his discarded jeans. Sasha's heart pounded with anticipation and her body hummed with impatience. He took out his wallet, then a condom. The wallet was tossed back onto the floor. He sidled back toward her, and she curled her fingers into the satin sheets in a bid to stop from plucking the packet from his fingers.

When he'd sheathed himself, he came back toward her and touched her again as he had before, bringing her to the edge of insanity with his fingers, his mouth kissing every inch of her skin. She was aroused and more ready than she'd ever been before. She wanted this man with every cell of her being. Their union was the most amazingly natural thing in the world. He hovered above her, and she opened her legs to welcome him inside.

"I was meant to meet you." He brushed the hair from her face. "We were meant to be together… like this."

She nodded, unable to speak above the roar of her blood as it surged through her, fueling her need for him.

He maneuvered the tip of his penis against her opening and then kissed her as he moved hard and unyielding inside her. She closed her eyes as relief left her on a gasp of breath. "Yes."

Gently, he moved. Then harder. Gently. Then harder.

Together they met each other's thrusts, their rhythm the most natural and beautiful thing Sasha could imagine. On and on until the sensations built and his penis grew impossibly thick inside her, filling her and taking her. She clung to his strong shoulders, urging him on.

Emotions whirled as her orgasm grew. Then they were there.

Over and above he took her, her climax merging into his and exploding as they came crashing down to earth together.

CHAPTER NINETEEN

JOHN COULDN'T TAKE his eyes off her. Her face lay in complete repose as she slept inches from him on their shared pillow. One slender arm rested limply across his stomach, her leg covering his thigh. The skin on her shoulder was smooth like silk as he gently played his fingertips back and forth across it.

He breathed deep and her soft, feminine scent filled his nostrils. A scent he believed entirely hers and not a blended perfume. Just Sasha.

God, he wished he could keep her with him like this forever. Safe and protected from the demons of the past…and the phantoms of the future. He clenched his jaw. How was he to do that? How could he help and protect her when he would have to leave soon and go back to his job and life before Templeton…before her?

Lifting his gaze from her beautiful face, John stared toward the French doors. He had to go back. He had people who relied on him. He had children at the school who needed him to help them through their exams. He'd no more let them down than he would her. So, what was the answer? He softly exhaled. Someone was going to be let down and right then, he had no way of knowing who it would be.

He closed his eyes and tried to clear his mind. He needed to sleep. Needed to take this moment of peace and embrace it. Soon, Sasha would wake and they would have to plan their next step. They knew more now. They had Sasha's truth and needed to act on it accordingly.

Next would be uncovering Kyle's truth…

The ringing of the doorbell and the harsh pounding at the door shot John's heart into his throat. Sasha's eyes snapped open, and she stared at him, her dark eyes wide and scared. "What was that?"

Bang, bang, bang.

"Mr. Jordon? This is Detective Inspector Garrett. Would you please open the door?" The shout came from downstairs, followed by the harsh clanging of the letterbox in his front door.

"Bloody hell." John sat bolt upright. Judging by the harsh tone of the inspector's voice, there was little chance of her disappearing anytime soon.

Sasha leaped from the bed. "What are the police doing here?"

He tossed back the covers and planted his feet on the floor. Where did he put his pants? "I've no idea."

"John, I'm scared."

He stopped and looked at her. "Don't be. Everything's going to be all right."

"How can you say that? Didn't you hear the way

the inspector sounded? Something's wrong." Sasha scrambled from the bed and ran from the room toward the master bathroom.

Bang, bang, bang.

"Mr. Jordon, you're leaving me no choice. I will have my officers break the lock in exactly sixty seconds."

Cursing, DI Garrett's threat left him no time to console Sasha. He located his jeans on the other side of the bed and dragged them on, his heart pumping. What the hell had brought the police to Kyle's home at this time of the night? Surely nothing else could go wrong now? He'd gotten Sasha to trust him, to relax enough to make love to her as though they had all the time in the world…and now this.

He strode onto the landing, buttoning his jeans as anger seeped into his blood. He rushed down the stairs, but when he reached the door, he lingered with his hand on the bolt. Sending up a silent prayer for the inspector to have made some kind of mistake, he shot a final glance toward the top of the stairs. Sasha had yet to appear. God only knew what was going through her mind.

He turned back to the door, unlocked it and flung it wide open. He scowled as he met the inspector's determined glare. "What's going on? It's past midnight."

"I know what time it is, Mr. Jordon." She brushed

past him, followed by two uniformed officers. "You need to come to the station."

John pulled back his shoulders. "What? Why?"

Her eyes dipped to his bare torso before she coughed and looked back through the open door. "If you'd like to get suitably dressed, we can talk more when we get there."

He glanced toward the stairs again. Where was Sasha?

"Is someone here with you, Mr. Jordon?"

He turned. The inspector stared directly toward the landing, her eyes narrowed.

Damn it. He didn't want Sasha dragged into whatever the hell was about to unfold. "Yes."

Her jaw tightened. "Who?"

"Me."

He and Inspector Garrett snapped their heads toward the stairs in unison. Sasha had gotten dressed and wore such an expression of guarded suspicion that made John's heart lurched painfully. Minutes before she'd been at such peace.

She descended the stairs slowly, almost nonchalantly, her chin held high. "Has something happened?"

He turned from staring at Sasha to face the inspector. Two spots of color darkened DI Garrett's cheeks as she regarded Sasha at the foot of the stairs. Clearly, this was not the situation she'd expected or wanted.

Another second or two passed before DI Garrett

spoke, her tone tight and laced with annoyance. "I'm afraid it has." She turned to John, her jaw tight. "I'm here to bring you in for questioning regarding the cache of class A drugs we seized from Funland earlier this evening, Mr. Jordon. It's unfortunate Sasha is here to witness it."

John froze as a lead weight dropped into his gut. His mind whirled. "What?"

"We were given an anonymous tip-off. We searched the fair and found a substantial amount of cocaine."

Anger hummed deep inside as Sasha's study of him burned holes into his temple. Freddy. He clenched his teeth. "There are no drugs at the fair."

"We've found enough to warrant bringing you in immediately." The inspector glared. "I'd like to think I won't have to ask my officers to arrest you, but I will if necessary. Now, if you'd like to get dressed, we can go."

John raised his hand. "Wait. Just wait." He dug his fingers into his temples. "This is impossible. There haven't been any drugs at the fair since I arrived. If there were, I would've known about it. Kyle wouldn't have kept that from me."

She lifted an eyebrow. "Are you sure about that? After everything you've told me about your relationship with your father, I'm not so sure you should place that much trust in him to have your back."

John clenched his jaw. She was right. How the hell did he know what Kyle would or wouldn't do as far as protecting his son from the law's attention? He'd brought him here to "sort things out." He'd said the drugs were gone, but who was to say he was telling the truth? John held the inspector's steady gaze. He could not let her see his doubt. "I'm confident Funland has been free of drugs the entire time I've been there. If you found something tonight, it was planted. Have you contacted Freddy Campton, by any chance?"

She tilted her chin. "I have officers looking for Mr. Campton as we speak." She turned to Sasha. "Would you like a lift home, Sasha?"

The use of Sasha's first name and his surname did not go unnoticed. He was an outsider. A man to be watched and suspected. He was a Jordon. Sasha's gaze pinned him. Questions stormed in the black depths of her eyes and her cheeks were flushed with either shame or anger. He couldn't have placed a bet as to which.

She blinked and faced the inspector. "I'd appreciate a lift home. Thank you."

John's heart picked up speed. The atmosphere had turned icy cold, and it was clear Sasha was taking the inspector's word on her accusation and believed he'd knowingly kept narcotics stored at the fair. Her fair.

"Sasha..." He moved to touch her elbow, but she stepped back, her gaze trained on a spot above his shoulder as a muscle worked rhythmically in her jaw. Swallowing, John dropped his hand to his side and curled his fingers into a fist. "This has Freddy written all over it. You know it has. Surely you don't believe—"

She nodded toward the front door. "Shall we go, Inspector?"

Detective Inspector Garrett stepped back and gestured with a wave toward the door. "You can ride with me while my officers take Mr. Jordon to the station."

With a curt nod, Sasha walked outside. John watched her go. He could only hope and pray she didn't do something rash and get herself on the wrong side of what was surely Freddy's smoking and vengeful gun.

He snapped his head around and scowled at the inspector. "So, you're telling me Freddy is out there? That he could've left the Cove after doing this?"

She planted her hands on her hips. "I don't know any more about Mr. Campton's involvement or whereabouts than you but, rest assured, I soon will. Now, if you'd like—"

"He did this. Freddy Campton's not a happy man right now. I fired him and this is his way of thanking me."

She nodded toward the officer standing beside her. "Are you going to get dressed or shall I get Officer Langdon to cuff you and take you to the station as you are, Mr. Jordon?"

Their eyes locked, and John drew in a long breath. "Give me five minutes."

She smiled tightly. "Absolutely."

SASHA CLOSED HER apartment door and collapsed back against it, her mind and emotions racing. John had been arrested, but not for a single minute did she think him guilty of keeping cocaine or any other narcotic at Funland. Yet, something inside her told her it was paramount that the less they said to each other in front of Inspector Garrett, the better.

On the ride back to her apartment, the inspector had been gracious enough not to mention the obvious sexual relationship she and John now had, but she hadn't been so subtle when she asked Sasha not to go anywhere anytime soon. In other words, the police hadn't dismissed her out of hand as having something to do with the seized drugs, either.

Anger burned.

How could anyone, including the town's inspector, think of her dealing in drugs? Maybe they hadn't...until it became clear she was sleeping with Kyle Jordon's son. Sasha pushed away from the door. Well, there was no way she'd regret her time with him. Nothing and nobody in her entire life had given her the sense of peace John did when they were alone and the rest of the world shut outside.

Snatching her bag from her shoulder, she strode farther into her apartment and took out her cell phone. She dialed Liam's number, glancing nervously at the clock. It neared twelve-thirty.

"Hello?" Liam's voice was curious but alert.

"Liam? It's Sasha. I didn't wake you, did I?"

"Of course not. Everyone knows how I love to work until the early hours."

She managed a small smile. "Well, I'm glad to hear it because I need you to go to the police station. Now."

"What?" All semblance of humor left his voice. "What's wrong? Are you there now?"

"No, it's not me who's in trouble. It's..." She hesitated and grimaced, not believing she was really asking Liam to do this. "It's John Jordon."

"John... Wait. You're surely not asking me to help the guy who's standing between you and the fair? The guy who happens to be related to the Cove's most notorious crime lord? Of course you're not. You wouldn't ask me to do that. That would be ridiculous." His tone dripped with irony.

Sasha sank onto her sofa and closed her eyes, her elbows on her knees. "I know, and I'm sorry, but Inspector Garrett's just arrested him for drug possession and I know he's being set up."

"How do you know that? You know what his father is. I know I teased you about liking this guy, but you can't afford to forget who he is. If the police have arrested him, it's time for you to step back."

"I can't do that."

"Yes, you can."

She squeezed her eyes shut and rubbed her fingers across the developing headache shooting from one side of her head to the other. "I can't."

"Why not?"

Because I'm falling in love with him. Because I trust him. Because he has to be good. I can't be wrong about him. Please, God, don't let me be wrong about him. "I just can't. Until I know for sure he had something to do with this…I have to believe he didn't. Liam, please."

Heavy silence filtered down the line as Sasha waited. Her heart beat hard and her hand turned clammy around the phone. If Liam said no to helping her, she had nowhere else to turn. What she was asking went beyond the call of friendship, but how could she leave John at the police station without representation when he knew absolutely no one else in the Cove?

Liam's heavy sigh rasped down the line. "Tell me what happened."

Her words rushed out as she told him about the inspector turning up at the house saying they'd found drugs at Funland.

"Wait." Liam's tone was ice-cold. "You were with him? At Kyle's house?"

Sasha stiffened as heat hit her face. "Yes."

Silence descended.

After a long moment, Liam cleared his throat. "Well, I see things have progressed since we last spoke. Fine. I'll go. If he refuses my representation, or I see or hear anything that makes me think Jordon is guilty, I'm out of there. Do you understand?"

Relief pushed the air from her lungs and she grinned. "Absolutely. Thank you so much. Anything you can do to help him—"

"I'll call you later. I want to see this guy for myself…especially now I know how quickly you seem to have gotten involved with him."

"Will you call me as soon as you've seen him?"

"Keep your phone on. I'll be in touch."

The line went dead, and Sasha dropped her head back against the sofa. Now that John would soon have someone with him, there was only one other man to be taken care of. She pushed to her feet and adrenaline pumped through her veins. If the police hadn't found Freddy yet, then she damn well would.

Leaping from the sofa, she stormed toward the front door, dropping her cell phone into her bag. She left the apartment and slung the strap of her bag across her chest, grappling for the key to the bicycle shed by the side of the apartment block. Her hands trembled but she finally managed to fumble the key into the lock. After several attempts, she freed her bike and wheeled it out.

She locked the shed behind her and dropped the key into her bag. She pushed away along the street. The night was clear and the full moon lit the stars above her as she pedaled from her apartment toward the main high street. She had no idea where Freddy would hide, but she'd start with the pubs in the hope someone had seen him…better still, had listened to him brag about John's demise.

Freddy didn't have Kyle's brains or discretion, which was most likely why Kyle never trusted Freddy with more responsibility than fetching and carrying—with, undoubtedly, the odd beating thrown in.

Sasha's nerves hitched. Would Freddy arrange or carry out something to physically hurt John if he were released without charge? God only knew whom Freddy could employ in the blink of an eye. Her mind drifted to the file box of contacts Kyle had left with John. Were they as loyal to Kyle's second-in-command as they were to the man himself? She swallowed. She had absolutely no way of knowing.

She pulled her bike to a stop outside the Coast Inn, fear and doubt humming through her. She alighted her bike and stared at the bar's facade. It was the only bar in Templeton that stayed open until two and the first time she would step inside at that time.

Leaning her bike up against a tree outside, she pulled back her shoulders and strode toward the door. She pushed it open and entered. Nerves leaped and danced in her belly as the weighted stares of the few drinkers inside assaulted her from every nook and cranny. She forced her chin high and walked purposefully toward the bar.

Dave was stacking glasses at the far end of the

polished counter when he turned. He did a double take. “What are you doing here?”

“I need to speak to you.”

His forehead creased with a frown and his gaze went on full alert. “What’s up?”

Sasha glanced over her shoulder. “Has Freddy Campton been here tonight?”

Dave followed the direction of her gaze before meeting her eyes. “No. Why?”

“I need to find him.”

“What’s he done? He hurt you?” Dave’s eyes turned icy cold. “If that damn fool has laid a single finger—”

Sasha grasped his fist where it lay on the bar. “He hasn’t done anything to me…but I think he’s setting up John Jordon and I’m not going to let that happen.”

“Now why in God’s name do you care about that guy? If he’s been nicked or in trouble, then I want you to stay the hell away, Sasha. No Jordon or Campton can be trusted. You’re a nice girl. A good girl. Why would you go looking for trouble? You always laid low as far as Kyle was concerned.”

She swallowed. “This isn’t the same.”

Dave slid his fist from her grip and crossed his arms. His intelligent eyes wandered over her face before his shoulders slumped and he shook his head. “Oh, hell, Sasha. You’ve gone and fallen for the man.”

Heat assaulted her cheeks. “I have not.”

He raised his eyebrows. "There isn't a thing about love you or anyone else can get past me, you know that. I've worked in this bar too damn long not to recognize that look in your eye. You're more than worried about the guy. You're terrified for him."

"Then help me. Ask these guys if they've seen or heard from Freddy. Someone must've seen him."

He studied her a moment longer before turning away and releasing a loud whistle from between clenched teeth. Sasha flinched and turned around. Every man in the place gave the huge bartender his immediate attention.

Dave planted his palms on the bar. "Anyone who has seen Freddy Campton today or tonight, I'd like a word. Sasha wants to speak to him so if any one of you lot intend drinking in my bar again, you'd better come forward with what you know."

Sasha's heart pounded as silence descended. Her mouth drained dry and her stomach knotted.

Then three men slowly pushed to their feet and approached the bar. The first one looked down at her from his tall height. "This have something to do with Jordon?"

She nodded. How had the monster towering at least a foot above her known that? She pulled back her shoulders. "Yes."

"If you find Freddy, are you going to get the cops involved?"

Sasha hesitated, unsure if the answer he wanted

was yes or no. She forced a steady stare. “Absolutely.”

Another tense moment beat along with her racing heart before the man’s face split with a wide grin. He slapped his hands together. “Then me and my friends will escort you there ourselves. It’s been a long time coming for Freddy Campton, and I will be more than happy to help things along.”

Sasha grinned and slipped her hand into the crook of her new friend’s elbow.

CHAPTER TWENTY

FREDDY WASN'T WHERE Sasha's new friend thought he'd be.

He'd gone. Disappeared into thin air.

They trekked from his house to the other bars in town, the arcade and every other haunt they could think where Freddy might hide, all to no avail.

Five hours later and Sasha stared out across the ocean from her apartment balcony, her knuckles aching from how tightly she clenched it. She sipped at her coffee, waiting for it to revive her. She hadn't slept at all and now the sun rose slowly over the water as dawn broke. Her body was drained, her mind numb. She could only imagine how John fared this morning.

Liam had said there was nothing he could do to prevent John from spending the night locked up but was hopeful of his release today. A small yet significant amount of cocaine had been found behind the numerous boxes held in the warehouse at Funland—in the exact place the anonymous caller had told the police they would locate it.

The only saving grace that Sasha pinned her

hopes on for John's release was Liam's confirmation the cops had zero evidence of John knowing the stash was there. They did, however, have evidence Freddy could well have planted it. DI Garrett had been more forthcoming with Liam than she had been with Sasha or John, and divulged Freddy had been spotted entering the fairground after closing. The eyewitness, a homeless vagrant seeking shelter in the public toilets outside, wasn't the most reliable witness, but the inspector was at least willing to investigate his claim.

It was only a matter of time until Freddy was caught and brought in for questioning.

Sasha drained her coffee cup and walked back inside. She needed to shower and change into fresh clothes before she headed to Funland. There had to be something useful in the file box Kyle left John. She could kick herself for not looking at it when John had asked her to. There could be something among the papers that would lead her to where Freddy might be hiding his cowardly ass. If not, then she would go directly to the person who knew him best. Kyle.

She headed for the bathroom and stripped off her clothes. The shower was hot against her cold skin, and she relished its rejuvenation. She wouldn't rest until she found Freddy and proved John's innocence. She closed her eyes and tipped her head back as the water ran over her face and body. He had to be innocent. The alternative made her want to run and hide after she'd finally started to trust him…love him.

Picking up a sponge, she washed the previous day and night from her skin and the insecurity from her heart. Today was a new day, and she wouldn't let her feelings for John be marred by the challenges ahead. Finishing up, she stepped from the shower and marched into her bedroom. She had work to do.

WHEN SASHA PULLED her bike to a stop outside the Funland gates an hour later, two uniformed officers greeted her. Her stomach dropped. *Damn it. Why didn't I consider the place would be under police restriction this morning?*

Inhaling a strengthening breath, she plastered on a smile and approached the two young officers. Judging by their youthful looks and underdeveloped physiques, they were barely out of police training.

She inwardly huffed. Gaining access to the fairground office would be easy.

She strode confidently forward. "Hi. Is there any possible way I could get into the office? I'd like to take some paperwork home to work on. I'm assuming you won't be letting me open the fair today?"

The older of the two stepped forward, his expression determined. "Good morning, Miss Todd. I'm afraid the fair is out of bounds until further notice."

She frowned and looked past him toward the

closed gates. "Surely I can grab a file or two. I'm more than happy for you to escort me inside and look over my shoulder while I get them."

"No can do, I'm afraid." He shook his head.

Fine, you want a fight, you'll get a fight. She fisted her hands on her hips. "It's not me under investigation, you know. I was with Mr. Jordon when he was arrested and DI Garrett even took me home. She didn't ask me any questions or tell me I couldn't do as I wanted today. I'm sure she'd agree for me to have access."

His expression wavered, and doubt flashed in his eyes. "The inspector has spoken to you?"

"Yes."

He glanced over his shoulder toward his colleague before facing her once more. "I'd have to clear it with her first."

Sasha crossed her arms. "I'm happy to wait."

He pinned her with a determined look before taking his radio from its holster at his shoulder. "Wait here."

The officer strolled away while his young colleague glared at her. His expression was undoubtedly the result of hours of practice in his bathroom mirror. She tossed him a smile and wandered a few feet away, pulling out her cell phone. She dialed Liam's number.

He picked up on the second ring. "Sasha. Good morning."

"Do you have any news for me?" Despite her

nonchalance with the officers, her stomach immediately knotted with nerves and concern. "Is John being released today?"

He yawned loudly. "Yes and yes. The police are concentrating on Freddy Campton for the moment and have no reason to keep Jordon past midnight tonight. He will have been under arrest for twenty-four hours and they have nothing to warrant keeping him there. They'll read him the riot act, telling him not to disappear, then let him go."

Relief lowered her shoulders. "Will they have a problem with him seeing Kyle?"

"Why?"

"I'm hoping the visiting permit John requested a few days ago will come through tomorrow morning. John needs to ask Kyle some questions, and there's no way John will leave without getting them. If the police won't let him go see his father, then I'll go in his place."

"Sasha, for crying out loud."

She frowned. "What? I worked with Kyle for years. He can tell me so much I need to know. I have to see him."

"About what? The drugs the police found? I thought you said this had Campton written all over it. Do you think Kyle had a hand in this?"

She shook her head. "No. The drugs from last night were Freddy. I'm sure of it."

"Then why do you need to see Kyle?"

Fear of the unknown and fear for John clogged

her throat. "He's the answer to me gaining some peace." She closed her eyes. "I hate that it has to come from Kyle, but he knew Granddad, he knew me and he knew my mother. The answers I need to move on are in the head of a man currently languishing in prison. I'm not prepared to wait another eight years for my life back. Not anymore."

Sasha pulled back her shoulders as thoughts of John and her future loomed large and beautiful in her mind. It was time to start living again.

Liam sighed. "There's no reason you can't take John's place if the permit comes through, but I don't like the thought of you going alone to see Kyle. You know his reputation. He could easily convince you he's the Angel Gabriel as much as Lucifer by the time you leave there."

Sasha smiled. "You forget I've worked with Kyle for a long time. There's little chance of him bringing me over to his side. Whether or not my mother's involvement brought the fair into his hands, Kyle was still the one who took it from Granddad without saying a word to me."

"Your *mother* had something to do with that?"

Sasha exhaled a shaky breath. "It's a long story."

"And one I want to hear about when we see each other."

"Maybe. In time." She looked over her shoulder. The officer who left to talk to DI Garrett had come back. He stood side by side with his colleague and they both watched her, their arms crossed. "I have to go. I'll call you soon."

"Make sure you do. Be careful."

"I will." She snapped her phone closed and walked back toward the Funland gates and the two officers. "Am I allowed in?"

Constable "Big I Am" stepped forward. "DI Garrett has confirmed access but ordered I check and clear anything you want to take away."

Damn it. Sasha's smile faltered. She didn't even know what was in the file box. She shrugged. "Sure, no problem."

He nodded curtly and waved her toward the fairground gates. The officer struggled to open the padlocked gate, and it took all of Sasha's self-control not to snatch the key from his hand. At last, he got it open and gestured her forward. She walked ahead of him on slightly unsteady legs. The dark and stationary rides, the silence only broken by early-morning birdcalls and the tarpaulin-covered stalls added a strange sense of eeriness she'd never felt before. She loved Funland. She wanted Funland. Yet, it seemed as time went on, the fair became more and more of a place that took from her soul rather than lifted it.

She swallowed. One way or another she needed to make it good and wholesome again. Failure to do so meant she had nothing left to work on. Nothing to throw herself into in a bid to eradicate the horror of her memories and make herself whole again.

John's face filled her mind's eye as she approached the office door. She blinked and he disappeared...much like he would soon disappear from Templeton.

Shoving her sadness into submission, Sasha took out her keys and unlocked the office door, flicking on the lights as she entered. The police officer stepped in behind her, and she tossed him a smile before heading straight to John's desk. Sending up a silent prayer there was nothing in the file to incriminate the man she was falling in love with, she unlocked John's desk and withdrew the file.

She lifted it onto the desk and glanced up through lowered lashes. The officer's face was stony as he studied her. She turned her attention to the file. She flipped open the lid, her heart thumping.

Hoping the officer wouldn't notice the tremor in her hands, Sasha carefully flicked through the papers. Each one was some form of employment record or CV with a small photograph pinned in the top corner. Her gaze darted over the names as she licked her finger and turned each paper over, one by one. She frowned and feigned concentration as though looking for something in particular when really she had no idea at all what she sought.

She took in the names and branded them on her memory in the hope they would eventually mean something to her—or John. Any small thing they could use to prove Freddy had a hand in the drugs the police found, or else, something to prove the opposite of John.

Face after face stared back at her as she continued her perusal. Employees she vaguely remembered from the past; ones she worked with now. Some she liked; others she despised. She flipped over another sheet and her heart stopped.

The tremor in her hands worsened as she stared at the face of the man she'd never forget as long as she lived. She tried to shut her eyes against the image, but they remained widely and cruelly open. Her molester smiled at the camera, his green eyes laughing, his handsome features jovial, as though the entire world was his for the taking.

Nausea whirled and rose to coat her throat in the bitter taste of hatred. She gripped the desk, all too aware of the officer watching her.

Help me. Help me.

Ice-cold perspiration burst on her forehead and the floor seemed to tilt one way, then the other. She stared, hypnotized by the slash of diagonal red ink across the page.

Location Unknown

"Miss Todd? Are you all right?"

The officer's voice drifted to her ears through an invisible wall of foam.

She looked up and nodded. "I'm… I'm fine."

He frowned and took a step closer, uncertainty etching his youthful face. “What is it?”

She snapped the file closed. “Nothing. I don’t need this after all.”

He glanced toward the file. “What’s in there exactly?”

Words stuck in her throat and she stood in a paralyzed state of shock as he drew the file toward him, his eyes locked on hers. He lifted the page of her molester and, as he did, Sasha abruptly stood, her chair falling to the floor behind her.

“Miss Todd?”

She huffed out a laugh, her heart racing as she fumbled to pick up the fallen chair. “Do you know something? I don’t know why I’m here.”

“What?”

She gripped the chair and shoved it under the desk, raised her shaking hands. “I should take the day off. Go to the beach. See some friends.”

He frowned and glanced toward the file box. “Are you okay?”

She grinned, her stomach whirling with nausea. “I’m great. I’m going to go, okay? Right now.”

His gaze turned from surprised to suspicious. “You want to go? You don’t want the file?”

Sasha’s lips wobbled as she smiled. “That’s right.”

“Then I’ll walk you out.” He lifted the box under his arm and gestured to the door with his free hand. “After you.”

Swallowing hard, Sasha glanced at the box a final time before striding toward the door on legs of rubber.

JOHN PUSHED OFF the rock-hard bed of the holding cell at Templeton Police Station and tilted his head from left to right in a bid to loosen the tension in his neck. It had to be nearing early evening, and he hadn't seen or heard from DI Garrett for hours. Every half an hour or so, the beady eyes of a cop peered through the slit in the locked metal door and then disappeared again.

John released a long breath as his waning patience wore thin.

They had nothing on him to keep him there so why the hell didn't they just let him go? He clenched and unclenched his fists as he paced the room. He was desperate to see Sasha and know she was okay. He couldn't stop worrying for her safety.

He loved her. He wanted her out of harm's way and happy.

His time in the cell had tormented him with thoughts of the fire in her eyes. The thought of her worrying, or more than likely acting out some form of justice on Freddy, sent chills of trepidation shooting up and down his spine. Sasha was strong, intelligent, street-savvy and totally unpredictable. God only knew what she'd do if she were angry about his arrest and Freddy's ensuing disappearance. DI

Garrett had yet to confirm they'd found him, so John could only assume Freddy was still AWOL.

Just as he considered shouting for an update, however small, the rattle of keys in the door brought him to a standstill. The door opened and DI Garrett stood on the threshold, her expression grim.

Her steady gaze wandered over his face before she stepped inside and gestured toward the door. "You and I need to have another chat, Mr. Jordon."

John took a step toward her. Her professional and determined expression gave him no indication as to what she was thinking or feeling. "Have you found Freddy Campton?"

"Yes. More than that, he has a lot to say for himself, so it's likely we'll have him in custody for quite a while longer yet."

John smiled, relief easing a modicum of the tension pulsing through him. "Well, that's good to hear."

He moved toward the exit when the inspector cleared her throat. "Let's get comfortable in interview room three, shall we?"

He halted outside the cell, the hair at his nape standing to attention. The tone of her voice alerted him to more trouble. He slowly turned. "What's happened? Where's Sasha? Is she all right?"

"I assume she is now, yes."

"Meaning?" He frowned as irritation hummed in his gut.

"Meaning, one of my officers escorted her into

the fairground office this morning. She said she wanted a file."

"A file?"

She nodded. "A file she knew exactly where to find...only whatever Sasha saw in there sent her running for the hills." DI Garrett's gaze grew intense as she stared. "Would you happen to know what file I'm talking about?"

Sasha ran? Left the fair? He couldn't imagine anything making her do that. He glared at the inspector. "Where is she now?"

"I hope she's at home. As for the file, it's in our possession for the time being." She nodded toward the corridor behind him. "Why don't we take a seat in the interview room, Mr. Jordon. I'd prefer anything else we say be on record."

His gaze locked on hers, his feet welded to the floor. "It's Kyle's file, isn't it? The file he gave me detailing the names of all his employees."

She brushed past him. "If you'd like to follow me."

John followed her, pulling his shoulders back and bracing himself for whatever was coming next. Whatever, or more likely, *whomever* Sasha had seen amongst that file of people had caused her to flee. He halted as realization dawned.

No. No, no, no.

He closed his eyes. How could he have been so stupid? How could he have not thought one of the people in that file could have been the man who'd hurt her, who'd touched her and made so many years of her life a constant battle to change and better everything he tainted?

"Mr. Jordon?"

He blinked and looked directly at Inspector Garrett. "What did Sasha say?"

The inspector tightened her jaw. "As I've already said, we'll talk more on record."

"Fine." John stormed forward.

They entered an interview room, where a plain-clothes officer already sat at a table bearing a black tape recorder. John dragged his gaze from the cop's steady scrutiny and took a seat on the opposite side of the table.

DI Garrett cleared her throat and sat beside the other cop. She nodded at him, and he removed a fresh tape from its cellophane packet and slipped it into the recorder. "This is an interview with Mr. John Jordon, currently residing at..."

Her voice faded into the background, overpowered by the thoughts and warnings screaming in his mind. He could have shown the contents of that file to Sasha days before. Why in God's name did she have to open it when he wasn't there to catch her when she fell? He screwed his hands into fists under the table and bounced his foot on the gray floor tiles.

His face was hot and his heart beat an erratic tattoo against his rib cage. How well did Kyle know the man who molested her? Did he still know him?

God, was he one of his damn cronies? The paid bloody help? Possibilities tormented him and ricocheted around his brain. He had to get out of there and back to Sasha. Take her in his arms and tell her everything would be okay.

"Are you with us, Mr. Jordon?" The inspector's voice cut through his reverie. "Can I get you some water?"

John lifted his chin and met her steady green gaze. "Have you spoken to Sasha?"

An imperceptible flicker of sympathy softened her gaze before she blinked and it hardened once more. "I think it best I ask the questions from here on in, don't you?" She leaned forward on her elbows and laced her fingers. "Let's start with the box Miss Todd was adamant she needed from your office early this morning. How and when did it come into your possession?"

John shifted forward in his seat and mirrored her posture, adrenaline pumping through his veins and mixing with the fiery need to pummel his father into the ground. "My father left it for me at the house when I came here. It's all the people who've worked for him in the past or work for him now. Each of their current statuses is shown on their individual CVs. I didn't consider the file anything more than providing me with a foundation for something I would have to piece together when I found these people."

"So you have no idea what Sasha—" she glanced

at the officer sitting next to her "—Miss Todd, would have seen in the file to make her react the way she did?"

"No." He gritted his teeth.

"Are you sure about that?"

He glared. "Yes, I'm sure. I care about her. Upsetting her is the last thing I'd do intentionally."

DI Garrett nodded. "I see."

Knowing he was giving away far too much of his emotions, John fought his heart to behave and scowled. "Did you ask *her?*"

DI Garrett narrowed her eyes. "Miss Todd claimed she was going to the beach." The inspector lifted an eyebrow. "Pretty out of character for someone who lives and breathes their work, wouldn't you say?"

John lifted his shoulders. *Good girl.*

Over his dead body would he give the police any information until he'd spoken with Sasha. He dealt in facts and facts only. So far as he was aware, he could be completely off the mark about her molester's face being in that file, and he wouldn't impart such personal information to anybody, DI Garrett included.

He faced her. "Do you have reason to think Sasha wouldn't be telling you the truth?"

A ghost of a smile whispered across the inspector's lips. "I ask the questions, remember?"

John held her gaze and said nothing.

She leaned back and crossed her arms. "I have

officers contacting every person in that file as we speak, Mr. Jordon. They're speaking to people, checking they're where Kyle says they are, according to the list of accompanying locations. They're even checking they are the people Kyle claims them to be. For all we know, half the people in that file could be using aliases."

John nodded. "I agree."

She lifted her eyebrow. "You agree?"

"Yes. I would even go so far as checking the ones he claims are dead are actually dead."

She smiled. "Glad to hear we're thinking alike, Mr. Jordon. If they are dead, I'll also be making sure they died under the same circumstances Kyle noted in his records."

John once more mirrored her posture and relaxed back. "I don't trust him, neither do you. Maybe when your officers have completed all their hard work, they'd like to share the results with me. It will save me a hell of a lot of time."

She glared, all semblance of friendliness disappearing on a puff of agitation. "I'll share information with you as and when I see fit."

He smiled, pleased he had her rankled. Sitting here, wasting time, was stretching his patience to breaking. Having a face-off with the inspector in this stuffy, drab interview room was like being questioned in the confines of a damn pressure cooker. He smiled wryly. Yet, at the same time, it was a satisfying way to release some of the rising frustration residing in a tight knot behind his rib cage.

"I find no part of this investigation amusing, Mr. Jordon, and considering Miss Todd's reaction this morning and your—" she quirked an eyebrow "—relationship status with her now, I would have assumed you wouldn't, either."

His smile dissolved and he sat bolt upright. "I don't. I don't find any of this funny. I want to get out of here."

His snapped response revealed the level of tension running through his body, but he didn't care. Inspector Garrett could know the depth of his feelings toward Sasha and so could the rest of Templeton for all he cared. What did he have to lose by letting the world know he loved Sasha? What did he have to lose but her rejection?

He jabbed his finger onto the tabletop and glared as fury pinched hot at his face. "One way or another, I want the truth. That's the only reason I'm in Templeton. I want to know who my father really is and whether it's you who finds that out, or me, remains to be seen. Now, am I being charged with something? Otherwise, I assume I'm free to get the hell out of here."

CHAPTER TWENTY-ONE

THE BUZZER OF her apartment door woke Sasha the next morning, and she lay still for a few moments, gathering her bearings. Dreams and nightmares had broken her sleep, leaving her body aching and her mind a mess. Blinking against the sunlight coming through the partially open blinds at her window, she stumbled from the bed, cursing when she stubbed her toe on the bedpost.

Buzz.

Scowling, she shoved her arms into the sleeves of her robe and stomped from the bedroom. Clearly, whoever was at her door had zero patience or politeness as they steadfastly leaned on the buzzer. Well, that was just fine by her because the mood she was in…

She reached the door and snatched it open. "Well, good morning…John!" She squealed and leaped at him.

Laughing, he caught her in his arms as she locked her naked legs around his waist. "Well, good morning to you, too."

She kissed his cheeks and jaw as he carried her

into the apartment, relief and excitement rushing through her. The door thudded firmly closed behind them and, grinning, Sasha pulled back. "I'm so glad to see you. I've been so worried…."

He stared into her eyes. "You've been worried about me? I've been going out of my mind worrying about you." He brushed the hair from her eyes. "Are you okay?"

Ignoring his question because she couldn't lie to him, she kissed him again. "When did the police release you?"

"Late yesterday evening, I wanted to come straight here but figured you'd be sleeping and wouldn't appreciate me hammering on your door." His gaze lingered at her lips. "I hope I did the right thing, because when I'm looking at you now, I'm thinking I should have come over and to hell with the consequences."

Sasha laughed as her stomach knotted. How had she ever lived before without someone looking at her the way he was right then? "You did the right thing. I…I needed to be alone."

His smile dissolved, and he lowered her to the floor, slipping his fingers into hers and leading her to the sofa. Silently, they sat and when he pulled her into the circle of his arms, Sasha gratefully leaned her back against the strength of his chest. Neither of them spoke as the atmosphere changed from euphoria to sullen silence. Sasha closed her eyes.

They both had so much to say, but she sensed John's internal battle was equally as difficult as hers.

She inhaled a deep breath and released her words in a rush. "The man who hurt me is still missing. Kyle has a profile of him in that file box. He must have known him."

His body stiffened around her. "And seeing that made you run, right?"

Sasha turned to face him. "You know about that?"

"The inspector told me and I put two and two together. I'm so sorry I wasn't there."

"Don't be." She pressed a brief kiss to his lips. "You're here now."

"We should find out more. We need to see Kyle."

She looked deep into his eyes and her eternal need to fight and be strong vanished. Instead, replaced by a need for him to take care of her. It was a dangerous place to be, yet one she didn't want to resist anymore.

He lifted his hand and gently drew his fingers down the side of her face to cup her jaw. "We're going to get all the answers you need." His dark blue eyes burned into hers. "Today."

"What are you going to do?" Her stomach trembled.

"What are *we* going to do. Kyle's visiting permit came through...he sent one for you, too."

"What?" Shock reverberated through her, quickly followed by a surge of panic. Sasha pushed from the sofa, her legs trembling. “Kyle wants to see me? Why?”

He stood and put his hands on her waist. “I don’t know, but we’ll soon find out. We can go see him together and get the answers we’ve been waiting for.”

She closed her eyes. “In my mind yesterday, I was halfway to the prison, but now it’s actually going to happen, I feel sick.” She opened her eyes. “Will he tell us the truth?”

His jaw tightened as he lifted his shoulders. “What has he got to gain by lying? He’s dying. Whatever he has or hasn’t done, he will never be held accountable for it. He didn’t want me to sell you the fair, and he knew the son of a bitch who hurt you. I honestly think Kyle wants to tell you how and why.”

Sasha pulled from his grasp and turned away, pressing her hand to the nausea churning in her stomach. “I’ll go get dressed.”

“I’ll be with you the entire time we’re there. There’s nothing for you to be afraid of, okay?”

She spun around. “What about you?”

He glanced past her toward the window. “What about me?”

She strode toward him and brought his hand to her lips. She kissed his knuckles. “This is the first time you’ve seen Kyle in twenty years. You can’t tell me you’re not equally, if not more, terrified than me right now.”

"I'll be fine." He continued to stare toward the window. "If we leave in the next half hour, we'll be at the prison right on the designated visiting time."

Sasha stared at the hardened line of his jaw before lifting onto her toes and touching a steadying hand to his chest. She pressed a lingering kiss to his cheek. "I'm glad I met you, John Jordon."

"I'm glad I met you, too." He dipped his chin and looked deep into her eyes. "When we've done this with Kyle, we need to talk."

Sasha's heart hitched and a heavy dread dropped low in her stomach. She stepped back and crossed her arms as though shielding her heart against a blow. "About the fair?"

He smiled wryly. "God, I wish the fair was what I'm struggling with right now."

His eyes were dark with sadness and his shoulders slumped. Sasha frowned, although deep inside she sensed what was coming because the same thoughts had blended with thoughts of her molester all through the night. She'd fallen for John and had spent more hours of happiness with him than she ever had with anyone else. Yet, how long could it last when Templeton wasn't his home and everything she wanted to make right was here? Would he stay with her? She wasn't sure she could go with him.

He smiled softly and took one hand from the clamp of her crossed arms. He tugged her forward and drew her against him. She let her head fall to his chest and the weight of his chin rested on her head. “I’m falling in love with you, Sasha. Big-time.”

Heat seared her cheeks as joy filled her heart. She grinned and pulled back and looked into his beautiful eyes. “Ditto.”

He winked. “Then we’ll deal with our feelings on top of whatever Kyle throws at us. I’ve got a funny feeling nothing gets past him and he’ll know what we feel for each other as soon as he sees us. He’ll know, and there’s every possibility it will give him more leverage than if we couldn’t stand each other.”

She frowned. “You don’t know that. I can’t even believe I’m saying this after everything he’s put me through, but Kyle does have some humanity despite his wrongdoings. He’s helped people in the Cove. I don’t think he’d use our falling in love against us. You’re his son.”

“I didn’t tell you why Kyle was incarcerated the first time, did I?”

Sasha shook her head as a horrible foreboding stole over her shoulders.

“He murdered my mother’s killer. He went after him and shot him dead.”

“My God.” She raised her hand to her throat.

“I’d lost my mother, then I lost my father. He never contacted me. Not once. When I came to Templeton, it was on his say-so and now he’s dying. He’s played me, just like he has everyone else, and now he'll know we're in love." Anger stormed in his eyes. "I have no idea what he'll do about it."

She stole her arms tightly around his waist. "He can't do anything about it unless we let him."

His eyes remained full of doubt. "We'll see."

JOHN KEPT HIS chin high and his gaze hard as he and Sasha waited for Kyle to appear in the visiting room. The constant tremor in the very pit of his stomach refused to abate, and he prayed his insecurity didn't show on his face. He glanced at Sasha, who sat rigid and upright beside him. She stared straight ahead at the closed door that would soon bring forth a man, his father, whom he hadn't seen for two-thirds of his life.

He turned and followed the direction of her gaze. He had no right to feel anything near fear. What thoughts would be running through Sasha's mind at that moment? What emotions clawed at her good and decent heart?

Although he longed to reach for her hand, they'd agreed during the ride there that they would strive to give Kyle zero indication to the nature of their deepening relationship. He was convinced Kyle would use it as ammunition. Sasha was yet to be convinced.

She had told him that she sensed this was confession time for Kyle. Confession time that would either help or hinder them for the rest of their lives.

The door opened.

One by one the prisoners filed into the room, and John's heart beat faster. The face he looked for resonated in his mind after years of pouring over the internet and TV images when Kyle was charged for drug offenses. John hated himself for doing so but was powerless to resist studying the man who sired him.

Kyle came through the door, and Sasha's sharp intake of breath beside him stretched John's taut nerves tighter. He sat straighter in his chair as his father came toward them. His forehead was smooth of anxiety and his mouth drawn into a careless smile that knotted John's stomach with irritation. However, there was no denying Kyle's weight loss, the yellow tinge to his skin and the fact the man who'd once walked upright and confident, now walked with a slight stoop as though he carried a leaden weight on one shoulder.

No one spoke as Kyle pulled out the plastic chair on the opposite side of the desk and sat. He placed his forearms on the surface and gripped his hands together. His gaze bore into John's with such focus, it was as though Sasha wasn't there. John met his father's unwavering stare. He wouldn't forget who this man was and the things he had done to him, to the new love in his life and to the tens of other people.

Kyle was dying, but for now, he was alive and still playing games.

Second by second ticked by as John's heart hammered with resentment and his mind rushed with questions and demands.

Sasha shifted in her chair. "Well, I can't say this is the most touching of reunions."

John continued to stare at Kyle. Hell would freeze over before he spoke first. Kyle owed him this. He owed him opening their first conversation in twenty years. At last, his father blinked and faced Sasha. "How are you, my dear?"

John tightened his fists under the table, relishing the feel of his nails digging into the flesh. The man might as well have punched him in the gut. Was he dismissing him? He'd agreed to this meeting and now chose to dismiss him and torment Sasha instead? Irritation turned to anger as John waited for Sasha to answer. Sooner or later it would be John's turn to speak, and God only knew what accusations and hatred would spew from his tongue.

"I'm surprised you have to ask me that." Sasha cleared her throat and leaned her elbows on the table. "Surely you know Funland still isn't mine. I'm also pretty confident you know Freddy is doing whatever the hell he can to get John into the cell next to yours."

Kyle's smile faltered. "What are you talking about?"

Sasha lifted her shoulders. "Oh, don't worry, it's not going to happen. He's sitting in Templeton Police Station as we speak, having planted cocaine at the fair in the hope of stitching up your son. Yet, you and I both know DI Garrett's capabilities as far as putting the guilty party where they belong, don't we?"

Kyle grinned. "She'll see through him like a plate glass window. Let him do what he wants, the place won't be his any sooner than it will be yours."

Sasha flinched, and John tightened his jaw, battling his anger into submission. He'd bide his time as he and Sasha had discussed. Until Kyle spoke to him directly, John would wait. They had Kyle in a corner, whether he liked it or not. The papers had been signed; his empire was John's in its entirety. The knowledge of that was the ultimate power for both him and Sasha, although she might not realize it. He'd spoken to Liam and the clause was invalid now that everything had passed to John. Whether his father accepted John's rebellion against his wishes or not, he was free to give Sasha the fair and whatever else she wanted…and he'd do it willingly.

Sasha emitted a wry laugh. "Let Freddy do what he wants? Isn't a battle between him and me what you had planned all along? What did you promise Freddy when you were arrested? The man is positively salivating with anger and frustration right now."

Kyle's face remained impassive as he turned to John. "And how are you?"

John exhaled as an eerie sense of peace descended over him. The years of anger continued to simmer like a fireball, yet strength assuaged his soul and he surrendered to it. He cleared his throat. "How do you think I am? I have more money than I ever thought possible, and I have your entire life's work to do with as I please. I'm just fine and dandy."

Kyle smiled. "I'm glad to hear it. That makes what I have to say all the more easier."

"Once I've had my say, of course."

A flicker of undeniable pride flitted through Kyle's blue gaze, and John inwardly cursed. The last thing he wanted to do was give his father any sense of satisfaction or pride in him. He wanted to annoy Kyle, do the opposite of what he wanted. He wanted to make him angry, frustrated and all too aware of what it felt like to be abandoned and seemingly forgotten.

Kyle coughed and leaned back. "Go ahead. Ask me anything you want to know. I'm fascinated why you came here today instead of when I wanted to see you with Freddy. What's changed, son? What made you decide to request that permit?"

The word *son* stuck like a knife in his gut, but John steadfastly ignored Kyle's questions. "Why did you ask Sasha here? Why don't we start with that?"

His father glanced at Sasha, and his smug smile slowly dissolved. "Like you said, I've had Freddy keeping an eye on things for me. I gather you two have been getting pretty close." His jaw tightened.

"That wasn't what I wanted to happen, but if you two…like each other then I've no choice but to come clean." He looked at John. "I want to wipe the slate clean."

John shook his head. "And you think whatever you are about to tell me will make up for two decades of absence?"

Color darkened Kyle's cheeks as he slowly closed his eyes and tipped his head back.

John glared at his father's leathery neck. "Well? We haven't got much time, and I refuse to let Sasha leave here without knowing what happened between you and her mother." He slapped his open palm on the table and clenched his teeth. "I won't leave here not knowing why you have a picture of the man who molested her in that damn file you gave me."

Kyle flicked his gaze back and forth between him and Sasha once more before exhaling a heavy breath. "Before I answer that, I want you to know I've made some dire mistakes in my life…taking the fair from Sasha's grandfather comes second only to leaving you alone after your mother was killed."

John's heart kicked painfully as perspiration burst out on his forehead. In all their years of estrangement, these were the words he'd waited for. Regret. Ownership. Apology. Tension ached along John's shoulders and neck as he stared at Kyle, studying him for an indication, no matter how small, that he was toying with him. That he was being insincere before he'd even really begun to explain himself and his actions.

Their eyes locked. Only an idiot would deny the genuine pain in his father's eyes. "I'm sorry, John. I'm more sorry than I ever thought possible."

John swallowed as words and accusations pricked like needles on his tongue. It was too soon to forgive. Too soon to acknowledge the lost years—but Kyle was dying. How long did they really have to lay the demons to rest?

He lifted his chin as pride and fear skittered over him. He stared at his father. "How do you know the man who hurt Sasha?"

Kyle's gaze lingered a moment longer on John's before he faced Sasha. "Your mother told me what Matt Davidson did to you and God knows how many other kids that came to the fair that summer."

John glanced at Sasha. Her body was rigid, but her eyes were alert and interested as she stared at Kyle.

"Tell me," she said as she straightened her spine. "Tell me what happened between you and my mother. Tell me what happened between you and…Granddad."

Kyle ran a hand over the back of his neck and leaned forward, his face a mask of suppressed fury. "Your mother came to me out of desperation. She was fuming with anger and frustration. Davidson had disappeared and she couldn't stand the thought he could live the rest of his life without paying for what he'd done...." Coldness streamed into Kyle's gaze. "For what he could still be doing."

"So you used that to con my grandfather? You used what happened to me to break an old man's heart?"

The skin at Kyle's neck shifted. "I didn't owe you or your family anything. I wanted the fair and was prepared to do anything to get it."

"You bastard."

Kyle's eyes flashed with annoyance. "That was then, this is now."

She glared, and John drew in a long breath through flared nostrils. "Where's Davidson now? Do you know?"

Kyle snapped his gaze to John. "No, but if I did, he likely wouldn't be breathing. The man deserves to die for what he did. You don't mess about with kids. Period." He faced Sasha. "Your mother told me if your grandfather knew what had happened, and that you seemed determined to stay at Funland no matter how much it hurt you to do so, your grandfather would want the fair out of your life. You might hate me, but I don't regret doing something that might have gotten you out of that place. Maybe one day, you'll open your eyes and realize your mother was doing what she thought best."

"Well, it didn't work, did it? Funland belongs to me. It's mine." Her voice cracked. "I won't let *him* make it a place I hate instead of love. It was my future, everything Granddad had planned for me. Why should I walk away and let that animal rip my destiny from me as well as everything else he's taken?"

Unable to stand watching her tremble, John reached across and closed his hand over hers. He held tight and looked to Kyle. His father's gaze stayed on their joined hands for a long moment before he looked up. Sadness, or maybe loss, lit his eyes, and John pushed his unexpected regret for a life his father no longer had from his heart. "So, you told her grandfather and then what? He agreed on a price? Any price just to get Sasha out of there?"

Kyle nodded. "Yes, and I'm pissed off I never found Davidson and made sure he didn't get the opportunity to hurt another little girl." He faced Sasha. "I'm sorry for what happened to you."

Chairs scraped and voices murmured all around them as they sat frozen in their seats. Nothing else needed to be said. Kyle coughed, a harsh racking that seemed to reverberate through him and rattle his bones.

John clenched his jaw, hating the instinct to move around the table and rub his father on the back and tell him he'd be okay. He didn't owe his father that—yet the overwhelming urge to thank him for at least trying to rid the world of evil danced on his tongue. He pursed his lips, trapping the traitorous words.

There was nothing he could do to stop Sasha when she stood and walked around the table.

She stole her hand over Kyle's back as he doubled over in his chair. Tears slipped over her cheeks as she smoothed circles over his father's back. All John wanted to do was go to her and offer some comfort after the truth Kyle had so easily delivered.

After what felt like forever, Kyle's coughing eased, and he raised his hand. "I'm all right. I'll always be all right."

Sasha looked into his eyes, a strained smile at her lips. "Thank you."

He smiled. "Thanking me is the last thing you should be doing. I still told John, no matter what, he wasn't to give you the fair."

Her hand slipped from his back and she walked around the table to her seat. She took John's hand and gripped it between both of hers. "I understand why you did that now. You were trying to look out for me the same way my mother and grandfather were."

John snapped his gaze to his father's and Kyle stared directly back. "I'm dying and the decisions I've made as far as you're concerned have been stupid at best. I know it's too much to ask that you forgive me or even to stop hating me, but I did what I thought best at the time. I loved your mother more than anything or anyone." He shook his head, his eyes turning steely, yet glassy with tears. "I couldn't stand by and let the man who killed her live. I don't regret that, but I do regret the repercussions."

John shook his head. "I can't forgive you. Not yet."

Kyle closed his eyes, nodding softly. "I understand. The time I had without you can never be gotten back. Maybe I was wrong to think you were better off away from me, safe and educated with a good future, but I came out of prison the first time a different man." He opened his eyes. "I wasn't capable of loving and caring for you. Prison changes a man. I didn't want anything else but to live a life where I was in control of what happened next, without fear of something happening to you. I figured if you were away from me, with good people who cared for you..."

John glared. "They cared for me because you paid them to. An eleven-, twelve-, thirteen-year-old boy who lives without his parents is never going to be all right. He's never going to be okay. How could you not know that?" Anger hummed through his blood, making him tremble.

Kyle nodded. "I can't turn back time any more than you can. I killed for love. I killed because of the rage inside me. How could you not know *that?*" His father's face darkened and his eyes bulged. "I only had you left. What the hell would I do if anyone hurt you, huh? You were better off on your own."

A bell sounded and they all started. Kyle immediately pushed to his feet and held out his hand to John. "Take care of her. Do what you have to in order to keep her safe. Do what you want with my money, the houses…." He glanced at Sasha. "Do what you want with the fair. Be happy. Both of you."

John's heart thumped harder and harder as he forced himself to take Kyle's hand. For the first time in twenty years, he felt his father's skin against his own. Time stood still as he stared into Kyle's dark blue eyes. "When I think of anyone hurting Sasha…I don't forgive you, but I understand."

Kyle smiled. "Then I'll die a happy man."

Slowly, their hands slipped apart and Kyle turned to Sasha. "Take care of him, too."

John slipped his fingers into Sasha's, his chin lifted as his father turned and disappeared into the throng of prisoners making their way from the room.

CHAPTER TWENTY-TWO

THE RIDE BACK from the prison was a difficult one. Time and again, Sasha tried to find the words to fill the heavy silence between her and John, but nothing seemed right or appropriate to alleviate the sense of anguish and shock surrounding them. She glanced at him for the twentieth time during the past forty minutes since they'd walked, hand in hand, through the prison gates.

They had so much to discuss, so much to absorb and come to terms with. Where did they start? Did they start together or apart? She longed to hold him and have him hold her, yet her head screamed to instill some distance so they had time to think rationally without emotional influence or distortion.

"Where shall I drop you?" John's voice was low and somber.

The harsh insinuation that he wanted to be alone slashed through her heart and she drew in a sharp breath. "Home. I think I need to be at home."

He huffed out a dry laugh. "Funny, that's exactly where I want to be right now."

"Mine or yours?"

His jaw tightened. "Mine. I need some thinking time."

"Well, Kyle's place offers more modern comforts than most, I suppose." She pushed his rejection aside and wrapped another invisible and protective layer around her heart.

He shook his head. "I'm not talking about Kyle's house, Sasha."

Her forced smile dissolved as her tardy comprehension hit hard in the center of her chest. "Oh. You mean your home. In Bridgewater."

"It's time I left Templeton." He glanced at her.

Their eyes briefly locked before he looked through the windshield once more. Words abandoned her, leaving her flailing and helpless in a pool of loneliness so much bigger than she'd ever felt before she met him. "I see."

"Do you?"

She turned to look out the window, tears blurring the passing houses as John drove them ever closer to the Cove. "Of course. You came to Templeton to understand Kyle better and now you do." She swallowed. "Your work is done and now you can go back to your life."

"Funland is yours...if you want it."

She snapped her head around. "What?"

He smiled wryly. "The clause is obsolete. Liam confirmed it yesterday. I can give it to you, along with the money to pay the inheritance tax that will undoubtedly be due, without repercussions. If you still want it, that is."

"I don't know what to say." Sasha stared, waiting for the rush of euphoria to overtake her. Instead, panic erupted around her heart as she fought the alien and horrible need for another human being. More than anything, more than the fair, she wanted John to stay.

"Then don't say anything." He pressed harder on the accelerator, his expression creating an unreadable mask.

Words escaped her as she desperately fought the god-awful pain squeezing tighter and tighter around her heart. He had his life and she had hers. They'd barely known each other more than a few weeks. He wouldn't ask her to change anything in her life, any more than she would ask the same of him. This was it. This was the end of whatever it was that had begun between them against a backdrop of their parents' lies, betrayal and deceit.

The purr of the car's engine grew louder in the ensuing silence. The interior of the car grew smaller and smaller. She pressed on the button to lower the window and gulped in the rush of cold sea air, blinking back the tears burning hot in her eyes.

The car slowed and Sasha's heart picked up speed when John pulled into a lay-by at the side of the road and cut the engine.

Don't stop. Keep going. Don't look at me. Don't talk to me. Just go. Please.

He stole his hand over hers, and Sasha forced herself to face him.

She turned and her breath caught in her throat to see such deep sadness in his gaze. "John—"

"I want you to have Funland." His gaze bored into hers. "But only if you can really say it's what you need to make you happy."

She swallowed. "It has to be."

"Why? I truly believe that place will bring you nothing but misery." He lifted his free hand and brushed the hair from her face. "Running the fair isn't the answer, Sasha. It won't put an end to what Davidson did to you."

She faced the windshield as her stomach knotted with determination. "You still don't understand."

"I don't think I ever will. That's why I have to go. It's why I want to get away from here and everything Kyle has touched, influenced and controlled. I know you love Templeton, but it's not where I'm meant to be. It…it feels wrong being here now."

Sasha stared ahead. How could she argue for Templeton's beauty when all he'd experienced was corruption and conspiracy? It didn't matter that their time together was so precious to her, it was clear it hadn't lessened his bitterness toward Kyle or his abandonment. It was clear being in the Cove hadn't given him a single day of happiness.

"Then you should go." She faced him. "I want to make Funland good again. I have to."

He slipped his hand from hers and shook his head, frustration seeping into his gaze and obliterating the tenderness that burned there a moment before. "Doing that won't undo what's happened. No matter what you do, or change, or paint, or pull down. It won't change what happened there."

Grief for the little girl she once was, for the little girl forced to grow up overnight, pressed down on her chest. "It will."

"It won't." He lifted his hand to her jaw. "Your happiness is out there for the taking. It's not in Funland. It's anywhere but there. Why won't you see that?"

Tears gathered and fell, slipping down her cheeks. "I'm scared. I don't really know anything but the fair. It's all I have."

He brushed the tears from her cheeks and leaned closer. He looked deep into her eyes before pressing a firm kiss to her mouth. "You have so much more. You have your liberty now. You know the truth. You know that staying at Funland is the last thing your grandfather wanted for you…." He kissed her again. "You have me."

Her heart hitched. "You?"

"If you want me." He smiled and pressed a kiss to her lips, her jaw and lower to her neck.

Sasha closed her eyes as a myriad of emotions whipped through her. She stole her hands onto the strong, muscular plane of his shoulders and held on. She tipped her head back and relished the pain and pleasure of his teeth nipping at her skin. How could she consider a relationship with him, when the real passion burning like fire inside her was to right the wrongs that happened that fateful summer? What did she really have to give such a wonderfully strong and determined man, when she continued to live so steadfastly in the past? He deserved a woman whose heart was filled with him, adored him and made his needs as high a priority as hers.

She eased him back and drew his hands from her face. "I need to know if I'm wrong about making the fair good again. I have to know if it's possible to stand true to what you love and not turn away when something evil threatens its very existence. Tell me you understand that." She kissed his mouth. "Please."

Sasha's heart pounded in her ears. She wanted him to say he'd stay in Templeton, stay with her and wait for her as they returned Funland to its former glory together, but she had no right. No right to smear her pain over what she hoped would soon be a bright and happy life for him.

He raised her knuckles to his lips and pressed a lingering kiss there. "I don't understand, but I won't stand in your way." He lowered her hands into her lap and shifted in his seat to face front. He slipped his hands from hers and gripped the steering wheel. "The fair is yours, but I'm leaving." He met her eyes. "You're a stronger person than me because I can't stand true to somebody I love when something evil threatens her very existence, and I'm truly sorry about that."

He turned the ignition and the powerful engine roared to life. Sasha stared at his hardened profile as he rejoined the traffic, her heart splintering a little more with each mile they covered on their way back into the Cove.

JOHN JABBED THE end call button on his cell and tossed it onto the sofa cushion beside him. He dropped his head back and pushed his hands into his hair. Three days. Three days since he'd dropped Sasha at home and they'd spoken their last words to each other. He'd lost count how many messages he'd left on her cell and her home phone. Lost count how many times he'd "dropped by" her apartment in the hope of changing her mind about pursuing her need to put Funland back the way it was before her abuse.

She never once opened the door to him.

How could she not see it was impossible to change the past? How could she not understand she would continue to hurt unless she made the decision to move on? He'd finally done it and was ready to live the life he should have been living before his father sent for him and made him pursue further ghosts, further hurt.

John stared toward the huge doors opening onto

Kyle's back garden. In the distance, the For Sale sign glinted in the midafternoon sun, lit up like a beacon for anyone rich enough to be passing the back of Kyle's mansion by boat.

His other properties were now up for sale, too. John smiled. Best of all, it was time to go and deliver the news to the husband-and-wife team he'd learned got things done in Templeton. The man who owned most of Templeton and the woman who protected it. If there were any two people who could ensure Kyle's money was used in the best way possible, it was Mr. and Mrs. Jay Garrett.

Unable to sit still or waste another moment brooding over the impossible dream Sasha might leave Templeton with him, John pushed to his feet. With adrenaline rushing through him, he snatched his keys from the kitchen counter and headed for the front door.

He drove through town and toward Clover Point, purposely avoiding looking at the picturesque views, the promenade, Marian's bakery and every place he'd grown fond of. It would serve no purpose to linger on the good stuff in Templeton. He'd store it in a box in his memory along with Sasha—firmly locked and marked Do Not Open.

Gritting his teeth, he pressed on the gas and ate up the steep incline toward the Garretts' home. A few minutes later, he drew the car to a halt outside their golden-brown cabin and let out a low whistle from between his teeth. "What a beauty."

The cabin was amazing. Enormous but not ostentatious. Grand, yet homey. He got out of the car and as soon as he stepped onto the gravel driveway, the front door swung open and a man John assumed was Jay Garrett came down the steps toward him… closely followed by his wife, DI Garrett.

John took a few steps closer, forcing a smile on his face despite the apprehension that this meeting might not go as he hoped. He offered his hand. "Jay?"

"Yes, indeed. Nice to meet you, John." A broad smile split Jay Garrett's face as he firmly clasped John's hand. "Cat's told me a lot about you."

John slid his gaze to DI Garrett and raised an eyebrow. "All good I hope?"

A soft smile played at her lips, her intelligent green eyes neutral in their welcome. "Good and bad, Mr. Jordon. Good and bad."

John laughed. "I didn't know I'd done anything bad in the short time I've been here."

"You just being here is enough for Marian to poison our minds." She smiled. "*If* anyone chose to take her seriously, of course."

The soft teasing in her eyes told John the inspector made up her own mind one way or another. He shrugged and shook her hand. "Well, I won't be arguing with the formidable Marian anytime soon."

"Intelligent man." She dropped his hand and gestured toward the cabin. "Why don't we go inside? I've been looking forward to your arrival."

She turned and led the way toward the cabin. John glanced at Jay, who smiled. "She likes to think she's the boss at home as well as the station."

John grinned. "Isn't she?"

He clapped John on the shoulder. "That's between me and her. If I told you the truth, she'd damn well kill me."

Laughing, John walked toward the cabin. The welcome he'd received had knocked him off-kilter, and he had a sneaking suspicion that since his phone call yesterday, DI Garrett had most likely spoken to Sasha as well as Liam Browne. Even though Sasha wouldn't talk to John directly, he couldn't imagine she would have she said anything negative about him.

He drew in a long breath and shoved away the pain that shot like a bullet into his heart. God, he longed to see her and talk to her, to convince her to leave Templeton and come with him. Deep inside, he knew there was nothing he could do or say to make her believe it was time for her to let Funland go. The determination in her dark and beautiful eyes left no room for argument. He could only pray she came looking for him if his belief that her mission would only bring further trouble was ever proven right.

The rich aroma of freshly brewed coffee greeted him as John stepped inside the cabin. As the coffee scent hit his nostrils, his eyes feasted on pure, unadulterated luxury. The cabin was probably worth equally as much as Kyle's place, but that was where the similarity ended. Rich, oak beams crisscrossed the enormous living room; huge sofas and bookshelves lined every wall.

He shook his head. "Wow, this is my idea of a house."

Jay smiled. "Ours, too. Why don't you take a seat? Do you want coffee?"

"Great. Thank you." John chose to sit on the armchair opposite the sofa where DI Garrett sat perched on the arm.

When he met her eyes, she was steadily studying him, the smile that had curved her lips when they'd been outside was somewhat diminished. She coughed. "So, we've read the papers Mr. Browne dropped here last night and we understand your proposition." She frowned. "A proposition that, if I'm perfectly honest, I'm more than a little wary of, considering who your father is. Plus, it's only been days since we found Freddy Campton guilty of planting class A drugs on property owned by you. What on earth could you have to say to me—"

"Us," Jay interrupted and raised his eyebrows. "Mr. Jordon wanted to speak to *us,* Cat."

She shot her husband a glare. "Fine. Us." She faced John, a faint blush darkening her cheeks. "That could make *us* consider what you're proposing."

John took the cup of coffee Jay offered and looked from DI Garrett to Jay and back again.

Never before had he felt so sure he was doing the right thing. Never before had he met two people who seemed so right together. A quiet yet palpable tension emanated between DI Garrett and her husband. He couldn't help wondering if the inspector realized Jay didn't take his eyes off her for more than two minutes at a time.

John inwardly smiled. He was confident Kyle's money would be spent in the right way once he left it in their capable hands. He took a sip of his coffee and then placed the cup on the low table in front of him. He leaned his forearms on his thighs. "I want to give you every penny of Kyle's money."

"Why?"

"Why?"

He grinned as DI Garrett's and Jay's voices joined, their disbelieving gazes not that dissimilar, either. He started again. "I want to give you Kyle's money—"

"Why?"

"Why?"

"Do you always echo each other? Or is it the prospect of anything of my father's coming into your hands bringing on this weird phenomenon?"

DI Garrett scowled at him and then Jay. "Is this guy insane or is it me?"

Jay shook his head and turned to John. He sat on the sofa, moving up close to where Cat was perched. He put his cup on the table and slid his hand onto the inspector's thigh. She appeared oblivious, and John guessed there weren't many times when these two were together and not in some sort of physical contact.

Ignoring the pull in his chest that felt far too much like longing, John flicked his gaze to Jay's. "Are you saying no?"

Jay frowned. "Why would you want to give us Kyle's money?"

"It makes complete sense. I want you to be the executors to his entire estate. I will give you power of attorney to every penny. There will be more when his houses are sold."

DI Garrett crossed her arms. "Why would you even think I want anything to do with Kyle's immoral earnings? You know I'm a cop, right?"

"Everything he has left after the police seized what he owed, is now his…or rather, mine. You and I both know their origin can't be proven, no matter what we might think. I want you—" he looked at Jay "—to use them to help the people at the center. Use the money to open more all over southwest England, if possible." He grinned. "It will fill me with more satisfaction than I could possibly tell you to know that after all the wrong Kyle has done throughout his years in Templeton, he'll leave this earth having done something irrevocably good."

Jay looked at his wife and their eyes met, identical frowns furrowing their foreheads.

When seconds passed with neither of them speaking or even looking away from each other,

John pressed on. "You've read through the paperwork. Liam's told you it's all perfectly legal and aboveboard, right?"

Jay shifted forward on the sofa and dragged his eyes from the inspector's. "Of course, but why us? You know how we feel about Kyle."

John lifted his shoulders. "It's because of those feelings that it makes complete sense it should be you and DI Garrett ensuring this money is used the right way. Simple."

They shook their heads.

"You're insane."

"You're insane."

John laughed as DI Garrett and Jay glared at each other as though it was the other's fault they kept saying the same thing. Satisfaction wound a warm knot in John's stomach. It felt good being there and giving Kyle's money to the woman who put him in prison and the man who obtained his damn crack house to make it a drop-in center.

"So…is it a yes or no?" He raised his eyebrows.

They searched each other's faces before they turned and grinned. "It's a yes."

John wasn't surprised when they answered in unison.

CHAPTER TWENTY-THREE

SASHA STOOD IN the doorway of the Funland office and stared out into the deserted fairground. Since its reopening a week before, she'd waited for a sense of coming home to whip through her…but it had yet to come. For days she'd avoided John's phone calls and his intermittent arrivals at her apartment. She'd ignored his incessant ringing of her doorbell, knowing seeing him or speaking to him again would just be too painful.

No matter how strong her yearning to talk to him, she stood firm.

Yet, her enforced separation was futile.

Another week had passed since he'd left Templeton, and her heart still lay heavy with a strange sense of bereavement, equal to that of when her grandfather died. She couldn't sleep or eat. Concentration and focusing on even the most menial tasks had disappeared the moment she walked away from John's car the last time she saw him.

Now it neared midnight on the eighth night since he'd gone, and she was lonelier than ever.

The last group of giggling, screaming and undoubtedly drunk teenagers had lumbered past her through the gates an hour before, oblivious to her presence. Much the same as she'd been oblivious to the cruel, heartbreaking aftermath of turning away from the most wonderful man she'd ever met.

Sasha turned back into the office, slamming the door behind her. She'd made her decision. John had laid himself bare to her and told her he was hers if she wanted him and she'd refused him.

She dropped into her chair. She was entirely alone. Funland was hers to do with as she pleased without having to answer to Kyle, Freddy or anyone else. So where was her excitement? Where was her passion and fire to get on with things and start making her dreams for the place come true?

"God damn it."

She slapped her palm onto the desk as frustration at her stupid, yearning heart and its unerring need to punish her. Her gaze fell on the two envelopes that sat on her desk, tormenting her. The buff-colored envelope contained the deed to the fair, all signed and sealed with her name emblazoned at the top. She'd squealed with delight when she opened it and then cried when she opened the second envelope that now lay next to it. The second envelope couldn't be more different than the first. This one shone in all its tempting red-and-white glory, was significantly flamboyant...and contained a ferry ticket.

The letter that accompanied the ticket was in her

apartment trash can, ripped to a million pieces so no one would ever see the blot of her tears blurring John's words. He'd left Templeton…and in his words, "would never come back."

He'd left, but not without pleading with her one more time to come with him and leave Funland and her pain behind. Left, but not without telling her his address and enclosing an open-ended ferry ticket out of the Cove, should she ever change her mind.

She swiped at her cheeks. Who did that? What sort of person gave another human being an open invitation to be with them, when the human being in question had so resolutely rejected them?

A person like John Jordon.

Her heart ached to go to him; her mind told her to stay exactly where she was and work on obliterating the evil that lingered in every inch of Funland since that fateful summer. Her heart beat for John; her mind burned with Matt Davidson.

She stared blindly through the windows toward the darkened fair. All day long the lights had seemed too bright, the rides and music too loud. Where was her joy in it? Where was the burning need to be there? It was as though it had packed up and slipped into John's suitcase when she wasn't looking.

"I have to do this, God damn it." She pushed away from the desk and marched into the kitchen.

She filled the kettle and flicked it on, gripping

the counter in an effort to steady the thundering pain in the very center of her chest.

So many people wanted her to leave Funland and all it entailed. Her grandfather, her mother, John… even Kyle, but if she did that, her molester had won. He would have taken the only thing she'd ever loved and destroyed it, right along with her self-worth.

Sasha reached for a cup in the cupboard and her hand froze around the handle.

The only thing I've ever loved is the fair…the only person I've ever loved is John. Am I wrong to stay here? Am I sacrificing the man I am meant to spend the rest of my life with for a place a monster violated the day he violated me?

"What am I doing?" she whispered. "God, what have I *done?*"

A sharp and powerful panic stole the air from her lungs and set her heart pounding. She turned and stared around the kitchen as if seeing it for the very first time. She stared at the counter on the opposite side of the room, her heart racing. Right there he'd made love to her, taken her body and heart in a single moment in time. Right there, her world had shifted and she fled from John and his power, blaming and lashing out, fearing what this new feeling toward someone else meant.

Trembling, she marched from the kitchen into the office and snatched up her cell. She punched in Leah's number.

"Hey, you." Leah's delighted greeting came down the line. "Long time, no hear."

Sasha swallowed against the dryness in her throat. "Listen. I've got something to say and I want you to hear me out. Once I'm done, don't hold back."

Silence.

"Leah?"

"I'm listening."

"John. John Jordon..." Sasha fisted her hair back from her face. "I love him. I love him more than I've ever loved anyone...except you."

"Good save. Go on."

"He wants me to leave Templeton. Leave Funland. Leave and be with him. He's given me the fair. For nothing. It's mine. He's also left me an open-ended ferry ticket to join him anytime in Bridgewater."

Seconds ticked by, and Sasha's heart picked up speed. She gripped the phone. "Well? What do you think?"

Leah's exhaled loudly. "What are you asking me exactly?"

Frustration bit hot at Sasha's cheeks. "What do I do?"

"Hmm..."

"Leah...this is serious."

"I know."

"Then tell me what to do!"

"You really need me to do that?"

"Yes. I'm dying here."

"Go, you moron." She laughed. "Go, now. The guy loves you. He wants you. You have nothing here but years of bad memories at Funland. Go make some new ones. Come back and visit, but hell, lady, the man is sex on legs with a heart bigger than the damn Cove. He *loves* you."

Sasha grinned, her heart near bursting from her chest. "What about you?"

"What about me?"

"Will you be okay?"

"Will I be okay?" Leah laughed. "I'll be fine and dandy. I'm going to hunt me down my own John Jordon, just you wait and see."

Sasha laughed. "I love you, Leah Dixon."

"I love you, too. Not get out of here. Send me a postcard."

"I will."

"Good. See you soon. I love you."

"I love you, too." Grinning so widely her cheeks ached, Sasha snapped her phone closed and grabbed her bag from the back of her chair. She stuffed the envelope containing the deeds to Funland into her bag, followed by the envelope containing the ferry ticket, before snatching up her keys. She locked her desk and headed for the door. Locking it securely, she marched through the dark and abandoned fairground and walked through the side gate and out into the open.

Replacing the padlock, she gave it a final tug

and dropped the key into her bag. With her chin lifted, she unlocked her bike and straddled it, her long-awaited feeling of coming home now burning bright and clear.

SASHA ENTERED HER apartment, tossed her keys onto a side table and ran into her bedroom. She snatched down a suitcase from the top of her wardrobe and yanked open drawers, tossing clothes inside before hurrying back to her wardrobe and throwing in anything she could get her hands on.

Once the case bulged with clothes and shoes, she raced into her bathroom and filled a bag with toiletries, hysteria stirring a laugh from deep in her chest when she haphazardly grabbed some sanitary towels. Had she lost her mind? She laughed out loud. Yes, and it felt amazing.

Tension hurtled through her, but it was excited tension rather than the heavy dread she'd been carrying around since she was twelve. She'd waited her entire life for John to find her; she could wait a few hours more to be with him…God willing, forever.

The continual doubts that he would still want her after her treatment of him continued to badger her conscience. Did she deserve such a man after she'd shown him how single-minded she could be? Did he leave Templeton on the ferry, shrugging off their relationship as a bad experience and one never to be visited again? No. He'd pushed a ticket through her mailbox. An open-ended ticket to share his life's journey.

She might be too late to begin the adventure with him at the starting line, but she'd take the first available ferry in the morning and catch him up at the next available stop.

JOHN STARED, UNABLE to believe what he was seeing. He blinked. Then blinked again. He turned to his class of eleven-year-olds, his throat dry. Their young faces were turned to the apparition smiling through the square of glass in the classroom door.

He swallowed and beckoned Sasha inside.

The way she tentatively pushed open the door and crept inside sent his heart leaping into his throat. He'd never seen her look so unsure about anything. He could only guess what this was taking for her to do this…to come to him.

The strength of his students' wide-eyed stares burned into his temple, but he couldn't take his eyes from her. Dressed in blue jeans and a simple, white V-necked T-shirt, John didn't think he'd ever seen her look more stunning.

Her luscious, thick, waist-length hair was loose and glorious about her face and the yearning to bury his face in it was stronger than ever before. She threw a hesitant glance toward the kids, the soft tap of her ballet flats loud in the rare silence of the room. His gaze dropped to the visitor's pass swinging from a lanyard around her neck. He'd find out later how she managed to convince the school receptionist to let her in. Right then, he didn't care. She was here.

She came to a stop a safe two-foot distance from him and lifted her eyes to meet his. "Hi."

"You're here." Somehow the words broke from his tongue. "You're actually here."

She smiled. "I am." She glanced toward the kids again. "Do you think we could talk outside for a moment?"

"Are you here to stay?"

"Yes."

"Forever?"

"Yes."

His heart beat a painful tattoo in his chest and his arms yearned to hold her, but he had to be sure she meant it. He had to be sure before he laid himself open to more pain when he hadn't recovered from the current agony ripping through him. He couldn't be abandoned. Not again.

He nodded and turned to his kids. "I want you to read through the first two pages of chapter five of your textbooks. I'll just be outside, so keep the noise down."

They stared at Sasha rather than him, one by one blindly reaching for their books, varying expressions of curiosity and envy on the girls' faces and varying expressions of prepubescent lust or disinterest on the boys'. Biting back a smile, John turned and gestured toward the door. "We can talk in the corridor."

A flicker of unease swept across her gaze before she turned and walked out ahead of him.

He shut the door behind them and the expected wave of excited chatter, screeching chair legs on tiles immediately ensued. With his hand at the base of her spine, he steered her to the last of the windows looking into the classroom to give them as much privacy as possible, without entirely obscuring his view of his class.

Her gaze locked on his, and it dawned on John, he was already hers for the taking, regardless of what she had to say or the brevity of his intentions to not get hurt more than he already had been.

"I'm sorry, John. I'm so sorry." A single tear escaped and slid onto her cheek.

He reached out and brushed it away with his thumb. "What happened to change your mind?"

"I woke up." She lifted her hand to his face, her dark, dark eyes boring into his. "I woke up from the nightmare. I'm here. I'm back in charge of my freedom again. I love you."

He turned his head and placed a kiss in the palm of her hand before lowering it and holding it tightly between them. "I love you, Sasha, but you have to be sure about this. I can't…"

"You won't hurt anymore." A choked cry escaped her, and she gave a wobbly smile. "I promise. No more hurt."

He smiled and blinked back the tears that burned behind his eyes. He stole his hands to her slender waist and pulled her close. “No more hurt for either of us. Ever again.”

She laughed. “Deal.”

Relief and love surged through his body and into his heart with such ferocity, John abandoned all thoughts of his kids for a single moment and hungrily covered her mouth with his. She was his… in heart, body and soul, Sasha Todd had come to him…as he would have soon to her.

The roar of applause and stamping of feet from his classroom forced them apart. They both glanced through the window at the beaming faces of his class before erupting into laughter. Sasha wiped the tears from her eyes. “I’ve found exactly where I’m supposed to be.”

He stole his arm around her shoulders. “Welcome home.”

Her grin was so wide, John didn’t know what else to do but kiss her again…and again.

* * * * *